Heaven on Hold

By Dorothy Mikat

Hope you find laughs within - Dorothy Mikat

Olympic Publishing

ISBN 978-1-4507-9826-6

Published in 2011

Cover design by Rick Mikat

Printed in the United States of America

Olympic Publishing
11209 White Lake Road
Fenton, Michigan
48430

For my sister, Janice
In hopes that she will find this work humorous

A Merry Heart doeth good like a medicine
Proverbs 17:22

Heaven on Hold

by Dorothy Mikat

It was the best of times, it was the worst of times; it was the age of wisdom, it was the age of foolishness; it was the epoch of belief, it was the epoch of incredulity; it was the season of Light, it was the season of darkness; it was the spring of hope, it was the winter of despair; we had everything before us, we had nothing before us; we were all going directly to Heaven, we were all going the other way.

Charles Dickens

Preface

Every generation has suffered through hard times while in the same era has enjoyed advances in the quality of living. Early in the twenty-first century, advances were appreciated in the fields of technology as applied to medicine, travel, communications, and space exploration. But during the same period, everyone experienced consequences of the economic recession. Most families had to make sacrifices. Millions of people lost their jobs and houses. How to come out of the slump was foremost on the minds of the victims. And so it was with members of a New York City book club.

~ 1 ~
Hard times in New York City

Candace dramatically shook the raindrops off her umbrella and wiped her feet on the café mat as she entered.

"Oh, the weather outside is frightful!" she sang causing heads to turn. Candace really didn't need her voice to draw attention to herself—her every movement and appearance did that. Her enviable figure was enhanced by her dark expressive eyes, full red lips, and long brown wavy hair that swept about her neck as she turned. On this day, she wore an attention-getting bright red, shiny raincoat that matched her umbrella and her persona.

Candace smiled at the patrons as she glanced around the room. As she did so, she slipped in what appeared to be a rehearsed dance step and fell gracefully onto the wet floor.

"Blast it!" she yelled as she jumped up and hopped around on one foot. "Ow! Ow! Ow!" At that moment, an unkempt and inebriated man staggered into the café. Seeing Candace hopping around accompanied by her verbal outbursts, he cried out, "Oweee! A rain dance! I can do that too." He imitated her with exaggerated hops and hollers.

"That's not funny. Get lost!" she yelled at him. "I've hurt my ankle, damn it!"

The burly café waitress escorted the inebriated man outside while the manager offered help to Candace. She took a few steps and let out a high-pitched screech. "Ow! Ow! Ow! I'll never be able to waitress tonight, and I really need that money. Oh how I need that money! Ow!"

The apologetic manager tried to help her to the back table where her book club friends were waiting, but she brushed him off. As Candace made her way, her five friends were watching her.

Allison glanced at her with a wry smile. "Our drama queen has made her arrival really obvious this time."

Mona sat with her arms folded across her chest. "Anything for attention," she smirked.

Brittany giggled. "You never know about Candace."

Even though she professed to being in pain, Candace talked with almost everyone she passed. "I like your sweater," she said to one man as she hobbled by and gave him a wink.

"Hello. Hello. Hello," she sang out as she approached the ladies who were waiting for her with their books on the table.

"Hi Candace. That was quite an entrance. You really ought to let me help you overcome your shyness," said Hannah facetiously.

"Very funny. Whatever it takes to be noticed!"

"Should we put ice on your ankle?" asked Hannah.

Candace glanced around the café, leaned forward and whispered, "I was just practicing my acting skills. You never know when a talent scout is lurking about—even in a small café."

Allison laughed. "If there is one in here, let's hope he doesn't see your heavy mascara running down your cheek." Candace quickly reached for a napkin and wiped her face.

Mona added, "If there is a scout, his attention is probably on that bum outside who's hopping around and now collecting money in his paper bag for his performance." The others laughed as they glanced out and saw him giving a perfect imitation of Candace's *dance*.

"Just my luck," said Candace as she pounded her fist on the table. "He's getting paid for my act." As she sat there, the concerned manager brought her a complimentary cappuccino. After she thanked him, she turned to the group and quietly said, "At least I got something for my act!"

"Despite your slip, you seem to be in good spirits. Does that indicate you did well on your audition last week?" asked Allison.

"Hell, no. My upbeat spirit is just one more act for you." She hesitated. "No, I didn't get the part I wanted." She lowered her head and her smile was replaced by a frown. "Everyone tells me I have talent, but then I always hear that I'm not quite right for the part."

Diana meekly looked at her and said, "Someday I'm sure you'll be discovered and be a star." Candace glanced up and thanked her. "I really hoped that getting a part in the new musical would pay my rent. My part time waitress job isn't doing it. I can barely scrape up money to pay for toothpaste. Anybody know of a cheap place to move and hang my hat? I'm afraid that soon I'll end up sleeping on the streets next to that loser outside."

"Is that why you did that faked slip...so that you could sue for money to pay your bills?" asked Allison.

"No. I wouldn't sink that low. It was just a fun performance."

"I wish I had room for you in my apartment," said Allison, "but Fred and I can barely turn around in our small space."

"I don't think you'd be happy sharing a room with my three little kids," said Diana.

Mona's frown deepened as she looked at Candace. "You're not the only one having trouble paying the rent. Me too!"

The others joined in: "Me too!"

Diana sat with a blank expression and appeared preoccupied. She looked down and fidgeted with her nails, which showed signs of her nervous gnawing. "What's wrong, Diana?" Hannah asked.

"I bet she lost her recipe for chocolate chip cookies," laughed Brittany.

"This is no time to be funny. Diana appears depressed. Come on, Diana. Share!"

"I don't want to bore you with my problems," said Diana.

"Thanks!" blurted out Brittany followed by her laugh.

Hannah gave Brittany a scowl. "Ignore her, Diana. So what's going on?"

"I'm really stressed out because of my financial state among other things. I've had a pounding headache for a week and haven't found any way to shake it. I almost didn't come today."

"Give me your hand," said Mona.

Diana looked baffled and said, "What for?"

"Just give it to me!"

Mona began to massage the recess between Diana's thumb and first finger.

"That hurts," complained Diana.

"Hush. Be patient for a minute." Then Mona asked, "How's your headache now?"

Diana opened her eyes wide and looked amazed. "My goodness! It's gone. How did you do that?"

"I took an acupressure class as part of my physical therapy training. I learned a lot of skills for curing many aches, pains and ills."

"It really worked, Mona. I can hardly believe it." Diana smiled. "When I get another one, I'll come looking for you!"

"Me too," said Candace. "That looked more effective than smoking a joint."

"And cheaper too," Allison added.

"Golly! How does that work? You didn't even touch her head," laughed Brittany.

"It's based on old Chinese principles of treatments involving magnetic energy paths," said Mona.

Brittany, the youngest member of the group, remained confused. "That doesn't make any sense to me."

"I'm not surprised," Candace said with sarcasm. She turned toward Diana. "How's everything else going for you?"

Diana appeared on the verge of crying. "You shouldn't ask. I'm still having a hard time adjusting to my divorce. I feel miserable when I know he's out having fun with his slutty girlfriend."

Brittany looked at Diana carefully. Diana's appearance contrasted sharply with that of the others. She could easily blend into the wall because of her quiet nature, her dowdy clothes, and the fact that she wore no makeup, and pulled her drab hair back and held by a simple rubber band.

"What you need to do is fix your hair in a new style, put on some makeup, and get the latest manicure. That's what I do to keep up my self esteem," said Brittany.

"You mean it takes goofy hair-doos to make you feel good about yourself?" asked Candace.

With her ever-present smile, Brittany answered, "My purple swatch of hair today matches my outfit. I'm in the mode. And yes, I do feel good about myself because I know I look good." She laughed again—that habitual, high-pitched laugh that was becoming increasingly annoying to Candace. Candace rolled her eyes without comment.

"I don't need to do that to keep up my self esteem," said Allison. "Exercising does that for me, and it's cheaper." She sat there in her jogging outfit, which she frequently wore to the meetings having jogged through Central Park from home. She was attractive in her own natural way with her ash blonde straight hair pulled back in a pony tail, her trim figure and glowing complexion.

"Aren't you afraid of getting mugged in Central Park?" asked Candace.

"It's safe during the day. There are lots of joggers there, and it's a beautiful place to stay in shape. But I don't go there after dark."

Mona looked back at Diana who still was looking glum. "This too will pass. You'll end up stronger with time, just like me."

"Ugh! Let's hope not," said Candace. "You've over-compensated and become too hardened."

"Oh yeah? Well, you're like one of the bitches who made me that way. I'd never trust you around a boyfriend of mine."

"Thems fightin words! If I'm a bitch, you're a super bitch."

"Girls, girls! Everyone seems on edge today. What's happening to us?" asked Hannah.

"The subject of men always brings out the worst of us," said Candace. She then looked at Diana. "You're just in one of life's slumps. You take men too seriously. I've developed the attitude that men are like buses."

"We know," said Allison. "When you lose one…" The others joined together to complete the sentence: "another will be around the corner in fifteen minutes."

Diana didn't like the attention her tears brought to her and she tried to suppress them. Hannah placed her hand on Diana's arm and looked at her with empathy. "Many of my patients have suffered through the same loss. You need to find new interests. You'll be surprised how much stronger you'll become as you work your way through this."

Hannah took a deep breath, and then said, "You all make me glad that I never married. From what I hear, men add to life's problems. I guess my height's largely responsible for that. I was always taller than the boys in my classes, and even now few men are taller than me. I know that most don't feel comfortable being with a larger woman than they are. So, I've resigned myself to the single life and concentrated on my career in counseling. I'm content without a man in my life."

Candace blatantly asked, "What do you do about your sexual needs? …Just do a series of one-night stands like I do? And then it's 'adios muchacho.'"

A bright blush appeared on Hannah's face. "Candace! Please!"

"Can I take that to mean yes? Come on. You can tell us. We're your friends."

"Lay off, Candace," Hannah said firmly as she looked away.

Mona sat with a constant scowl. "Let's start our book discussion. I'm getting tired of this conversation." Her comment was ignored.

Diana lifted her head from the table. "I'm sorry. I didn't mean to unload on everybody, but I'm feeling worse today because it's my birthday. It sure is an awful feeling to be alone on my birthday with no one to celebrate with me."

"What do you mean, 'no one to celebrate with' you?" Candace abruptly stood and belted out, "Happy Birthday to you." Her projection was so good that it drowned out a loud siren on a passing fire truck. She won the attention of the entire café. As she neared the ending, she jumped upon her chair and sang the last "to" with a broken high note followed by a brief pause and then a final loudly emphasized "**you**".

The patrons in the café responded with applause and "bravos". Candace gave an exaggerated bow and stepped down. Diana blushed but smiled widely. "Thank you, Candace. That made my day! I hope a talent scout is here and heard your performance."

After the club ordered their coffee and snacks, Candace looked directly at Hannah. "Hey, I didn't mean to embarrass you. How goes it for you, Big H?"

"Don't ask," responded Hannah. "I just got news two days ago that my house is going into foreclosure."

The others looked shocked. Allison asked, "How can that happen to you? I thought psychologists had it made in any economic time."

Hannah sighed, "My big mistake was not having adequate malpractice insurance. I cancelled it because I'd never had a claim, and it was getting way too expensive. So, my biggest loss was from a client suing me. My attorney thinks he purposefully came to me with the plan to sue for money to rid himself of debts. This has been devastating to me both financially and emotionally. I haven't slept well in weeks."

"That's terrible," said Diana. "Some people have no conscience about hurting others for their own gain."

Allison agreed. "That's for sure. I have to watch my pennies now too. My husband just got notice of a pending lay-off. I'm trying not to think about it until it happens. "

Hannah muttered almost imperceptively, "Denial is a powerful defense."

Mona looked over at Brittany with a sneer. "You must still be doing well. You're dressed in your usual expensive and high fashioned clothes that we all envy."

Brittany giggled. "I'm lucky. I get these clothes at a huge discount because of where I work." She hesitated and her demeanor changed. "Unfortunately, my job isn't secure either. Fewer people are shopping and buying expensive clothes from our department. I hope they don't lay me off too. My boyfriend depends on me for support. If I lose my job, I lose Charley. I guess I should be as worried as you gals." Another giggle.

Candace put her hand on her hip, and glared at Brittany. "Why do you let that bum live with you? He's taking advantage of you. Kick him out if he doesn't get a job."

Brittany was quick to defend her man. "It's not that he sits around all day doing nothing. He reads a lot of philosophy books. Did you know that the central message of Buddhism is *Every man for himself*? He's trying to make me stronger and not let people take advantage of me."

The women all looked down, trying to hide their wry smiles.

"Yup! He sounds like a real winner," said Candace.

"I love him, and he makes me feel good about myself."

Candace rolled her eyes again. "You could love a dog just as well, and it wouldn't cost you as much."

"Nothing could take the place of a guy you love," laughed Brittany.

"Maybe so, Bee Bee. But what's so damned funny about that?" asked Candace. "Don't answer. Apparently everything is a big joke to you." The smile came off Brittany's face, and she became silent.

Allison looked at Diana who still appeared depressed. "Did you come out okay financially with your divorce settlement?"

Diana began to tear again. "Are you kidding? I'm struggling. My ex is way behind on child support. I didn't even have the money to buy the book for this month's reading. The library didn't get a copy for me until two days ago." She pulled out a tissue and wiped her eyes.

Brittany broke her silence, and with her mask-like smile asked, "Have you tried to get a job?"

"Even if it were easy to find work, do you know how expensive child care is these days? I wouldn't even break even."

Hannah sighed. "It looks like we're all having money problems. No wonder everyone seems down today."

"We're as down as the Dow Jones," said Mona.

Candace rose slightly from her chair and put her hand over her heart. With much drama she belted out her own words from *The Music Man*:

Oh, we got troubles.
Right here in New York City.
With a capital T and that rhymes with P
and that stands for...poor! ...or pathetic.
Oh yes friends, we got troubles.

That brought smiles from the group. "Laugh and the world laughs with you," said Candace.

Brittany looked puzzled. "I don't understand."

"It's like we all have our Goliaths to conquer, and when we do, we become stronger and can laugh again."

"I still don't understand."

"Don't you know the story of David and Goliath from the Bible?" asked Allison.

" Oh, yeah. But what does that have to do with us?"

Candace shook her head. "Nothing at all, Brittany. Nothing at all."

Candace started her song again...*Oh, we got troubles. Right here in New York City*...She stopped and straightened up. "Hey gals. If we don't pull ourselves out of the doldrums, this book club isn't going to survive. It's going to become an economically depressed support group!"

"Well, let's face it. We're in the same economic crisis as is the whole country," said Hannah.

"Some people still seem to be doing well," said Allison. "I don't know how they're doing it."

Mona sat up straighter. "They've probably stashed away supplies and money for a rainy day, like we should have been doing."

"Or they're involved with a product or service that everyone yearns for and can't resist buying. Look at cigarettes. People always find a way to buy them even if they can't pay the rent," said Hannah.

Mona continued to harbor a spirit of gloom. "We just didn't prepare for these times."

With her inappropriate smile, Brittany said, "If only we could invent a product that would make us rich quick."

"If only..." repeated Allison.

The rest of the group chimed in. "If only!"

"Easier said than done," said Hannah.

Candace pounded her fist on the table. "That's what losers say! Sitting around crying about our problems doesn't solve anything. We need to act."

"You're the expert at acting. Show us how," said Mona.

Candace frowned at Mona. "Sarcasm is another tool of a loser." Candace's excitement caused her to knock over her water glass that spilled onto her library book. "Oh, sh…ugar!" she yelled out, modifying her language when she saw children at a nearby table staring at her. The group continued their conversation as they ignored Candace blotting up the spill.

Hannah sat up straight. "Hey gals. If we want to work together on this problem, we need to behave as a team. Now, we're all smart women. If others have found ways to make money, we should be able to put our heads together and do it too."

Brittany blurted out, "We could become a lottery club. That would increase our chances of winning big." Everyone grunted at her suggestion, and Hannah added, "The chance of any win in a lottery is less than finding a needle in a haystack."

"That bum outside looks like he's raking it in. He's still hopping around and collecting money for his performance. Furthermore he looks happy," said Allison.

Hannah smiled. "My mother used to say, 'When ignorance is bliss, tis folly to be wise'."

Brittany looked impressed. "That's something to think about. I think I'll tell Charley that one and see what he says."

"Please let us know his reaction," Candace scoffed.

"As far as people getting rich quick, the first thing that comes to my mind is people who created fads and made it big. Do you remember the guy who invented pet rocks? I heard that he didn't even think he'd make much money on that idea, but he very quickly became a multimillionaire."

"Actually, I bought one myself, and I love it," said Brittany.

"Somehow I'm not surprised." Candace gave her a smug look. "Hannah does bring up a good consideration though. Many unusual fads have made millions for their creators."

Brittany became more animated. "We could do something similar to the pet rock…like paint faces on the rocks and label them as children. Childless couples could talk to them as they would their own." No one commented.

Candace moved nervously around in her chair. "Moving right along... I was just thinking of the movie *Ghost Busters*. Remember that one? I read an article that said about half of the people in the

United States believes in ghosts, and some are really afraid of them. Maybe we could create a ghost buster agency."

"Interesting thought, but I think it would be complicated to develop and probably not lucrative," said Allison.

Candace tensed. "Well, if you have a better idea, let's hear it."

Diana quietly said, "An idea just came to me that I think could work —it involves a different kind of cleaning service."

"Ugh! That sounds too much like housework. I avoid that whenever possible. That's what killed my mother, you know," Candace said with a grimace.

"Cut the crap, Candace. Let Diana finish," said Allison.

"Well, I saw a program on television where some women developed a business for crime scene cleanups. Apparently there's a real need for that service. As you know, the scenes can be pretty gruesome. A lot of people have a hard time dealing with cleaning up blood and all that stuff. But, I think we could get used to it and make good money. Also, we wouldn't have to invest a lot of upfront money to start it."

Allison had an expression of horror on her face as this idea was presented. "That sounds gross. I couldn't work in a place where someone had just been murdered or raped. We'd find ourselves cleaning up not only the blood and gore but my vomit too!"

"Yuk!" commented Brittany.

"Like I said, we could get used to it and soon take it in stride," said Diana. "That's what doctors have to do."

Hannah frowned. "It also sounds like hard, dirty work. Would we really be happy with such a career?"

"If we made money, we'd be happy," said Mona. The others laughed.

Candace abruptly dismissed the suggestion. "Any other ideas?"

Diana hung her head and forced a smile while trying to conceal her disappointment for the general lack of interest for her suggestion.

Candace proposed starting a fine arts studio for children. Many objections were voiced. With an angry tone, Candace said, "Oh, forget it! You guys think of something better. I give up. Maybe I should just go it alone." Again her overly dramatic gestures caused her hand to knock over a large saltshaker spilling its contents onto the table.

"Quick! Toss some salt over your left shoulder or you'll have bad luck," blurted out Brittany.

"F you!" responded Candace.

Allison grimaced. "Candace, you really should enlarge your vocabulary. You're overusing four letter words."

"Would a six letter word like *stupid* be better?"

"A slight improvement, but still limited."

After a moment of silence, Candace turned to Mona. "Have you come up with any ideas?"

"I was thinking we might offer massages in public places, like airports or even in Times Square. There are a lot of tense people there who would enjoy a relaxing massage. Also, it would help us release our frustrations with heavy poundings on those flabby people who need to be shaken up…and we'd be paid for doing it!"

Allison grimaced. "The thought of touching a bunch of sweaty and smelly bodies makes me want to puke. Count me out!"

Candace tensed and sarcastically said, "Why don't we just hold out canisters with signs saying *Help the Poor*!"

"Even though I've heard that's profitable, our *friend* outside being an example, I don't think any of us would be willing to lower ourselves to that," said Hannah.

Other ideas were thrown out such as making and selling unique jewelry, presenting improvement seminars for women, and operating playgrounds for young children.

"I guess there's no easy answer," said Allison.

Brittany had been staring out the window. The sight of an imposing Mercedes sports car pulling into the adjacent parking lot broke her thoughts. "Now there's someone who must have found a way to be rich," she laughed. As the man stepped out of his car, she said, "I'd recognize an Armani suit anywhere." The others looked out.

"He's obviously well to do," said Hannah. "He probably works in the stock market."

Allison's jaw suddenly dropped. "Is he wearing a clerical collar?"

"Well, I'll be…" said Candace.

"I thought preachers sacrificed material possessions and became poor," said Diana.

"This one doesn't look like he's suffering from any sacrifices," said Mona.

Hannah smiled as she said, "I once heard that an easy way to become rich fast was to start a church."

Mona looked skeptical. "That's hard to believe. Where did you hear that?"

"There were some claims that Scientology was founded on a get rich quick proposal. I understand that they've done quite well financially."

"Apparently people are anxious to generously give money if they think they'll get a great eternal reward for doing so," said Hannah.

Candace's eyes widened. "Also, aren't there are lots of tax benefits that further increase income?"

The others were quiet as they watched the preacher walk briskly with his head held high.

"He doesn't seem concerned about the rain getting those expensive Italian shoes wet," giggled Brittany.

Mona scowled. "He probably runs one of those crooked revivals where the leaders go around with microphones and hidden hearing devices and deceive poor people out of all their money?"

"I don't think it takes those extremes to become rich in the church. I suspect that the preachers just give people what they emotionally need and the people are happy to pay for it," said Hannah.

Candace sat more erect and almost rose out of her chair with a burst of excitement and flailing arms. This time she hit the back of Mona's head. Mona pulled back in defense. Hannah quickly intervened. "Listen, we should think about this more carefully. We might have the perfect solution. We were just considering what most people want or need. A church would provide for all those needs. Furthermore, in this time of economic depression, people especially turn to religion for hope and blessings."

Allison became more animated and spoke rapidly. "We have Candace here who could provide quality entertainment during the services. Hannah has been trained to offer support or therapy in times of crisis. Mona could relieve people from physical pain. All in all, we have a ready made team all set to help and offer hope to others for a better life…you know—all that good stuff."

Brittany added, " And people are happy to give to a cause. I myself have felt those warm fuzzies when I drop a few coins into the kettle of the Salvation Army at Christmas time. That feeling is worth the price of the donation if not lots more." She laughed.

Diana slouched as she quietly said, "And then there's me. As usual, I would have nothing to offer such a business."

"Hey. It takes a good organizer to run a well oiled home. This project would need the best of organizers, and that's you," said Hannah. "That's your gift."

"Wait just a minute," said Mona. "We're not qualified to form and operate a church. Ministers have years of formal training."

Candace was quick to object. "Maybe that's true for some churches, but not all. Even training can't change boring personalities and limited thinking. I know we're smarter than the average preacher, and besides, we have interesting personalities."

Mona sat with her arms folded, and a defiant look. "Well, I say you can't do it."

"I love to hear those words. I can't resist a challenge. Do you remember that old song about the ant?" Candace, knowing that a song would be really annoying to Mona, stood behind Mona with her arms about her and loudly sang about the ant determined to move a rubber tree plant. "Everyone knows an ant can't…"

"Stop! You're hurting my ears. Please have mercy on us all and stop," said Mona.

Candace wasn't one to easily give in, and she continued while Mona put her head on the table and covered her ears. The others couldn't help but laugh and joined Candace in the chorus… "But he's got high hopes…" and finally… "Whoops, there goes another rubber tree plant!"

As if to further aggravate Mona, Candace smiled at her. "And so, Mona, you need more high hopes!"

"And you need to put a lid on it," Mona said as she continued to scowl.

Candace laughed and turned to the others. "How about the rest of you. Are you ready to hope along with me?"

It was mutually agreed that they should all attend a church the next Sunday to formulate ideas. The hour ended and the book selection for the month was never discussed. As the group was leaving, Candace offered more encouragement. "Remember the words of President Kennedy: *Life is either a daring adventure or nothing.*"

Hannah shook her head. "No. It was Helen Keller who said that".

"It sounds more like something Frank Sinatra would say," said Brittany.

"It doesn't matter who said it. But if there is a God, I don't think he'll like this idea for an adventure," said Allison.

~ 2 ~
Leaving the Café

Allison's husband, Fred, was waiting for her outside of the café. He was leaning against a signpost with his shoulders slumped and his head hanging low.

"Fred, what are you doing here? What's wrong?"

"They laid me off today. There wasn't enough work to keep us all busy. I don't know what to do." His upper lip quivered.

Allison put her arms around him. "We'll find a way to work things out. Maybe we can both flip burgers for awhile until something better comes along."

"That might keep us from starving, but that's about all."

"We were just talking in the book club about all of our financial problems. We tried to think of get rich quick schemes to help us all."

Fred gave a disconcerting huff. "Just like everyone else in this country is trying to do." He hesitated briefly and then quietly asked, "Did anyone in your group have any brilliant idea?"

"We tossed around several ideas. The one that got the group most excited was to start a new church."

"That's the funniest thing I've heard all day. That's one crazy group you belong to."

"Don't be so quick to dismiss it. It just might be the answer."

"I don't see how. What about that Great American Novel you've been writing for several months. Isn't that more likely to bring us in money?"

"That's nowhere near completion, and the publication process is a lengthy one. It's getting hard to even find an agent to accept manuscripts now."

Fred grunted. "Start a new church? I must admit the idea is a creative one. I can't imagine how it could be done quickly enough to help us now."

"Maybe you underestimate the power of the women in my crazy book club as you call them."

Allison comforted Fred with her arm around him. "By the way, we decided to all attend a church this weekend to get a better idea of what would be involved. Will you come with me?"

As they walked away, Fred weakly smiled and said, "I suppose, but while your group thinks about it, let's go to the grocery store and stock up on rice and beans."

"Card declined!" the cashier called out as Diana stood in the checkout line at the grocery store. She could feel the heat of a blush on her face, and fought to hold back tears. She glanced back at the long line behind her, and hoped no one from her book club was there who saw her.

"I might have cash to pay for some of it," she whispered to the cashier. She searched desperately throughout her purse, and pulled out a few small bills and a handful of coins. Her nervousness caused her to fumble, and the coins flew out of her hands and scattered widely over the counter and floor. The disgruntled sighs from those waiting their turns were obvious. She knelt on her hands and knees to retrieve the money while wiping the tears that trickled down her face.

After leaving the market, she thought, *Soon I'm not going to have enough money to feed my kids. I need to work hard and quickly to support the plan to start a new church.*

* * *

Diana decided to attend a late morning Sunday service. She recalled as a child getting dressed for church in her finery complete with a hat, and so she adorned herself.

Travel took longer than expected. She arrived at church only minutes before the start of the service. An usher welcomed her and started to lead her down the aisle to a seat.

"I'll sit in the back," she told him. "I'm here just to observe."

"The back rows are all filled. There are lots of empty seats in the front where you can see better." Without waiting for a response, he led her down the aisle.

The parishioners seemed unnaturally quiet as they waited for the service to begin. Unaccustomed to high heels, she walked unsteadily, her shoes sounding loudly against the tile floor while her ankles fought to keep from turning as she followed the usher. To add to her discomfort, she glanced at the congregation as she passed. She saw no one wearing a hat except for some teenagers who wore baseball caps. Only a rare man wore a suit, and most of the women were in slacks.

"There! You can have this pew all to yourself." She felt that all eyes were upon her as she sat alone. She took a notebook and pen from her purse.

I'm here to see how a normal church operates, Diana told herself to help get her mind off the anxiety she was experiencing. She looked around and noted the stained glass windows providing a reverence accompanied by quiet organ music. Within a minute, the organist started the opening hymn. She heard some commotion but ignored it. Midway through, Diana was still searching for a hymnal when she glanced around and noted she was the only one still seated. She quickly stood. After the music ended, a minister came forward and said, "Let us close our eyes and pray." The prayer was lengthy and Diana grew tired of standing. She opened her eyes and discovered all those behind her were seated or kneeling. She tried to quietly sit. And so it went through much of the service: her timing for standing, sitting and kneeling was out of sync with the others.

After the opening rituals, a lanky man in jeans and with several tattoos on his arms, moved to her side. She was aware of him staring at her. When she glanced at him, her attention focused on the long toothpick dangling from his mouth that he rhythmically moved from side to side to the beat of the music. She tried to subtly move farther from him.

The pastor officially welcomed everyone and suggested they all greet their nearby neighbors with a handshake. The man next to her eagerly grabbed her hand. "Hi lovely lady. I'm Jimmy. I don't think I've seen you here before."

"Hi. I'm here just to observe," she said.

"Well, look into my eyes and tell me what you observe."

She gave him a weak smile. He continued to firmly hold her hand until the pastor spoke again.

Throughout the service, Jimmy stared at her while moving his toothpick from side to side with his tongue. When the sermon began, he moved closer to her. Within a few minutes, there was a loud snore from a few rows back. Her overly friendly neighbor used that as an opportunity to make contact by tapping her on the arm as he laughed. To her chagrin, he suddenly leaned back and put his arm around the back of the pew where she was sitting.

She kept trying to inch her way from him, but when the gap became obvious, he leaned towards her and made some comment. Then his arm actually moved around her shoulder. This surprised her and she let out a loud gasp. The preacher looked directly at her, thinking she had just reacted to what he had said. He commented, "Yes. That certainly was a shocking thing for the prophet to experience." He saw that she was taking notes and believed it to be from pearls in his sermon. He frequently looked to her for further feedback. Jimmy was aware of the preacher's focus and eased away only to return when the sermon ended.

To break contact with her neighbor, she feigned a cough and leaned forward to open her purse for a tissue. She tried to keep her head down for as long as possible, and then took the opportunity to slide farther away. He moved with her.

The offertory was announced. Diana had forgotten about that. She opened her purse and couldn't find any bills—only small coins.

When the plate reached her, her few coins fell onto the plate with loud clangs. Her blush intensified.

When the service ended, her would-be friend became more brazen. He put his arm around her waist, and offered to walk her home so they could discuss the Good Book together.

"If you'll excuse me, I need to use the restroom," she said.

"I could use a break there myself," he responded.

She kept the door to the ladies room slightly open and watched him enter the men's room. She hurried out of the church and hid behind a delivery truck until she saw him leave the building scratching his head.

~ 3 ~
Visits to the Past and Present

Candace frowned as she entered the café.

"What's wrong, Candace?" asked Diana.

"I just had a run-in with a cop on a horse. He led the dumb animal into a big mud puddle and drenched my clean slacks and shoes with mud. I was mad and I yelled a few minor swear words at him."

"You did?" said Diana in disbelief.

"Yes. He yelled back that I should have respect for his uniform. I told him that I did, but it was him personally that I was yelling at." She laughed. "He merely trotted away."

"I'm surprised he didn't give you a citation," said Hannah.

"He should have given me an award certificate for not being subject to his stupidity!" Candace glanced around the table and then said, "There, Allison. What did you think of my nine letter word?"

Allison smiled. "You're getting there."

Candace smirked and then said, "Where's Mona? It's not like her to be late. We have a lot to discuss today."

Hannah frowned. "Mona called me after our last meeting. She thought that starting a new church was a ridiculous idea and doomed to fail. She added that she wasn't coming to any more of our meetings."

"I'm not surprised. Talk about negativity! We don't need that. I say good riddance!" There was a brief silence and then Candace continued. "Mona sure was a downer! But we could have used her for healing services... if we get to that. I hope none of you share Mona's doubts?" The others shook their heads.

Candace's demeanor then brightened. "Hey, did everyone go to church on Sunday?" The women nodded, but no one spoke up. Candace looked at them. "Well? If no one wants to start, I will." She sat up straight and had a sly grin on her face and then started to laugh. "I was just thinking of going to church once when I was little. My grandmother took me there. That was the first and last time. She told me that she couldn't keep me quiet. The more she tried, the louder I became. Finally, my screaming forced her to pick me up with my arms and legs flailing. She hurried me out. She was so embarrassed that she didn't return to church for months."

"That sounds like the Candace we know," said Hannah.

A challenging look appeared on Candace's face. "What do you mean?"

"Just a friendly comment. You're always full of energy."

After an awkward moment of silence, Candace appeared to relax, and she said, "May I continue?"

"Please do! Your comments are always appreciated, Candace," said Allison.

Candace appeared skeptical but continued. "Well, the church I went to seemed like a joke. The members participated but almost reluctantly. They recited responses that were printed in a book. Even the prayers were printed out. Repetition! Repetition! Repetition! Is that how people usually pray?"

"Not in the church I attended," said Hannah.

Candace ignored Hannah and continued. "And the minister—what an uptight piece of work." She looked at Allison. "I hope you appreciate that four letter word. I was going to use a three letter word but thought you wouldn't like it."

"Thank you, Candace."

Candace continued. "And the hymns sounded more like funeral songs to me. I just couldn't hold back. I put some spirit into that service, let me tell you! I changed those dirges into belted out hymns. That woke up a few people!"

The women looked at each other in silence. They smiled as they visualized the scene.

"My experience was in sharp contrast to yours," said Hannah. I really enjoyed the church I visited. There was a lot of backslapping, wide grins, and loud welcoming. Everyone seemed comfortable and happy to be there. There was a dynamic choir dressed in magenta robes and singing gospel music with gusto. The only problem I saw was that the people looked so poor. They were happy but didn't look like they had much to put in the collection plates."

"So, we have to use similar tactics that will draw a wealthier clientele," said Candace without emotion.

"Can we put that another way? Like, how can we involve all classes of people to be blessed?" said Hannah.

Candace answered, "Call it what you'd like. We just need to pay our bills and perhaps have some extra for recreational activities."

Hannah continued. "And the sermon was anything but boring. In contrast to the poor people in the congregation, a man dressed in what appeared to be an expensive suit, gave the sermon. He had a prominent gold watch and rings. He reminded me of the man we saw outside the café wearing the clerical collar."

"Just as we suspected!" said Candace.

Hannah talked rapidly as she continued. "The preacher roused the audience with his dynamic words. With almost all declarations, his words inspired someone to yell out, 'Amen' or 'That's right.' I almost did so myself."

"Halleluiah!" yelled out Candace as she slapped her knee.

"Exactly," laughed Hannah. "There was a lot of moving about and clapping by choir members as they sang hymns. The congregation joined in with swaying—almost dancing in place. Everyone let themselves go. It looked like a good place and time to release inhibitions and stress. I can see why people like to go there. And by the way, I didn't see any empty seats there."

"That's what we want to see," said Candace. "That's our model!" She turned towards Diana who had been quietly listening to the others.

Diana's voice was so soft it was almost a whisper as she began. Candace soon blurted out, "Speak up, girl. We want to hear what you experienced."

Diana blushed but began again. "I don't want to talk about it. It was a total disaster."

"Nothing exciting to report, huh?"

"I wouldn't say that. Disaster is my only word to summarize it. I don't want to relive it by talking about it."

Allison intervened with her experience. "I went to a church that brought back a lot of bad childhood memories. I was forced to go to church with my family. Sunday morning was the worst time of my week. Everyone was mad at each other, as we got ready. We had to share a single bathroom. I remember so clearly hearing my family bang loudly on the bathroom door telling me I was taking too long and to get out of there. And then when I got to church I was bored to tears—same thing last Sunday. I became so restless I could have screamed. But, one plus for me was that it used to offer the opportunity to meet and talk to nice single guys that went there. You know how a good man is hard to find. Church increases the odds of finding one. That's how I met Fred."

"I don't belong to any church," said Brittany. "My family is Jewish, but we never went to Synagogue. It was a real eye-opener for me to go to a regular church Sunday."

"Where did you go?" asked Candace.

"I went to the biggest church I could find." She laughed.

"What's so blasted funny about that?" said Candace.

"Everything in it was funny. I didn't understand most of what was happening, but the costumes were interesting. The ministers or priests, or whatever you call them, were dressed in long black robes with white overtops. They were sort of an A-line style, gathered at the yoke and with tight pleats extending over the shoulders forming three-quarter length sleeves The guy who appeared to be the chief wore a funny hat that looked a bit like a dunce hat, but it had fine embroidery on it. His scarf had pretty embroidery too. I was thinking that the seamstresses where I work could improve on the design for us—maybe making the gown shorter, pinched at the waist, and with a lower neckline. Forget the hats though!" She giggled again. "Although hats I suppose could be optional. In many churches the women wear hats or some head covering, don't they. Why not women preachers also?"

Candace stared at her with a grimace. "I'm not sure that costumes will be the enticing feature that draws attendance. We'll give it thought though, Brittany."

Candace became more excited with the idea of starting a profitable church. "Well, I think we could create a church that everyone would really enjoy—one that would be not only interesting but inspiring, uplifting, and fun."

"Fun?" said Allison. "I've never thought of attending a church as a fun experience. In fact, I've heard some people refer to it as a duty—a sacrifice to give to their creator."

"Well why couldn't it be fun? Do you really think our creator, if there is one, wants a bunch of long faced people sacrificing to him? I'll bet he would prefer happy people having fun while they attend church and think about him."

"That makes sense," said Diana.

Allison leaned forward and wrinkled her brow. "We're putting a lot of emphasis on fun, but I suspect there's a lot of hard work preparing for services. First of all, I think we'd need a special angle to attract people to attend."

"That would be easy," said Candace. "In this age of enlightenment, we could start a nudist church. We could advertise that it was for special praise to our creator for the beautiful bodies he endowed us with." She stood, held her head high, chest forward, and with exaggerated hip movements and swinging arms she paraded herself around the table.

"Candace, you are absolutely bonkers. If you're serious, you can proceed alone," said Diana.

"And I think you are probably one of the few in this society that would qualify as having a beautiful body," offered Hannah.

"Anyone can get a body like mine if you're willing to pay for it," laughed Candace.

"None of us could afford that even if we wanted to," said Allison.

"Okay. Okay. That was far out. "Our talents would speak for themselves."

"That's easy for you to say."

"Well, I know we can make it all work. First of all, we would be an attraction for the 25 million tourists that come to New York City every year. Most of them hover around Times Square just looking for entertainment. There's not much to do on Sunday mornings. Second, we have a big advantage because about half of the United States population doesn't belong to a church. They have no allegiance to any religion, so they're ripe for us."

"You mean we're going to form the Church of the Unbelievers?" commented Hannah.

"I don't know what our church will be yet. Rich is my only goal," said Candace.

Candace was too restless to sit. She started pacing around the table as she spoke. "If we're within walking distance to Times Square, we could become listed as a must see attraction for visitors. And the streets around there are always crowded—a captive audience for us, so to speak, especially when there are no competing shows on Sunday mornings." She glanced at Hannah who was grinning. "What's so amusing?"

"I was just thinking that the *Naked Cowboy* might give us serious competition." Everyone laughed. Candace replied, "His attraction lasts for only a visual moment. Ours will be long lasting! ...Well, at least for an hour."

"How can we start a church when none of us is a minister?" Brittany asked.

"We can just wing it," said Candace as she moved about in her chair barely able to conceal her excitement. Her animation caused Allison to frequently back away to avoid being hit by Candace's flailing arms. "I could finally become a star on stage! And the rest of you could get your own recognitions."

"Thanks a lot Candace," said Allison sarcastically.

"You know what I meant."

"Yes, Candace. We do! And we always should keep in mind the good we would be doing by giving people what they want and need."

Hannah said, "Let's not deceive ourselves. Let's admit it: Doing good for others is hardly our main goal."

Candace grunted. She then commented, "One positive thing is offerings would be strictly voluntary. The services received would cost people far less than those from a professional counselor or entertainer."

"The big question we haven't considered is where we could hold the services," said Allison.

"I'm ahead of you. I have a plan that I'll tell you about later," replied Candace.

~ 4 ~
Planning for the Fun of it

"Look what I have here!" Allison said with excitement as she hurried into the café.

Candace interrupted her. "You're late! We were beginning to wonder if you too didn't like the idea of starting a new church and had given up the ghost."

"No. No. That wasn't it. I'm sorry I didn't call. I went with my husband to file for unemployment benefits. But look what I have." She proudly waved a gold embossed certificate in front of them. "From now on, please refer to me as *The Reverend Doctor Miller*!" The others reached for it in disbelief. But it looked official, verifying her as an ordained preacher.

"How did you get that, and how much did it cost?" asked Candace.

"I just had to fill out my name and address on an Internet site. Certification was immediate and free. But to get the printed certificate, it cost me five dollars." She laughed as she said, "What a rip off!"

The others laughed with her. Candace moved excitedly around in her chair. "I just can't believe it's that easy. Does that mean you can get all those tax deductable benefits now, and can perform all kinds of ceremonies and be legit?"

"Yes it does! The Internet also makes accessories easily available—but at a small cost. You can get official name badges, priestly robes, brochures on how to perform various rites, sermons on various topics, et cetera."

"Unbelievable! I had no idea it was that easy. Good work, Allison. Tell us the site we should go to. I think we should all be ordained," said Candace.

Allison smiled broadly. "I'm happy to share. This really is starting to be fun."

Candace stood up abruptly. "That's what it's all about. Fun while making money! So, let's move forward. Is everyone in agreement?"

The women were excited and each gave Candace a high five sign. They talked rapidly and at the same time as they applauded the proposal.

Hannah tried to quiet them since the nearby patrons appeared disturbed by the loudness.

"I'm opposed to a formal and strict format with repetitive prayers and regimens," said Allison. "That becomes old fast. I'd like to see variety in our performances."

"Performances? Are we putting on a show?" asked Brittany.

"You'd better believe it," Candace said. "Our aim should be to put on *The Greatest Show on Earth*! Our show should be so great that it would even draw hard-core atheists to attendance. Those attending should see it as a happy and emotionally stirring thing to be there."

"Candace is the only one of us that I think could put on such a great show," said Diana. "I still wonder how I'll fit into all of this. And what role can I play? I can't carry a tune, and I'm not socially outgoing."

Hannah frowned at Diana. "You've got to stop being so negative and self-degrading."

"I'm only being realistic," she responded.

"Not true! We need to help you with your self esteem issues," said Hannah.

With an upbeat voice, Candace said, "You'd make the perfect person to hear confessions! You'd just have to sit there and listen…and enjoy all the juicy dirt. What could be more fun than that?"

"Maybe." Diana looked at Candace and said, "I wish I could belt out those hymns and move people into a frenzy, like you do."

"All of us envy Candace's talents," said Hannah. "But, people need more than entertainment from a church. Some people just need human contact, and some have no other place to find social outlets, like me."

"Is one hour on Sunday enough to satisfy that?" asked Allison.

"We can plan other get-togethers later…all with admission charges of course."

Allison frowned. "But what about the people who come because of feelings of guilt and are there to suffer and feel a relief from that guilt?"

"Some religions punish by making the sinners say lots of prayers."

"We might try something more effective for the masochists," said Hannah. "How about making them eat spoonfuls of Habanera peppers?" Even Diana saw the humor in that.

"I'm surprised at you, Hannah," said Allison in jest.

"Next thing we'll hear from her is to put toothpicks under their fingernails, and make them pay for it on top of it!" said Candace.

"Let's get serious," said Hannah. "We could have sensible confessional sessions that we would rename—something like *counseling*. When someone confesses a sin, we'll ensure that they'll feel punished and forgiven by paying for that sin. We could print a poster with suggested donations for each sin's forgiveness. The greater the sin, the greater the suggested donation—maybe ten dollars for telling a lie, fifty for stealing, five hundred for adultery."

"Let's hear it for adultery!" laughed Allison.

Candace slapped her knee as she yelled out, "Yeah! Yeah!"

Allison mentioned that officiating at special ceremonies shouldn't be difficult. They could either buy the Internet brochures or copy from some printed established church rites. Generous fees for the rites would of course be expected.

"Hey, wait a minute. Candace, have you done anything about finding a place for us to hold the services?"

"I know the owner of an off-Broadway theatre. It's never in use on Sunday mornings and frequently not in use for weeks at a time. I plan to talk to the owner. Hopefully he'll let us use the building as a tax deductable charity for him."

"Candace, you were just born to be in business. *Nobody does it better*," Allison sang.

"Hey, your voice isn't half bad," said Candace. "We'll be able to use you! And Diana, you graduated as an interior designer. We could use your artistic talents to design handouts advertising our program. You know—like something including *Sunday morning Broadway church services conducted by talented preachers who are known for their roles in popular Broadway shows*."

"None of us have been in Broadway shows," said Diana.

"Didn't I ever tell you that I was a chorus dancer and singer in a Broadway show? Unfortunately, it only ran for a week, but I appeared in it," said Candace.

"Hmmm," was the group response.

"Allison, you're a writer. We need some prayers composed that would have universal appeal. They could be memorized and not just read by rote like some dull prayers."

"I suppose I could do that," Allison volunteered.

Candace had been thinking ahead and continued with her mental list of needs.

"We also need designer collection plates—expensive looking plates that would cry out for generous contributions."

Brittany volunteered for that. "I know fashion and everything associated. I could design the plates, and I have contacts that could produce them. I want to take part in the ceremonies too. I want to be the one who does weddings and funerals. They seem like fun."

"We'll see Brittany," Candace said to appease her for the moment.

"Do you think we need at least one man in our group? There are still people who believe it's the men who have the special calling to preach. And a good-looking man on stage might be a draw for love-starved females," said Hannah.

"True! True!" said Allison. "And there are even more women who are attracted to the bad boy image. I wonder if we could find a physical hunk who projects inner piousness while also giving off that come hither look. If he just sat on the stage with us, he probably wouldn't need to say much. Or we could have him participate with a simple prayer."

"He could serve an even more important function—giving hugs as people leave the church," offered Brittany.

"That's the first good idea I've heard from you," said Candace. Brittany frowned as Candace continued. "People thirst for hugs. Our church might be the only place some people can get the contact. And teenaged girls! A hunk would be a real draw for them."

"Not only would women enjoy hugs from a man, but I think men would like hugs from us gals too," said Allison.

"I agree," said Candace. "We might become known as *The Church of Hugs*."

Allison leaned forward with excitement. "Hey, we could keep track of how many hugs we give, and advertize it like fast food places." She held her hand up as if towards a billboard. "*Two billion hugs given*! *Come in and help us reach three billion*!" The group then burst into laughter.

"I've seen people on Times Square with signs saying *Free Hugs*. I've never seen anyone approaching them for hugs," said Diana.

"Getting a hug from a disheveled street person is quite different from a hug by respectable clergy!" said Allison.

"Seriously girls, we need to come up with an enticing name for our church—something unique that makes it stand out from conventional churches," said Hannah.

"How about the Church of Saint Aphrodite," suggested Brittany.

Candace laughed. "Better yet, The Church of Saint Aphrodesiac!"

Hannah didn't appear amused. "No, no! In any case we can't use the name Saint. People would just interpret it as another branch of the Catholic Church."

"Okay. Let's shorten it to Aphrodesiac Church."

"We're wasting time," said Hannah. "Get serious."

After a brief pause, the group started throwing out other ideas, but there were objections to each suggestion and no consensus.

Hannah finally said, "Let's just take a temporary name for now and move on with plans." She recommended the name *Heaven on Hold Church.* "That would be certain to attract curiosity."

The other members accepted it as a temporary moniker.

Diana sat with her head down in contemplation.

"What are you thinking, Diana? You look concerned," said Hannah.

"I'm just wondering if we could really pull this off. It sounds like it might get big."

"Let's hope it does get big," said Allison. "And if it becomes too big for us to handle, we can call for volunteers to help. Most religions stress service as a step towards pleasing their creator. It shouldn't be hard to get people to usher, tend a nursery, prepare coffee and donuts for the after service socializing. Incidentally, those treats would be tax deductable and of course generous donations would be suggested for them."

"That's right," said Candace. "The bigger, the better. Let's get started on specifics. I think we should make two weeks from now as our goal for opening day."

That suggestion hit the group with a jolt.

"Two weeks! How can we ever do that?"

"Wow. Just making an outline sounds like a two week job."

"Not possible!"

Allison spoke up with a sense of urgency. "Hey gang. I'm with Candace. Let's give it a try. I say let's get going on this. My mortgage payment is due in 16 days."

Diana added, "And I need money to feed my kids now."

~ 5 ~
Place of Worship?

Candace had her convincing ways. She arranged for a meeting with Marc, the wealthy owner of an off-Broadway theatre.

"Hi, Can-Can," he said as he greeted her with a hug. "Long time no see. I've missed you, Babe."

Candace smiled broadly. "How'd you like to see more of me?"

"Anytime. Anyplace."

Candace shared with him the plan of starting a new church. "We need a place to hold our Sunday services. I thought of your theatre when it's not in use."

"What? You leading church services?" He started to laugh. "Gimme a break. Tell me, have you ever been inside a church?"

"Come on, Marc. I'm serious. You must agree that New York needs more religious direction? The five of us ladies want to provide that."

"Ladies? This I've got to see. I'm sure you'd light up the stage, or should I say pulpit—just like you light up me! Still, you'd have to give your best performance ever to pull it off. That's for sure."

Candace ignored his comment. "There would be tax advantages to you for donating use of the building for church services on Sunday mornings. Besides, the Lord loveth a cheerful giver," she said, recalling one of the few words from scripture she had heard as a child.

Marc studied her expression and realized that she was sincere. "Well, there's a lot for me to consider. First of all, the woman who sold the theatre to me was a devout Christian. She put a legal clause in the sale that no shows could be performed on Sundays."

"I hardly think that a church service would be considered a show," said Candace.

Marc laughed. "Well, that's technically true, but we both know you and what your performance would be considered. But, it might work. I'd have to clear that with my attorney." He looked at her again with suspicion. "A church service verses a show. Hmm. Is there really a distinct difference?"

Candace put her hands on her hips. "Marc. Gimme a break."

He paused and then said, "What about cleanup after the services? Who would do that?"

"We'd stay after and do that."

"Also, I'd need to charge you something for utilities."

"Of course. I'm sure we can scrape up enough to pay for those."

Marc was silent for a few moments. "Hmm. Are you sure you know what you're getting yourself into?"

"I can only imagine, but I think it'll be fun while doing something worthwhile for the city."

"And worthwhile for your purse?"

Candace looked away, and then said, "Come on, Marc. It would mean so much to us."

"I'd need more than tax advantages for such a favor." He looked directly into her eyes and asked, "Just how much would you personally be willing to give for such a favor?"

Candace smiled knowingly.

"Weren't you recently married, Marc?"

"What does that have to do with business deals?"

This wasn't the first time Candace had exchanged favors. That was how she got her brief appearance on the Broadway stage, and Marc knew it. For Candace, it seemed like a fair trade. She looked at him intently. "I can give you what you want."

Marc smiled. "I'd like the down-payment now, Can Can."

"Marc, you know I don't like you to call me Can Can. I feel like a bathroom fixture. If you want to use a nickname, how about Candy?"

"Ha! Candy is dandy but liquor is quicker. But I guess in your case, liquor is dandy and Candy is quicker!"

Candace frowned as she started to unbutton her shirt, revealing a black lacy bra that appeared to be trying to contain her bulging implants.

After the down payment was rendered, Marc looked at Candace. "Was that part of the protocol of your church?"

"I believe the *Good Book* says 'The end justifies the means' ".

Marc laughed. "Don't waste your time trying to locate that reference in your *Good Book*. Nevertheless, that proverb has always been part of my religion!"

~ 6 ~
More Considerations

"I could give a sermon any time, any place," said Candace as she abruptly stood and mimicked a clergyman. "Brothers and Sisters: I come before you on this beautiful Sabbath Day to tell you all that it's important to give all your money to me!"

"That is our ultimate message, but we should be a bit more subtle than that," said Allison while laughing.

When the laughter quieted, Hannah said, "Concerning who should really give sermons, Candace, you're going to be center stage for musical entertainment. We can't have you do everything."

Candace snapped back, "How about yourself, then? Do you think you could do better?"

"I wasn't volunteering."

"I'll do it," said Brittany.

"You? Give a sermon? I don't think you're right for it yet," said Candace.

Brittany became indignant and stuck her tongue out at Candace. "Who made you queen of the town? Just because you can sing doesn't mean that you should rule over the rest of us."

Candace inhaled deeply. "Those of you who think Brittany should take charge, say aye." Silence followed. She looked at

Brittany. "Satisfied?" Without waiting for a response, she said, "Moving right along…"

Brittany bit her lip as if trying not to cry. She excused herself to go to the restroom. When she was out of sight, Diana said, "I'm concerned for Brittany's feelings," said Diana. "We need to make her feel a bigger part of this. What responsibility can we give her?"

Candace said, "I've been concerned more about her than for her. She's ditsy and her judgment isn't very good. Maybe she'd be satisfied with greeting people as they come in. She can't mess that up…at least I don't think she can. And remember she did arrange for our robes design and production. I guess we haven't shown much appreciation for that."

"How about her arranging the social hour after the service?" suggested Allison.

"That's a good idea," said Hannah. The others agreed.

When Brittany returned, the women were still discussing the deliverance of the sermon.

"Perhaps Allison would do that well. She's a writer or the texts could be taken from the Internet. They could be memorized, and I'm sure that Allison could present with enthusiasm and seeming spontaneity," suggested Hannah.

"I don't know if I'd feel right offering spiritual advice. Are you sure I wouldn't be struck by a bolt of lightening trying to do that?"

"Sermons don't have to be spiritual. They can just be an inspiration to do something good, such as giving generously for the growth of the Kingdom."

"What hymns have you selected, Candace?" asked Hannah.

"It's a surprise."

The others glanced at each other. Hannah spoke up, "I just hope they'll be appropriate."

Candace rolled her eyes. "Not to worry!"

"Who's going to accompany you?" the others asked.

"I've taken care of that. My actor friend, Jason, was overjoyed when I asked him to play the theatre organ for the services. Playing a theatre organ is regarded as quite a privilege, you know. Jason's primarily a jazz musician, but he's versatile. He likes upbeat tempos, unlike the common funeral type music heard in many churches that both he and I detest.

Allison said, "We're lucky that you've had so much experience and know so many people." Hearing such a sign of appreciation, brought a broad smile from Candace.

"To change the subject, we need some good PR. Newspapers freely announce church services. I'll bet they could squeeze us in. They couldn't deny us if there's time. They can't discriminate," said Candace.

"I'm going to check that right away. That might bring more people in than street ads," said Allison.

At that moment, their conversation was dwarfed by the loud sound system of a passing double decker tour bus. "Hey, that gives me another idea for PR. Those buses are full of sight-seeers. We should plaster our notices all over them, and when they stop, we could jump on and sing or give some promotional speech," said Candace.

"Good idea, but that would take a lot of our time and we don't have much to spare at this time," said Hannah.

"Well, let's do as much as we can." Candace continued. "We should distribute thousands of flyers and we'll also need printed programs for Sunday. We have to appear professional and ready to give our guests what they came to receive."

Hannah said, "Already we're accumulating expenses. How are we going to pay for everything we need to just get started?"

Allison said, "Many businesses will donate things to churches and other groups—things like day-old bakery items for the after-hour socials and floral arrangements left after funeral services. That would help keep our costs down."

"That's a great idea," said Hannah, "but we still have to pay for printing services, utilities and so forth. Do any of them give discounts to churches?"

"We can ask," said Allison.

"I already checked on printing costs and they're out of sight," said Diana.

"Did you try using any of your feminine charms to get credit?" asked Candace.

"What do you mean?" said Diana.

"You know...just sway your hips seductively as you go in, bat your eyes, look seductive, and lean over the desk with a low-cut top. It's always worked for me." Candace rose and demonstrated. "Give it the ole college try, Diana."

"The print shop is only a block away. Maybe I should leave now before I talk myself out of it."

"Go for it."

The Ole college Try

"I can't let the group down," Diana kept telling herself as she left the café.

She was glad to see that there were no other customers in the shop when she entered...only the middle-aged printer who initially had his back turned.

"Let's see. Candace said I should walk in swaying my hips." With exaggerated hip movements, she entered. Her cloggish boots and long grey skirt didn't lend well to a sexy walk. The printer turned toward her.

Noting her awkward movements, he said, "Hello. Are you okay?"

"Yes, I'm fine," she responded as she batted her eyelashes. "You sure look handsome," she said with a distorted and unnatural smile. She raised one shoulder trying to look as seductive as she had been instructed.

"Thank you. Now what can I do for you?"

"I need one thousand flyers and programs printed like these," she said as she handed him the papers.

"Sure. We can do that. I just need a one hundred dollar deposit, and they'll be ready in two days."

She leaned over the counter as Candace had recommended but her turtle neck shirt failed to reveal any interesting skin. She batted her eyes again. "How about such a big, strong man giving me a credit account til I get my business started?"

"We don't give out credit or discounts here. I'm sorry."

Diana felt humiliated, but she continued. "Isn't there any favor I could do for you in exchange?"

"I'm sorry but no. That's a firm policy."

Diana was so embarrassed from her unsuccessful behaviors that she started to cry. At that moment, another customer entered the shop.

"Hi George," the printer said as he recognized his frequent patron.

"Hi. What's the matter with this young lady? Did you mess up an order?"

"No. She doesn't have money for an order, and I can't give credit."

"George, you helped me out when I was getting started. Can't you stretch your credit policy and help her out. She looks honest."

With some hesitation, the printer looked at her crying, and finally agreed saying he would bend the rules this once.

Diana left her order and hurried out trying to get the shop out of sight as fast as possible. She returned to the café and reported her success.

Candace laughed and said, "My method always works."

Hannah then changed the subject. "I still think we're rushing into this too fast. We need to be better prepared. I can see that we need some serious rehearsals."

Candace objected. "What's there to rehearse? We'll have a canned sermon and prayers and musical numbers. Serious rehearsals, as you put it, increase tension. When overly prepared, people are more fearful of forgetting a crucial word or part. Spontaneity always proves best. I have faith that we'll be successful without wasting our time on rehearsals. What we really need is someone to be in charge of decorating and ambience." Allison and Hannah volunteered.

Brittany finally spoke. "I guess there's no place for me in your services."

"Oh, we put you in charge of organizing the social hour after the services."

Brittany gave Candace a piercing smirk. "Couldn't you think of anything less important?"

"Oh, shove it," said Candace.

Hannah tried to be more diplomatic. “Brittany, that might be the activity that is most lucrative for us. That alone may be what keeps people returning. It’s a very important job.”

Brittany didn’t respond.

Additional assignments were given. Towards the end of the meeting, Candace said, “Girls, we still haven’t found our ideal hunk to appear with us as a fellow preacher. I suppose we could do without, but it would be so much more fun to work with a stud.”

Allison looked up, smiled and seemed excited. “I think my husband would be willing to do that.”

The women all looked downward trying to avoid eye contact with Allison for they had met her husband Fred. Although personable, he was overweight and slightly balding, not what they had envisioned as their ideal hunk. It was Candace who blurted out, “Fred isn’t exactly what we had in mind.”

Allison defended Fred. “He may not seem like a sexy hunk to you, but to me he’s the ideal!”

Candace looked down at her hands on the table. In a low voice, she said, “It’s good that you think so.” She then glanced upwards. “Allison, how about you and I going on a man hunt after this meeting? We can put our views together.”

“Where do you suggest we go?”

“Hey, we’re in the Broadway area. We should easily find many hunks to choose from on the streets. We just have to keep our eyes open.”

Hannah said, “You gals better find one quick. We still have a lot of last-minute details to take care of.”

“You worry too much,” said Candace. “I thought psychotherapists were above that.”

“I suspect most of the group thinks I’m just being realistic and practical.”

“Whatever! Anyway, let’s go, Allison.”

Candace picked up her backpack. “Oh, could we stop by the corner market for a moment. I’m all out of fresh fruit. I can’t live without it.”

“Let’s limit it to ten minutes,” Allison said while looking at her watch. “As Hannah said, we’ve got a lot to do today.”

With smugness, Brittany said, “May the force be with you!”

~ 7 ~
In search of the Ideal Man

The women walked briskly out of the cafe. They scrutinized every male they passed. There were many vendors selling brand-named purses and watches—others drawing quick cartoon sketches for visitors. They tried to visualize each of them as priests, but somehow none seemed right. Their eyes lit up when they saw a lean, muscular man with his hands in his pockets and his back to them. When he turned however, he had large tattoos on his arms and chest and was missing a front tooth. "Uh, uh. Not good!"

Just before arriving at the market, an unkempt man was leaning against a post. "Oh mama. I like what I see," he called out to them.

"Forget you, Creep!" yelled Candace. She turned to Allison and said, "Maybe it'll be harder than I thought to find the ideal man."

"It doesn't look promising so far."

They hurried into the market and rushed to the fresh produce section. Allison's eyes suddenly opened wide as she spotted the back of a man wearing ripped jeans and a cut-off tee exposing his muscular arms. No obvious tattoos. His well-rounded buns couldn't be ignored. He was squatting, as he appeared to be checking out the melons. Allison nudged Candace who had already noticed him. They looked at each other and simultaneously whispered, "Perfect!"

Without hesitation, Candace moved in close. "Do the melons look ripe and ready?" she asked. As he turned, his eyes focused on her engaging breasts that she had purposefully projected before him. He smiled. "Yes, the melons appear ripe and ready. And look pretty good to me."

The women were momentarily stunned by his good looks. Not only did he have a becoming physique but also had the facial features of a Greek God—a masculine straight nose, high cheekbones, broad jaw, and full lips. His smile was engaging, his voice quiet but deep as he answered. His eyes darted around the market as if trying to see if there were others watching him. He cautiously rose to his feet. Candace felt no need to waste time on small talk. "What do you do on Sunday mornings?" she blurted out.

"Usually sleep one off," he said.

Candace gave him a flirtaceous smile. "Hey, I think we may be on the same wavelength. How'd you like to help some damsels in distress? We're starting a new church and need a man to sit with us up front. You wouldn't have to do much—just provide moral support, and maybe offer a short prayer that we could have printed out for you."

He looked at them with suspicion. "A new church? Why are you doing that?"

"New York City needs more spirituality, don't you think?"

"Maybe. I've never been much into religion. It doesn't sound very exciting. I don't know how I'd fit in there."

"You'd fit in fine. We just need you to sit with us."

"Who's managing all this," he asked.

"I'm Candace, this is Allison, and three of our friends—and you are…?"

"Harry."

"Well, come on Harry. I guarantee you won't be sorry."

"I'm sorry already. What if one of my friends see me there?"

"Won't they be sleeping one off at that time?"

The *Greek God* continued to look skeptical.

"Hey, look at it this way. It's going to be fun, and while having fun, you'd be getting heavenly rewards for such a work, and don't we all need those? If we get enough donations, we might cut you in on the take."

At that Harry's eyebrows raised. "Is this some business enterprise you're starting?"

"Not exactly. We just want to do something nice for the area."

"You gals don't look like preachers to me. Come on now. What are you really doing?"

"As I said, just trying to do something nice for the Big Apple."

"Where is this church?" he asked.

"Not far from here. We're meeting temporarily in the *Old Templeton Theatre."* Candace boldly threw her arms around him and directly looked into his eyes. "Pleeeze."

Harry succumbed. "Okay. You talked me into it, but you better sit close to me and tell me what to do. I don't want to look stupid up there."

"Agreed! We're all a team and we help each other. We're having a planning session tomorrow evening at the *Café Fantastique*. Why don't you come and meet the other ladies. We'd value your input."

Harry hesitated. "I'm not sure I can make it, but I'll try."

Candace selected her melon and a few other fruits. The three went to the checkout lane together. Harry was there first. As the cashier rang up his charges, Candace noticed that her melon was priced much higher than that of Harry's.

"Your total is nine dollars and twenty-five cents," said the cashier.

Harry fumbled through some bills and gave her nine dollars.

"Twenty-five cents more," said the cashier.

"Can I use the coin behind your ear?"

The cashier appeared puzzled. "What?"

Harry reached up and took a quarter from behind her ear.

"How did you do that?" asked Allison.

"It's magic," he replied.

Harry left the market with his few groceries including a choice cantaloupe. He glanced around to see if anyone else in the store or outside area was checking him out.

Outside of the supermarket, Allison said, "Be still my heart! If I weren't married, I'd be first in line for a hug from that hunk."

"You'd have to be super strong to push me away from that line. Mmm. Mmm. Actually, he seems agreeable and pleasant—likable really. Who would have thought that we'd find a Greek God wandering around in a New York City market and disguised in disheveled clothes!"

Allison smiled but then became serious. "When we first got close to Harry, it looked to me like he was exchanging labels on the fruit."

"I thought the same thing. And I may have been the recipient of a bad trade. He probably needs money as much as we do."

"Ah well, he sure is a charmer."

"He doesn't seem that bright. But that should make him easy to manipulate.

~ 8 ~
The Setup

Church entertainment at its best!

Join us for a celebration of blessings from our Creator.

Nondenominational worship service

Led by ordained preachers with Broadway experience

Come, shake hands or enjoy a hug from the talented performers

No Admission Fee

June 22, 11 a.m.

Old Templeton Theatre / Off Broadway

Diana smiled with approval as she looked at the printed announcements she had created. Her ex came by the home to take the children for a visit. He saw the printed notices on her desk.

"What's this?" he asked.

"It's an announcement for the new church that my friends and I are starting."

"I didn't know you had an interest in religion."

She frowned. "I have to do something to get money to pay the bills."

"Good luck," he said sarcastically. He turned his back to her and left with the children.

It was another jab meant to hurt her. She still yearned for his acceptance. She desperately wanted him to care about her as she thought he once did. Tears flowed down her cheeks from the wounds that had not yet healed.

Harry arrived late for his first meeting. He was wearing the same holy jeans and cut-off tee. Candace jumped up when she saw him enter the café.

"Over here," she waved.

He smiled broadly. "Sorry I'm late. I couldn't get away from a business meeting."

Hannah looked over his attire and whispered sarcastically to Diana, "It must have been some high-classed meeting!"

"You're forgiven. I want you to meet the other members of our group," said Candace. As she introduced them, Harry acknowledged each woman with a charming smile. His eyes focused longest on Diana.

"Diana was just about to show us the announcement she made for the services."

Diana shifted about in her chair and quietly stammered, "It's not very good. I just printed it off quickly as a suggestion." She passed copies around.

"What do you mean 'not very good.' This is great," said Allison. The other women agreed and enthusiastically expressed approval. Harry said, "I think it's perfect. You're a very talented lady, Diana."

Diana looked down and blushed.

"We should all take to the streets, and hand out these notices three days before our service," said Candace.

"I have a suggestion for widespread distribution. We could throw off thousands of the notices from the Top of the Rock. We could make it snow in June," suggested Harry.

"I can see you have a very creative mind, Harry," said Hannah.

Harry smiled. "Aw shucks, ma'am. I'm just a simple man with simple thoughts."

Brittany giggled and said, "Phooey! We know better than that."

"If we did as Harry suggested, wouldn't we get arrested for littering?" asked Hannah. "Also, it's expensive just for admission to take the elevator up to the top."

"You have to spend money to make money," said Harry.

"Tell us all about it, Harry," said Hannah.

Allison grimaced. "Let's avoid anything that would get us in trouble."

There were still other expenses that needed to be covered.

"Our costumes will be costly. My dressmakers may give a little discount but such time-consuming work is still expensive," said Brittany.

"Does anyone have any spare money or credit source we could draw from?" asked Candace.

There was a long silence. Finally, Diana said, "I have an antique sapphire ring that has been in my family for generations. I've never had it appraised, but my mother said it's worth a lot of money. I could take it to a pawnshop and get money for it, and then retrieve it within two months once our money is coming in."

Allison said, "We couldn't ask you to do that. What if our business fails?"

"It's not going to fail," said Candace. "We just need financial help now to start our project. It's just a loan. I think we have no choice but to accept Diana's generous offer."

"Wait a minute, Diana. Let's face reality. I think you need to think carefully about the risk. Our business could bomb," said Hannah.

Candace looked sternly at Hannah. “Don’t be so negative, Big H. Don’t you teach your patients to be optimistic for success?” Hannah smiled sheepishly.

After a brief pause, Candace continued, “Well then, let’s get moving. Can we be ready for next Sunday—six days from now?”

The others still looked worried. “Maybe we should wait another week. There’s a tremendous amount to be done.”

Candace answered, “Let’s consider the first week as a trial run. If we’re as successful as I think we’ll be, after the first service, we should be able to get many volunteers anxious to serve and increase their points with the Man in the Sky.”

Then Hannah said, “There’s something else we should settle. We haven’t selected our treasurer yet. Who will do that?”

Allison suggested that Brittany might handle that position. The rest of the group tried to be discreet as they negatively responded.

Brittany spoke out in angry tones. “Thanks a lot, you guys. I don’t know why I’m trying so hard to be part of the team. You obviously have no confidence in me.”

Hannah tried to smooth things over by giving her credit for the costumes. “The costume design and upkeep is a full time job alone,” said Hannah.

“Who then?” asked Allison.

“I can do that,” said Candace. Subtle grimaces could be seen on the women present.

The group agreed that she was already taking on too much.

Harry spoke up. “What about Diana? She’s already contributed needed money from the hocking of her sapphire ring. She’s also demonstrated that she’s responsible and organized.”

“Could you handle being treasurer, Diana?” said Allison.

Diana beamed with joy that she should be considered. “I guess I could if everyone felt they could trust me. I’ve had tons of experience managing household finances.”

“Okay. Let’s give her a try. Now, does everyone have a clear idea of what their responsibilities are?” asked Candace.

“We think so.”

“As I said earlier, let’s just do it. We can meet again on Wednesday and iron out any difficulties. Candace turned to the others. “Well, there’s nothing to worry about. Everything’s beginning to fall into place. *Everything's comin up roses!*" she belted. Suddenly she became quiet as if in deep thought.

"What's on your mind, Candace. You look concerned about something," said Hannah.

"I was just thinking of something silly that Marc told me about the theatre."

The women looked intently at Candace. "Share!" they said.

"I think he was just trying to dissuade me from using his theatre, but he told me that several people had reported seeing ghosts there at odd times."

"Ghosts?" The women laughed thinking that Candace was teasing.

"I'm not kidding. Marc said that a ghost-like figure of a man in a dark suit was seen by several people in housekeeping and among the ushers prior to the theatre opening."

"Do you think that's true? And do you think there actually are ghosts that haunt this earth or spirits that help us?" Allison asked.

Brittany was the only one of the women who felt certain there were such beings. Diana shyly looked at Harry. "What about you, Harry? Do you think there are unseen spirits or witches that surround us?"

"I'm sure that there are," said Harry. "I know of instances in which people we may have known and who have died, still live in this world. They can put themselves into another dimension and walk unseen or seen amongst us."

Candace started to laugh. "Harry, you're weird."

"Don't laugh at something you know nothing about," he said.

Allison looked at Hannah who was sitting with a blank expression on her face. "Hannah, you've had some astronomy classes, haven't you? Do you think ghosts exist and travel in space? If so, can they travel at the speed of light?"

"We live in a world that operates by the laws of physics. The concept of ghosts doesn't fit into that world. But then again, if there are angels or ghosts, they probably would operate in a dimension beyond ours and not be bound by our laws of physics."

"It seems that there are many people who have seen them or evidence of them," said Diana. "I personally haven't had any encounters, but I'd like to believe we are being watched over and protected by either ghosts or angels."

Harry leaned forward and looked intently at Diana. "Actually, studies have been done that show it's a rare person who doesn't want to believe in an afterlife and spirits from the Great Beyond."

Candace opened her eyes wider and said, "Hmm. Should we introduce a type of séance in our services?"

"Let's stay away from weird," said Hannah.

"Right! At least not in our main services, but if there seems to be interest, we could hold quiet mini-meetings during the week," said Allison.

Harry interrupted. "You gals aren't qualified to lead such a service."

"And you think you are?"

"I know I am."

Candace looked at Harry with a piercing glare. "You get weirder and weirder the more you speak."

"I still think there may be a place for some kind of spiritual counseling. It might be helpful for those grieving over the loss of a loved one. A belief that the departed still is with them would be comforting to practically everyone," said Diana.

Diana hurried home and ran up the stairs to her bedroom. She opened the bottom drawer of her dresser. Under a pile of lingerie, there was the small purse hidden from casual view. She opened it and took out her prized ring. It looked even more beautiful than she had remembered. She slipped it on her ring finger and moved her hand around so that it reflected light from all directions. *Why haven't I ever worn this? I feel happy just looking at it. Mom always said it was very valuable and could be a bartering tool if times got really hard—like if we needed food for survival. Is this one of those times? Do I really need to pawn this for my survival? No point in thinking about it now. I already promised it to the church.* Without further thought, she drove to the nearest pawnshop.

Allison used her creative decorating skills to design and make unique pillows to adorn the theatre. From several old down quilts, she made colorful and eye-catching beautiful pillows. She had to scrounge around for stuffing. She finally mixed Styrofoam balls and pellets and feathers from the quilts, and enclosed them with quick long stitches. The pillows were meant to be spread across the stage to complement the floral arrangements on the stage and in the foyer as well as spread throughout the theatre on chairs. Allison made so many that they soon overwhelmed their already small living quarters. Fred started to become annoyed with them and with all the time Allison was devoting to her project. "It's time to stop now," he ranted. "Soon we won't have room to walk from room to room."

~ 9 ~
Flowers in a Frenzy

Traffic was heavier than usual on the morning of the first church service. During the long trip to the funeral parlor, Hannah's thoughts were focused on the conversation from the last meeting concerning ghosts. An eerie feeling came over her. *This is silly,* she thought. *I know there isn't such a thing as ghosts.* Still she couldn't get her mind free of those intrusive thoughts.

Arriving later than planned at the funeral parlor, she quickly opened the main door, and almost ran through the lobby trying to find someone to assist her. Suddenly, a pale *being* in a dark suit came into the foyer as if it had floated through a closed door. She let out a screech and stumbled. In her frenzy, her face hit against a hallway shelf upon which there was a large ornamental urn holding fresh flowers. It started to topple and turned upside down. By instinct, she reached for it and caught it in midair as its contents spilled over Hannah's head. She sat stunned with a reddened face.

"Are you okay?" the man asked.

Hannah's vision was slightly blurred from the impact on her head which made the man appear ethereal. She cowered against the wall tightly holding the vase. At that moment, a young boy ran through the foyer. Seeing Hannah in a daze sitting against the wall, he stopped. "I'll help you up," he said.

She gratefully reached for his extended hand. A sudden electrical jolt made her jump. He chuckled. "Gotcha," he yelled as he ran into one of the showing rooms. This brought Hannah out of her stupor. "That kid just reminded me of why I never wanted to have children," she murmured.

"I apologize," said the funeral director. "That child has been giving us trouble for the past two days." Hannah studied the man for a moment, and convinced herself he was just a man. "I'm sorry. You startled me," she said in a loud voice. The man put his finger to his lips indicating she should speak quietly. He relieved her of the vase that she was holding. She bent down trying to gather the dispersed flowers. "We can take care of the mess later," he whispered. "Who are you here to visit?"

Because of the mishap, Hannah felt reluctant to tell him she was here for the unclaimed flowers she had called about earlier in the week. She blushed and then quietly related the reason for her visit.

The attendant composed himself and smiled at her. "Oh yes. I remember speaking to you. There are many flowers, but there's a complication. The deceased will be sent to another state for burial later today. His widow is here now, and she's reluctant to leave. We can't let you take flowers until she's gone."

Hannah threw her head back in disappointment. She knew that time was short to get the flowers to the theatre and arrange them. "How long has she been in there?"

"She came early this morning. I think she's lonely and doesn't want to go home to an empty house. I'm sorry, but we can't disturb her."

Hannah looked at her watch, and took a deep breath. "I'll wait in the foyer," she told the attendant. After several minutes of pacing the floor, there was no sign that the widow was ready to leave.

When the director disappeared, Hannah crept quietly into the room where the deceased was displayed. A woman, dressed in black was sitting close to the casket. She was unaware of Hannah's presence until Hannah forced a sneeze. The woman jumped and turned around.

"Excuse me. I didn't mean to disturb you," whispered Hannah.

The woman scowled. "You didn't think I'd still be here, did you? I knew you'd show up."

"You did?" Hannah asked innocently.

"I know all about you and Sylvester. He thought it was a secret, but a wife always knows."

"Madam. You're mistaken. I didn't know your husband."

"Nobody really knew him. I'm still trying to figure him out, the mean old bastard."

"I'm sorry about that," said Hannah.

The woman scowled. "You should be!"

Hannah was becoming more anxious about the time and repeatedly checked her watch. She tried to think of words to prompt the widow to leave. "You'll probably figure more out with time. Sometimes it's not good to linger here too long."

"Are you trying to get me to leave so you can finally have him all to yourself?"

"No. Really, I didn't know your husband."

"You don't have to pretend anymore, you floozie. You were out with him having fun while I was left at home with his stinky socks."

Hannah knew that no words would convince her otherwise. She tried to conceal her growing restlessness and attempted to be patient and show understanding. "I can tell that you must have been very devoted to him, and find it hard to be without him now, but sometimes it's best to cut the ties quickly and move on."

"Move on? Where do I move on to, now? An empty house? Even a bastard is better to live with than being alone."

Hannah became desperate. "I have an idea. I'm on my way to church. Maybe we could go there together and take some of your lovely flowers with us as a tribute to Sylvester."

"Sylvester never liked flowers."

"I'm sure that wherever he is now, he is watching down and appreciates all your thoughts and the flowers as an expression of your love."

"Humbug."

"It's said that when people die, they become perfected. Sylvester, now in his perfection, I'm sure appreciates any of your fond gestures. He wants you to move on and live your life with a fond remembrance of him."

The widow didn't answer immediately. Hannah looked at her, and she appeared to have fallen asleep.

Hannah raised her voice. "I know you'll feel better when you leave here."

The widow slowly opened her eyes. "What did you say?"

Hannah almost yelled, "I'm a psychologist. You'll feel better when you leave here."

"Do you really think so?" She hesitated. "I don't know. . ."

"I'm sure of it."

"I don't have any place to go."

"Come with me to church."

With a pathetic look on her face, the widow asked, "How could we get to your church? Is it far?"

The funeral director had been eavesdropping. He also was anxious for the widow to leave, and so he came to the front where the women were seated.

"Ladies, if you wish to leave with the floral arrangements, I can arrange for a car to take you."

Hannah stood up. "Perfect!"

That was the signal that was needed. The widow slowly stood and grabbed her cane.

It was nearly time for the service to begin. Hannah, now in a sweat, helped carry flowers out to the limousine. The widow walked slowly. She kept stopping to look around and talk to the director.

Hannah rushed back to the widow, took firm hold of her arm, and briskly pulled her toward the awaiting car. "We need to hurry so we don't miss the opening."

Those words didn't appear to register. Hannah could no longer feel empathy nor block her intrusive thoughts. It took great effort to not say aloud, *Hurry! Hurry, you old bag.*

~ 10 ~
Sunday

Gloomy, dark clouds hovered over the theatre Sunday morning, and the smell of impending rain permeated the air.

"Please don't rain. Please not today," Candace pleaded. Her cries went unheeded. One hour before the services were to begin, a few sprinkles of rain dotted the sidewalk in front of the theatre. This was soon followed by thunder and then a torrential downpour. Lightning flashes were intense and struck close-by.

"One thousand one, one thousand…" was all Brittany could speak out before a loud clap of thunder shook the lobby doors. She jumped and covered her ears. "It's a sign. It's a sign. God doesn't want us to do this." She went into a panic mode and started to run madly through the lobby. Candace grabbed her.

"One more stupid reaction like that, and I'll be forced to slap some sense into you," threatened Candace.

Brittany cowered at Candace's strong words and became quiet.

Allison also tried to calm the scene. "This is merely a cloudburst—great for the dry spell we've been in—just a minor inconvenience for us today."

This further agitated Candace. "If you call this a minor inconvenience, I say *F-you!"*

Diana started to cry. "I thought we were trying to bring more spirituality into the city. How can we do that with the conflicts between us?"

Candace put her hands on her hips and rolled her eyes. "Now we have to deal not only with stupid freaks but cry babies," said Candace.

"If that's going to be your attitude, let's forget the whole thing and go home," said Allison. Her comment had been impulsive, and she wished that she could retract it. After devoting so much time and effort into preparations, she especially wanted her designer pillows to be admired during the service.

There was silence until another loud clap of thunder rattled the doors. Brittany started to open her mouth, but once more had her attention diverted by Candace. In a more subdued voice, Candace said, "I guess I'm on edge. I want everything to go well, but things seem to be going against us. We've put too much into the plans to just dump it at the last minute. I apologize." She smiled and said, "If I believed in prayer, I guess this would be a good time to ask for help."

"Thank you, Candace. Let's all try to be more understanding of each other this morning. We need to all work together to make this program work," said Allison. The others nodded in agreement.

There was another bright flash of lightning followed by unnerving thunder. Brittany tensed again but did her best to hide it.

"Damn! I guess we can forget about good attendance today. We should have sold advance tickets yesterday for today's performance," lamented Candace.

The women stood peering outside through the ornately etched theatre doors. They agonized as they watched the few trees in the area bend and sway in the storm. At times the downpour was so heavy, they couldn't see the other side of the street.

"No one will venture out in this," said Candace. "And where's Harry? Wasn't he supposed to be here before now?"

"Maybe the rain is delaying him. Actually, I wondered if he'd even show up," said Allison.

"He'd better," said Candace. "I hope he remembers to wear a nice suit. It's important to have a conservative clergyman on the stand."

"That's the least of our worries," said Allison.

"Well, I'm sure we'll have our organist here. I've rehearsed some numbers with him. I know he's desperate to perform rain or shine and for any group large or small. Also, a few of my theatre friends will be here. I've gone over the music with them. They're always looking for an excuse to perform. All we have to do is open the doors to the church, and hopefully the great music will draw a crowd—even if only to get out of the rain."

"My husband will be here too. He's behind us all the way," said Allison.

" Great! An audience of one," replied Candace with sarcasm.

"Here he comes now. Come in and dry off, sweetheart. I think you've met everyone here now." The women nodded in recognition.

The rain had failed to dampen Fred's spirit. "What can I do to help?" he asked.

"Just stay in the foyer and help welcome anyone who may venture in," said Candace. "Do we have anyone lined up to pass the collection plates? Maybe Fred could be in charge of that. By the way, where are the plates?"

That was the moment Brittany had been dreading. She looked up sheepishly. "I feel so awful. The special plates I ordered didn't arrive. I looked all over for substitutes this morning, but couldn't find anything suitable."

"What?" Candace screamed. "Why didn't you call us earlier? Now what are we going to do?" Candace looked so angry she appeared ready to hit Brittany.

Brittany started to cry. "I'm sorry. I couldn't find anything else. I tried."

"Didn't you have any bowls or pans?"

"I do but they don't match each other."

"What else, Lord? What else?" Candace rolled her eyes. "At least you're not laughing about it," she said sarcastically.

The leaders looked around trying to find something to hold collections. Eventually, their attention was drawn downward.

"We could pass our shoes," said Diana.

"That's gross," said Hannah.

"And we wouldn't look very presentable running around without shoes," said Fred.

"What about socks then? Probably no one would notice our not wearing them." Allison looked at Fred's socks, and hoped he didn't have any holes in them.

"Actually, I have three new pair of large woolen socks in my backpack," said Fred.

Candace looked forlorn. "I guess we don't have any choice"

At that moment the hearse with Hannah, the widow, and flowers stopped in front of the entrance. The driver ran around and helped escort the widow out.

"What's this all about?" asked Allison. "Is this the only way we can get an audience?"

Hannah got out and started unloading the flowers. Although she tried to shield them from the downpour, they still got drenched and drooped. She ran in with two displays. "Can someone help me?" she pleaded. Allison and Fred ran to assist.

Allison hesitated and stared at Hannah. "What happened to your face? Were you in a fight on the way?"

"It's a long story. I'll tell you about it later."

Diana helped escort the widow to a seat. The widow took off her raincoat, and then looked around. In a loud voice she said, "This doesn't look like a church."

Diana smiled. "It's the New Age look."

"Why isn't anyone else here? Is this a scam? Let me out of here."

"You're okay. People are late because it's raining. They'll be coming soon."

"I never should have let them bring me here," she yelled.

Hannah came running to try to calm her.

"We'll be starting the prayer service in a few minutes. Do you need something to drink?"

"I know you. You were Sylvester's lover. Now you want me to drink poison so you can get his money. Help!" She started to raise her cane to attack. Hannah quickly retreated.

Diana tried to calm the woman. "If you want to leave, I can get a taxi for you."

"I don't trust taxi drivers. They rob you blind."

"The music will be starting soon. I hope you enjoy it. I'll leave you alone so you can meditate and feel the spirit." Diana backed away, feeling that she didn't want to say anything to make the widow more paranoid.

The preachers quickly slipped into their white silk robes designed by Brittany. The colorfully embroidered low cut tops were pinched at the waist and flared at the hips. There wasn't any resemblance to church priestly attire, but the women thought they looked fashionable and stunning.

"Brittany, I must admit you did a good job in designing these robes. The embroidery is gorgeous and so colorful." Candace smiled. "But they're all the same color. I think at least mine should be vivid red with white and gold embroidery. I need to stand out more since I'm the lead performer."

Brittany's smile disappeared. "Who designated you as number one?"

"It goes without saying. My talent is the one that will make us famous."

The group was not happy with Candace and her inflated ego, but this was not the time to debate since the service was to start soon. "Let's drop this for now," said Hannah. "What about Harry? He can't be expected to wear one of these. They're too feminine."

Candace said, "He can wear his suit. That'll look okay. He doesn't need to stand out."

"A plain choir robe would fit in better," said Allison.

Brittany looked disappointed. "I should have designed a robe for him too. I didn't think about it. I'll have a costume made for him for next week."

Hannah went back to the foyer and picked up some floral arrangements. She placed the largest on the stage and the smaller ones in the foyer where they could be seen upon entering. They helped to present a more church-like atmosphere in contrast to the otherwise garishly decorated theatre. Allison arranged her pillows around the flower stands.

"We'll not only sound good, but look beautiful too," Allison said.

"If only the rain hadn't drooped the flowers. Do you think there are too many arrangements? Did we overkill?" asked Hannah.

"You can never overkill with flowers."

Allison sat in a theatre chair. "These seats are much nicer than the wooden church pews I grew up with. Wow, if I weren't part of the cast, I'd want to come here."

"That's exactly what we're trying to encourage," said Candace. "Oh good. Marc just arrived. He's going to operate the lights and sound system for us. Actually, I think he didn't want to risk us messing up his equipment. Also, I know he's skeptical as to whether we can pull this off. I'm sure he wants to be here to see the outcome."

"Good morning, ladies. Don't you all look chic! Were those robes designed by Oscar himself? And this place looks fantastic. Those bouquets must have cost you a fortune. And where did you get those beautiful pillows? Maybe I'll hire you as my personal decorators."

"I think your theatre is perfect for us. Thank you so much for letting us use it," Hannah said.

"And enhance it!" added Allison.

"I understand it's for a good cause. People around here need to have their spirituality boosted, and need to *keep the faith*!" Marc and Candace exchanged glances.

Jason, the organist, came in as Marc went up to the lighting box. Jason appeared manic—hyper in his movements as he shook off his coat and folded his umbrella. "Oh rain, rain, go away. Come again some other day," he said as he laughed. He was anxious to perform and have a captive audience. He too had been struggling to find positions for performance. This job could add to his resumé and might help him land good paying jobs. He looked at the women in their priestly robes. "You gals look stunning! I wish I had a costume like that."

"It might have fit the mood better than your faded jeans and sweatshirt," said Candace.

Jason ignored the comment. From the foyer, he looked surprised when he heard a voice from inside: "Where am I? I need help."

"Who's that?"

Candace laughed. "One of the ladies needs help with decorations."

"I'll go help," said Diana.

Jason almost ran to the organ to warm up. He had been briefed by Candace on selections. He began playing some Bach sonatas. The acoustics were great and there seemed to be appropriate vibrations striking every seat. "The sound is so good. Perfect!" said Candace.

Members of the choir next began to arrive. The rain didn't dampen their demeanor. Candace welcomed them and said,

"I think it's time for you to robe up. And you greeters should get ready and position yourselves. Oh, just in time. Here comes our *just for show* dolt."

"Hi Harry. Do you feel the spirit this morning?"

Harry beamed. "I feel the spirit just looking at you ladies. You look great. What do you want me to do to help?"

"Just put on a robe, sit with us on stage, and try to pay attention."

"A robe? You didn't say anything about that. I'm not going to wear one of those girly tops. I don't wanna wear somethin that people will mistake me for gay."

"Your robe will be like the choir's. It's not a dress. It's a priestly robe of distinction."

Harry frowned but said nothing further. Candace introduced him to the others whom he had not yet met. Again his eyes focused most heavily on Diana which made her squirm.

Fred looked at Harry intently. An unpleasant sensation came over him.

Jason's music was getting louder. He pulled out all the stops as the theatre doors were opened and everyone was in place. He hesitated briefly between selections.

"Where am I?" could be heard from the congregation.

Hannah told Harry about the widow. He walked over to her while the others watched. She initially appeared frightened, but as he interacted with her, they saw her relax. He gave her a hug and kissed her on the cheek. Then she started to smile.

"I knew he'd have a good effect on the ladies," said Candace.

Later, Diana approached Harry. " That widow seemed to like you. What did you say to her?"

"I just told her what she wanted to hear."

~ 11 ~
Curtain Up

Strong winds accompanied the storm—so strong that they occasionally slammed against the drenched people as they trickled into the theatre just minutes before starting time. Debris accompanying the forceful blows were so strong that they left several persons rubbing their derrieres for comfort. An occasional person fell face first on the foyer floor. As Hannah and Brittany tried to help them to their feet, they dropped their programs which the winds blew and scattered throughout the foyer. One of the guests commented that it looked like a cyclone had been through.

Brittany dressed in her expensive attire, now looked disheveled. Her abundance of gold jewelry appeared out of place. One man, who appeared in jeans, looked at her necklaces and said, "Are we dressed okay for the service?"

"You look just fine. You blend very well with the rest of us," said Hannah "I don't think the Lord wants church services to be fashion-shows. Everyone is welcome."

Those entering were heard to make comments about the charm of the theatre, its décor and beautiful organ music.

It was eleven a.m. It was disappointing to the preachers as they sat up front and looked out at the congregation and many empty seats.

"We'll still give the few here more than their money's worth," said Candace. "And perhaps today will be worthwhile if it serves only as a rehearsal."

Candace nodded to Jason as a signal to wrap up the prelude music. She then walked to the podium and said, "Welcome everybody. Are you all prepared to have fun at this worship service?" The audience responded with slight smiles. The widow who was seated alone surrounded by empty seats called out, "Where am I?"

Candace continued, "Hopefully our opening hymn will start you on that road to really feel the Spirit. Take it away, Jason," she said with a dramatic sweep of her arms.

Jason belted out the introduction, and then Candace with the talented choir members began singing, *The Battle Hymn of the Republic.* The jazzy arrangement caught the audience by surprise. Most sat quietly without joining in singing. Candace did what she could to get the congregation involved. She increased her arm movements, and began strutting back and forth across the stage while colorful strobe lights followed her. She frequently beckoned the audience to sing along. The congregation and other preachers appeared ill at ease. They tried to go along with Candace's mood, but they appeared awkward.

Harry sat in front next to the other preachers except for Diana who sat in back. He smiled warmly as he quietly observed both the women and congregation. When he saw two teenaged girls looking at him, he gave them a wink that made them giggle.

At the conclusion of the hymn, Hannah again welcomed everyone and mentioned personal counseling and confessions available immediately following the service. She then said, "Let us now bow our heads for an opening prayer."

Candace nudged Harry to rise and pointed out the printed prayer he was to offer.

Harry rose from his chair slowly—so slowly that Candace wondered if he would make it to the podium. She whispered to Diana, "Maybe he was a poor choice. I should have asked him if he could read." The other women were holding their breath, wondering how he would come across. He looked up and smiled as he looked at the congregation. He then bowed his head. His voice was quiet—almost reverent as he began to slowly read the words before him. He hesitated several times as if pondering the message. At one point his voice became shaky and emotional. Candace opened her eyes to check out the audience. She saw several people wiping tears from their eyes. She leaned towards Allison and quietly said, "For Heavens sake! I'll bet the audience thinks he's been overcome by the spirit. It looks like they've connected with him. I don't believe it."

When he uttered his final *amen*, there was an audible return of *amens* and an occasional *halleluiah*. Hannah then announced, "Our very talented vocalist, The Reverend Candace Arthur, will now sing her own rendition of *How Great Thou Art*. The choir will join her for the last verse."

Candace put her all into the hymn. Her *all* included dramatic movements of both her body and voice. So intense was the performance that the few in the congregation now responded. When the choir joined in, people stood and started singing with them. Even the widow stood unassisted. **Yes**! This was the response they had hoped for.

When the hymn concluded, Hannah returned to the podium. "Our sermon for the day will be presented by The Reverend Doctor Allison Miller."

Allison had memorized much of her sermon from an on-line site. She appeared confident as she began. "The message for today concerns living a full life as the Lord intended for us." She looked around the theatre at the audience. Their eyes were focused intently upon her. "There is a tendency for most folks to get stuck in ruts…to live only half-lives. Thoreau recognized this as he said he did not want to come to the end of his life and realize he had never really lived."

Although she presented the message with good eye contact and dynamic animation, the message didn't compare with the entertainment presented at the beginning of the service. Several members of the congregation soon began to nod. Seeing this, Candace signaled the choir to sing a loud *hum* after each pause in the text. That perked up the congregation who sat up straighter and with closer concentration as well as seeming amusement. Allison soon caught on, and she turned back towards the choir after each pearl she gave, awaiting the *hum.*

When Allison ended her sermon, Candace stepped forward.

"What the Reverend said was so right. Songwriters have long agreed with her message. We're going to share a song now that emphasizes the wisdom of her talk. Hit it Jason!"

Candace began to sing the lead song from Cabaret: "What good is sitting alone in your room?" She began quietly and reverently making it sound like a hymn. She slowly upped the pace and sang louder. "Come hear the music play."

"This has got to be a first," said Diana as she looked at Hannah. "A rousing Broadway hit performed as part of a church service. How do you think the congregation will accept it?"

Hannah nervously shifted about in her seat. "Somehow this music doesn't appear fitting for a church service." But the audience started to become involved and slowly swayed and clapped. This encouraged Candace to become even more animated. She again strutted boldly across the stage as she belted out the words. Hannah hoped her thoughts of caution would vibrate the message to Candace: *Back off. Back off. Don't overdo it.* Her thoughts failed to reach Candace who exaggerated her actions and sang all the louder.

Contrary to what Hannah expected would happen, the audience loved the show and actively participated. Even the widow joined in by clapping her hands and dancing around in the nearby aisle. Hannah herself soon became taken in. When the song was ending, she thought it was a good time to pass the collection plates. She yelled into the microphone, "Remember, The Lord loveth a cheerful giver and will bless one hundred fold to those that sacrifice for his kingdom." Before she was able to back away, Harry quickly grabbed the microphone.

"Brothers and sisters: Today you will see an unusual form of collection plate, in fact it's not a plate at all—it's a sock." He looked around at the congregation who sat with puzzled expressions. "You probably wonder why we have chosen a sock to collect donations. First of all, is there anything more humble than a sock? It gives its all to us offering protection and comfort. And what does it get in return? We just walk all over it. Still it continues to serve us without complaint."

Candace stared at Harry with her mouth slightly open. "This has got to be a bad dream," she murmured. Harry continued his unrehearsed sermon.

"The sock is usually taken for granted and at times even met with disgust, but it's not the sock's fault. It's ours. We don't appreciate all it does for us."

Candace nervously shifted around in her chair. She was about to rush forward and grab the microphone when Harry dramatically raised his voice.

"The sock protects us from the bitter cold of winter. We all know that when the feet are cold, we're cold all over. And the sock protects our feet from blisters. That alone should bring it special recognition. Our performance in everyday life depends on the sock. We all know how we can't accomplish much when our feet are uncomfortable. It can make us or break us. It deserves our appreciation."

"Do something," whispered Allison to Candace.

"It's too late. The damage has been done."

Harry continued. "Today we pass socks for donations; and as we do, we encourage you to think of the example of the sock, and to continue to serve without complaint even though appreciation is not always expressed. Think also of the many blessings we have that we take for granted. Give generously so our ministry can continue, and we can help provide the poorest of the poor with socks of their own."

Harry took his seat. Brittany leaned over toward him. "Your talk was absolutely brilliant." Harry smiled at her. Candace and the other women stared as if in a stupor.

Jason played loud music while the socks were passed. Harry noted that the widow opened her purse to give her donation. Her purse appeared full of money but she gave only a single bill.

As the socks were nearing the back of the theatre, a thin, unkempt man entered. His ragged clothes were dirty and he carried a bulging large plastic bag. He took a seat in the rear.

Allison saw him enter. With a smirk, she turned to Harry. "Is this your idea of a Santa Claus. Is he going to reach in that bag and fill the socks?"

"Very funny!"

When a sock reached the homeless man, he appeared surprised. "Thank you," he said. He held it up to take a better look. He then looked down at his own threadbare socks. He bent over and slipped the collection sock over his tattered one. He shook his foot as he felt the bills and coins. He smiled. He left the theatre, limping from the coins in the sock. Fred was dumbfounded. He didn't know if he should follow the man and ask for a return of the money or let it go as witness of good intentions by the church. He let him leave without bother.

When what remained of the offertory was presented at the podium, Candace nudged Brittany who was scheduled to give the offertory prayer.

"I lost the printout," Brittany whispered to Candace.

"Just make it up then."

Brittany had minimal exposure to prayers. She only recalled hearing them at a friend's house as a child. She reluctantly went to the podium.

"Now I lay me down to sleep. I pray the Lord my soul to keep. Amen." She followed this with a nervous giggle.

"There's a girl who should sit alone in her room," murmured Candace. "She's a total disaster."

Candace didn't want to give the congregation too much time to think about the prayer. She stood and signaled Jason and the choir to start the music. They repeated the rousing rendition of *The Battle Hymn of the Republic*. Candace belted out the words with volume that almost drowned the entire chorus. It seemed that the whole building was resonating. The audience responded more this time but still appeared to feel self-conscious being few in number.

All through the service, Harry closely observed the reactions of the congregation—what energized them, what brought out their emotions. Preacher Harry was called upon to give the closing prayer of thanksgiving. His quiet words again conveyed a spiritual essence to many. Fred kept his eyes open as he watched Harry—*Observer observed.*

For the closing hymn, Jason initially held back on his accompaniment as Candace softly began, "He's got the whole world in his hands." She quickened her pace and increased her voice volume until the chandeliers were rattling. The audience began to rhymically clap their hands. A small group of people entered from the streets and they too were clapping and singing. They actually cheered at the conclusion. Now was the time for the hard sell.

"Thank you all for joining us today," said Hannah. We can't continue without your support so if you feel so inspired, there are donation socks in the foyer that will help us to serve the Lord and provide for the needy. Also, if you have problems to discuss with one of us, or if you have sinned and feel a need for forgiveness, counseling will be available off the main foyer after the service and by special appointment. And please join us for coffee and refreshments in the foyer. Thank you all for coming."

That was Jason's clue to shine with his talents. He enlivened another Bach composition, which he creatively combined with *The Battle Hymn of the Republic.*

"Only Jason!" murmured Candace.

The choir and clergy led the parishioners out to the foyer area. Candace looked around. "Brittany, where are the refreshments?"

"You didn't tell me I was responsible for them."

Candace struggled to contain her anger. "Good one, Brittany," she said as her face turned red. "We'll talk about this later, Miss Laughing Hyena. Go get my purse. I need a joint."

Brittany didn't appear remorseful as she said, "Get it yourself."

Candace's face turned red as she angrily looked at Brittany. She managed to control herself and walked away.

The preachers formed a line to shake hands with everyone as they left. Some parishioners weren't satisfied by a handshake and drew close for a warm hug. Even though Candace took center stage, it was clear that Harry was the one they loved the most. The lineup for him was longest. Candace couldn't help but hear comments made to him:

"Your words meant so much to me."

"I was one guilty of taking socks for granted. Now I understand them symbolically, and they mean so much more to me."

"What a brilliant way to remind us to be humble and appreciative."

The women glanced over at Harry and saw him also befriending children. He was using the same magic trick that

Candace and Allison saw him do in the supermarket—grabbing a quarter from behind the ear. The children loved it.

"I wonder if he knows any other tricks?" said Allison as she nudged Fred.

"We'll see you next week," Candace said, "and remember to invite your friends."

Marc came running down to the foyer after most of the crowd had dissipated. "Great, great show, everybody. Even I enjoyed it. I might have you write it into an off-Broadway musical."

"That's not our forte, Marc. If you find anyone capable of doing it, we're open to consider it though."

Candace then saw Fred. "Hey! Why'd you let that homeless bum get away with our money?"

"I couldn't go after a limping homeless man. I think he needed the sock and money more than us."

Candace rolled her eyes. "That wasn't for you to decide. We earned every penny in that sock."

Diana gathered the remaining socks and slipped the offerings into a zippered pouch.

Candace approached Harry as he was preparing to leave. "You really impressed everyone. Did you enjoy it?"

"It was okay. I was nervous all the time though," he said as he smiled shyly.

"You didn't look nervous. You were quite the star. We're counting on you to be at our meeting on Wednesday."

Fred looked at Harry. "No, you didn't appear at all nervous or shy."

Candace looked happy. As she gathered her props she said, "Now wasn't that fun?"

As they were closing the theater, Hannah noticed the widow sleeping peacefully in her seat. "Now, what do we do?"

Harry graciously said, "I'll get her home." He walked over to her. She jumped as he gently shook her.

"It's time to go home. I'll help you."

She smiled at Harry. He got into a taxi with her. She directed the driver to her home. Harry's eyes opened wide as he saw the upscale home in which she lived.

"I forgot my wallet," said Harry. "Can you pay the fare?"

The widow reluctantly took out some money and carefully counted it.

"Could you spare a bit more to get me home?" he asked.

She smiled at Harry. "Take what you need," she told him as she opened her purse. Harry took a wad of bills. He kissed her on the cheek and bid her adieu.

~ 12 ~
Where did we go Wrong?

"Only one hundred, forty two dollars and fifty cents…and a black button!" Diana reported at the Wednesday meeting. "If we divide that between the five of us, we would only get about $20. And that's without subtracting all our expenses. We're deeply in the red."

Brittany laughed. "I wonder if we could locate the person with the missing button and return it."

"Wipe that smile off your face, Brittany. You're a big part of the reason we didn't get more," said Candace.

"What? It wasn't my fault we didn't rake it in."

Candace rolled her eyes without comment.

"I thought we had a sure thing for getting rich quickly. We've duped ourselves," said Hannah. The others chimed in:

"Yeah. I thought for sure we'd haul in thousands today."

"Where did we go wrong?"

"It was the bad weather."

"There wasn't enough time to prepare."

"We should have had a rehearsal."

"Maybe we should abandon the idea now before we get further in debt."

Candace blurted out, "No! I'll tell you where *we* went wrong. First, the floral arrangements were drooping and looked sad. Bringing that crazy widow didn't help attendance either. The announcement and handouts were pathetic. The emceeing was terrible—uninspiring. And then there's you, Brittany—you didn't bring any donation plates and then completely forgot to organize the social hour, and I mean the *forgot* in quotation marks! How could anyone forget such simple assignments? And that hideous attempt at an offertory prayer…not to mention that stupid laugh of yours at the end."

Brittany continued to smile, which further enraged Candace. The others were stunned. After having put so much time and effort into preparations, the critical words of Candace came as a shock. Diana burst into tears.

Hannah came to their defense. "Candace, what you said was out of place. We all worked hard in what little time we had to prepare. I think the basic program was nice. We just didn't have time to spread the news of the new church. And a rehearsal would have helped immensely. The rest of us appreciated each other. As for Diana, she probably worked harder than any of us."

Candace said, "Wait. I was about to get to you. Your plea for donations was nothing but pathetic. And I think the audience was about to fall asleep listening to you announce the program. You gave me a poor lead-in that I had to desperately work to overcome."

"Well next time, maybe you should announce your own act."

"Maybe I will. And Brittany, that's the first time I've heard a preacher giggle while giving a prayer. You'd better seek a new career."

Brittany again merely smiled. "Stop that stupid smile or I swear I'll knock it off your ugly face," yelled Candace. Diana stopped sobbing when she saw she wasn't alone in being attacked.

"What a bunch of cry-babies! Allison, are you going to cry too when I tell you how dull your sermon was? No wonder the donations were so little."

Hannah boldly said, "We all know that you're the only one who's perfect, Candace."

"You guys are full of it," Candace said.

"Well our full of it isn't as disgusting as yours," said Allison.

Candace stormed out of the room and slammed the door. Within two minutes she returned appearing like nothing had happened. "Girls, let's discuss this as adults."

Hannah looked at her. "Candace, you said yourself that we should consider that service as a trial run. Why take it so seriously now?"

There was hesitation before Hannah continued. "There were many factors that led to a poor outcome including the weather. We didn't plan far enough ahead. And the guests didn't have a chance to plan ahead to come to this. They weren't yet invested personally to make bigger donations. Also, we need a system for giving receipts so they can use the tax deductions. That should increase the size of the donations."

Diana said, "Maybe we shouldn't have advertised *no admission fee*. That might have given the impression that the show was strictly free with no donations expected."

"Maybe those who did come will tell their friends about us, and the turnout will soar," said Allison.

Diana appeared to be contemplating. "Is there anything else we could have done to bring in more money?"

"The hugs seemed appreciated. I think people in general are hug deficient. I heard of one famous woman only known for giving out hugs. People stand in line for hours just to feel her accepting embrace. We could become known for giving them in our church," suggested Hannah. "Everyone needs human contact. This might be the only place they can get it…and be willing to pay handsomely for it."

"Indeed. That would help cure my deficiency too," Diana said.

Harry arose abruptly from his chair and rushed over to Diana. His strong arms lifted her out of her seat, and he gave her a prolonged, close hug. Diana's face turned beet-red.

"Did that help cure your deficiency?" asked Harry.

Diana was speechless. "It would cure mine," interjected Allison.

"If the hug thing is true for most people, how could we let that be known—that it's available here for all?" asked Candace.

Allison suggested, "In the next newspaper ad, we could advertise: *Have you had your hug this week? Get yours in our church this week!*"

Having regained her speech, Diana said, "I don't know. I feel shy about hugging strangers. Are you sure everyone would like that?"

"Didn't you?" asked Harry.

Diana looked down and didn't answer.

"I'm sure that most people would. And if women felt wary of hugging another woman, we have Bad Boy Harry. They could take their choice. And Harry wouldn't have to speak. He could just give them a nice warm embrace without words," said Candace.

"Who gave me that negative title?" Harry asked.

"Can't you tell when someone is joking?" said Candace.

"A joke is supposed to make people laugh. I didn't see that response from anyone here."

"Oh, just forget it," said Candace.

Hannah changed the subject. "Giving hugs would take care of one basic need. What about other needs like the need to feel appreciated by someone. How could that work?"

"We can make volunteers feel appreciated by our thanks. We got several names in our guest log. Let's contact them and ask for help with ushering and greeting. That would also guarantee a greater turnout next week," said Allison.

The others thought this was a good idea.

"Did we get any requests for counseling?" asked Hannah.

Allison shook her head. "Not that I know of. I think people need to know us better and feel that we can be trusted first."

"Okay. I'm glad that no one really wants to give up on the church. I know if we stick with it, we'll soon be rich women," said Candace.

Harry tried unsuccessfully to hide a smile. Candace glared at him. "You don't think we can do it, do you?"

"I think you're just amateurs. That's all."

"Advice from Mr. Success! So, is there a school we should attend to learn to be as good as you?"

"No school could teach you that!" Harry said as he laughed.

Candace was not amused. "Very funny, Harry."

Hannah was anxious to move on. She suggested that they should plan a potluck social during the next week to keep people engaged."

"Good idea," said Allison. "And we can advertize that during next week's service."

"First, we need to have a social hour after the service with at least coffee and cookies and with a donation plate obvious for the treats! Who can we depend on to organize that?" asked Candace.

Brittany quickly commented, "I've been really overwhelmed with other jobs lately. I wouldn't have time."

The others hadn't even considered Brittany for the job after she forgot to organize it last week.

Candace frowned at her. What about you, Allison? Could you squeeze in a few minutes to collect bakery treats and arrange coffee, tea, and juice," she said while still glaring at Brittany.

"Sure. I'd be happy to."

"Check on bakeries to see if they'd donate day old cookies or pastries for the cause. Maybe Diana could help."

Hannah suggested that they continue with the theme of living life to its fullest. "Most people operate in ruts of routine. Let's encourage them to get out and make the most out of life. Instead of routine sermons, our presentations should be more like motivational talks. People pay lots of money to attend those."

"I feel some songs coming on," said Candace. "I'm going to live 'til I die," she started. And then went into, "What good is sitting alone in your room? Oh I love it!"

"I do too," said Brittany. Our big screens could blast out the simple word, ***Live***!"

"Thanks for your contribution," said Candace with sarcasm.

Harry finally spoke up. "Ladies, although the service provided much entertainment, I don't think it was unique enough to draw people away from other churches. The few people who came made it harder for them to respond to the dramatic presentation. We need better PR."

Hannah agreed. "Harry's right. We need something really eye-catching to get people's attention and more exposure. Allison, you're the creative writer. Any ideas?"

"I think newspaper ads are our best bet along with hand out flyers. We might say something like, *Bored of your humdrum church services? Come visit ours. We guarantee you'll stay awake!*"

"I like that idea," said Diana. "That might do it!"

"Sounds like a winner," said Brittany. "By the way, our beautiful collection plates arrived yesterday."

Candace scowled at her.

"Does that create another problem?" asked Hannah. "Actually, the sock collection devices seemed to work out well. Harry pulled us out of that problem. Do you think that we might become known for that? Official plates now might spoil our image."

Allison said, "I know! We can use the nice plates for the official collection but use large socks for other donations such as for confession donations, therapy sessions, social hour contributions, and so on."

"That would work," said Harry.

~ 13 ~
Second Sunday…Whoops!

The sun was shining on this beautiful Sunday morning. And the theatre was stunning—decorated with cascades of dazzling flowers complemented by the attractive pillows. The cast arrived early for the second service.

"Great arrangements, Hannah. Good job," said Allison.

"Thanks. It took more footwork this time. Some of the families took all their loved-ones' flowers home with them. How can anyone be so selfish?"

The others all smiled at her wry humor.

"Is everyone ready to hand out hugs today?" asked Candace.

"As ready as ever," said Hannah.

"I'm not sure this will come off smoothly. I really don't know if desires for hugs are universal," said Diana.

"We'll know soon enough."

Jason sauntered unsteadily into the theatre. He was unshaven. His eyes were bloodshot and he appeared in a daze. When Candace saw him, her mouth opened momentarily. She quickly composed herself and greeted him with a big hug. He beamed. "What did I do to deserve this," he asked with slurred speech.

"We just appreciate you so much, Jason. Are you okay?"

"Never better!"

The other women also gave him a hug. Diana pulled herself away from Jason abruptly. "I smelled alcohol on his breath," she whispered to Hannah.

"I did too. How will he ever be able to play for the service?"

"I don't think he can."

Brittany said with disgust, "That alcohol smell got all over my costume. Will soap and water take it out?"

"That's the least of our worries, Brittany," said Hannah. "We'd better keep an eye on Jason and be prepared to take action if necessary."

Diana looked puzzled. "What could we do to help? None of us are skilled musicians."

Hannah told Diana that she had taken piano lessons as a child and thought she could at least play a melody on the organ if necessary.

Harry came shuffling into the foyer. The women all ran up to him and almost overcame him with hugs. He responded with a big grin. "Ladies! Ladies! Control yourselves…or should I say *don't*?"

Candace became animated as she said, "Hey! See how happy people are to get hugged. Harry, you really fit in with our team. You're going to be a regular with us, aren't you?"

He smiled broadly as he said, "I wouldn't miss it."

Instead of quiet Bach music, Jason, in an awakening burst of energy, once again pulled out all the stops. His efforts vibrated into the street, and beckoned those nearby to join in the celebration. The congregation was unaware that he was inebriated. The women preachers relaxed when they heard him perform, but remained vigilant of him throughout the service.

The attendance wasn't much greater this Sunday. Most of the seats were again empty. Nevertheless, the speakers were dynamic. Candace and the choir brought down the house (the few in it) with their musical renditions. The parishioners appeared more comfortable with participation. They became energized and clapped and swayed to the music.

Allison's sermon was brief and to the point. Even though it was short, Jason fell asleep at the organ. Before the final end of the sermon, Jason's head fell and hit the keyboard blasting out a long deranged seventh. The horror of the noise startled the preachers who sat frozen not knowing how to respond. Jason quickly lifted his head and looked all around trying to reorient himself. That unexpected blast, however, seemed well timed to the congregation and even planned. It emphasized the speaker's message at that point. Enthusiastic *Amens* were given in response.

The sparse attendance meant only one thing to Candace—little income again this week. In an effort to increase the donations, Candace went to the podium.

"Brothers and sisters: We live in times of moral decay. The Good Book has predicted this to happen. As church-going people, we need to do all we can to stop this trend. All of us have done wrong. Confessing and being sorry is the answer. After the service, we will have counselors available to listen to your confessions so that you can free yourselves of the burdens you carry. I hope you all will participate."

After the donations had been collected and the service concluded, the leaders assembled in the foyer for the grande hug finale. Hannah and Diana positioned themselves near the office door by a sign reading *confessions*.

Candace, being the most outgoing, approached the first to leave and offered a warm hug. Several smiled as they received this special token, but there was a wide range of reactions. The teenaged boys weren't appreciative, and when they saw what was happening, they ducked around the others and made a beeline for the outside. Some adults did the same. Others beamed with pleasure.

When all of the visitors left, the group gathered to discuss the service.

"What happened with the confessions?" asked Candace.

Diana's eyes widened. "I had only one lady approach me as she was leaving. She confessed to a lie. It didn't really seem that bad of a sin, but she paid the suggested ten dollars, and appeared to be relieved of her burden. I was surprised that it didn't seem that hard to listen. I simply encouraged her not to do it again."

Candace frowned. "Did we only get one confession? I thought I made it clear that confessions were good for the soul"

"You did, Candace. And we all got that they would be good for our pockets as well!" laughed Allison.

"So why did only one person take advantage of our offer?"

Hannah thought that the suggestion was presented too abruptly; leaving not enough time for people to consider the benefits to something they hadn't practiced in the past.

"Do you think men would more likely confess to another man, especially if the sin involved a sexual misconduct?" wondered Allison.

"Maybe Harry could be available," offered Diana.

Candace sat up straight. "You're full of sage advice, aren't you Harry?"

"I can rise to any occasion."

"That remains to be seen," responded Candace.

In an effort to change the conversation, Diana asked Candace how many hugs she thought she had given today.

"A lot, but not enough to increase the donations. We should have done our hugging when everyone first entered."

Allison smiled. "I must have given at least twenty-five hugs. All of us combined would have made more than one hundred. One man I hugged wasn't a very huggable type. He was overweight and sweaty, but you should have seen his reaction when I put my arms around him. He was so happy that he laughed. I watched him leave and before he did so, he dropped another offering in the donation sock near the door."

Candace slapped her hand on her knee. "That's just the reaction I was hoping we'd see from everyone. And I'll bet that man will be here next week!"

~ 14 ~
Not Enough

"Well, we almost doubled our take from last week—two hundred and thirty two dollars," announced Diana. After expenses, there still isn't enough to pay us for all our time and efforts."

"Groan!" said Hannah. "What made us think that starting a new church was the easy way to get rich quick? Maybe we should cut our losses and give up now."

Candace pounded her fist on the table. "No, no, no! I must admit that I underestimated people and their willingness to pay for top-rated entertainment. A show like ours would cost well over a hundred dollars per person in a legitimate theatre. I thought it would be obvious to everyone. Either our message hasn't reached enough people or we need other ideas to get a great landfall. One thing for sure is that we can't give up now."

Allison's face was without expression and she looked down. "Everyone is concerned about paying the bills in these hard times. We should have expected low offerings. Donations are probably the first to go in most people's budgets."

"Church donations are different," said Hannah. "People usually regard those as necessary expenses during hard economic times. Blessings are expected from such sacrifices. It's the other non-essentials that get cut when money is tight. My counseling job is a good example of that."

"Still, people need a break from their hum-drum lives. Cheap entertainment should offer as a stress reliever that helps people survive," said Diana. Candace agreed.

"There's no doubt that we have great talent and enthusiasm, but let's face it. We aren't as unique as we need to be to attract a big following," said Allison.

"I don't understand it. We put so much effort into our performance. The word about us isn't spreading. The income this week wasn't worth our efforts," said Brittany.

"Thanks for the great revelation, Brittany," said Candace.

"Maybe the poor attendance was a fluke on Sunday. I agree with Candace. Let's continue as we were and see what happens on Sunday," said Allison.

"What are we going to do about Jason?" said Allison. "We can't have him arriving in a drunken state again."

Candace assured the others that she would have a serious talk with him.

Hannah concurred. "Still, we need to at least have a backup plan."

Diana looked at Hannah. "Didn't you say that you took piano lessons as a child?"

"Yes, but that hardly qualifies me as a church organist."

"Could you at least play the melody line to get us through a service if necessary?"

"I might. It would help if one of you had some backup instrument to accompany me."

Harry laughed. "I played the cymbals in my high school band."

Candace rolled her eyes. "Well, since you're so smart, I'm sure you can think of a way to blend the instruments and make heavenly music."

"I could if I wanted to!"

Candace rested her fist on her chin. "Hmm!" She hesitated a moment and then said, "Next, we've got to think of better ways to increase attendance and revenue."

Harry was ignored when he said there needed to be better PR.

Hannah thought that the group should think about other ideas to enhance revenue. "Many churches have gift shops in the foyer area. Ladies especially can't resist souvenir shopping."

"Right on!" said Candace. "I can make CDs of songs I've done in church."

"I'm sure those would become best sellers," said Diana. "If we can start bringing in more money, I'll buy several." Candace beamed on hearing that complement.

Allison's eyes lit up. "In keeping with a religious theme, I could write out inspired prayers in a book form. That might be my best seller that I've dreamed of so long. And my husband would be happy that my writing was finally bringing in some money."

"By all means, do it!" said Hannah.

"I think autographed portraits of us would sell well," said Brittany.

Hannah encouraged Brittany, and suggested that she check into the logistics and expenses of such a project. She added, "Many people think there is power in prayer accompanied by candles. We could sell candles with our church name printed on them."

"Having a nursery available during the services would benefit not only the parents but us," said Diana. "As I've looked around at s mothers struggling to keep their young ones restrained, I'm sure attendance would increase if the parents were free from distractions from their children."

"I don't want to end up babysitting," said Brittany.

"We wouldn't have to babysit. We could call for volunteers or have the parents rotate the care. From there, we could expand to a day care program. We could charge for that but at a cost less than other centers charge. Mothers who need the money would then be more free to have paying jobs and thus have more to donate to the church."

"All of those ideas are great," said Candace. I think we should use them all."

Harry had been silent for much of the time. After new proposals were presented, he finally spoke up. "What we need most is better PR."

Brittany reminded him that they had used good PR ideas last week. "I don't know if we could do any better."

Candace turned to Harry. "Have you had any experience with PR?"

"A little—enough to be more effective than what's been done so far here, I know."

"Well, let's make you chief PR person," said Candace.

"What do we have to lose?" commented Hannah. The women skipped rapidly over the idea and returned to the subject of money.

Candace suggested that Diana write small checks to each of the five women. She thought the others should still be considered as volunteers. Harry looked disappointed. "Hey, if you expect me to bring in more from good PR, shouldn't I get a cut too?"

"Right now, there's not enough in the treasury even for the five of us to make ends meet. I agree you should get something. We'll talk about that later." Harry said nothing but his frown indicated he was not happy with the arrangement.

"Let me give the next sermon," Candace said. "I think it's time for a Hell and Damnation sermon to get people to take their hands out of their pockets."

"I think emphasis on Heaven and the Holy Spirit would encourage people to give more generously than fears of damnation," said Diana. Hannah agreed with Diana while the others ignored the topic.

"We haven't discussed our healing potentials as a source of revenue," said Allison.

Everyone straightened up in the chairs. "Yeah," they responded almost in unison.

Candace started to sing. "Do you believe in magic?" She continued saying, " Miraculous healings get everyone's attention. That's for sure. I once went to a kind of healing revival. The preacher held his audience in an almost hypnotic state while convincing them he had the power to heal anything wrong with them. He covered failures by claiming the people didn't have enough faith. I was amazed at how strong were his suggestive powers. And the big thing—people were emptying their pockets for a mere chance to be touched by him."

"Would any of us be able to be that convincing?" said Allison.

Diana spoke up. “I could give a true testimony of how acupressure helped my migraines.”

“Not everyone considers acupressure to be a form of spiritual healing,” said Hannah. “And aren’t we getting back to the subject of spirits intervening in our lives?”

“Spiritual healing involves a different type of spirit, doesn’t it?” asked Diana.

“Who knows?” said Candace. “Let’s stay away from how the healings work and just do them!”

“I’ve had some experience with successful healings,” interjected Harry.

The group looked at Harry with skepticism. “That doesn’t surprise me. Tell us about it, Harry,” said Candace.

“There are some healings that can’t be explained by natural phenomena. It takes intense practice to get in touch with the healing spirits.”

“Here we go again. You don’t look like the type to be in touch with the heavenly spirits,” said Candace.

Harry spoke up. “Maybe you don’t have the gift of discernment.”

The others were reluctant to comment after that come-back.

Harry continued, “You have to move in stages to gain the faith.”

“There’s so much deceit in healing practices. I think there should be a limit as to how far we go to get donations,” said Diana.

“I’m not referring to deceit. I’m speaking of truth,” said Harry.

The women looked at him in disbelief but said nothing. After a brief pause, Candace offered her favorite quote: “Doesn’t the end justify the means? If people feel better for something we do, does it matter how it comes about or that they pay for it?”

Allison said, “I’ll have to think more about that. I do think we’re getting more and more weird now. One thing for sure, though, we shouldn’t advertise these services. They’d have to be made known from word of mouth.”

Candace looked at Allison as she straightened her back with a defensive posture. “Why not advertise them? Some of the most successful healers pay for whole page ads in local newspapers.”

"I thought we were trying to come across as more traditional but with an entertaining flare."

"Bah! Hannah, you were the psychology major. Do you think healing sessions would work and be a good source of added income?"

"Sure. I think everyone wants to believe in magic and miracles to some extent. They may not openly admit it, but there is some universal hope for escape to a more perfect world. Paying for this makes the belief even stronger."

"Those of us giving counseling, should keep our eyes open for people likely to benefit from such a magic show!" said Brittany.

"What are you smiling at, Harry?" asked Allison.

"I'm just amused by your conversation. How little you ladies know!"

"And you have all the answers. Is that right?" said Candace.

"Maybe not *all*, but most."

Allison looked concerned. "Maybe healing services would work, but I think we should establish ourselves in a more traditional way first. We need to build confidence in the congregation before we go so far out on a limb."

The women finally agreed to table the plan for healing services at that time.

~ 15 ~
Chapel Bells from the Chapel Belles

The ringing of Candace's cell phone interrupted the meeting. The other women watched and listened as Candace conversed. Her expression became gleeful. "Sure, we'd be happy to do that for you, but Sunday is the only date we have available. Could you work with that?" After a brief hesitation, Candace broadly smiled. "Great! We'll get together with you after the service next Sunday and discuss details." She gave a thumbs-up sign to the group.

"What was that all about?" Hannah asked.

"Guess what!" exclaimed Candace. "That cute couple I've seen usually sitting in the back just told me they want to be married in our church. They said they had never felt so close to any religion as they do to ours. And they want us to perform a unique wedding ceremony."

"That would be a forgone conclusion," murmured Hannah.

Allison smiled broadly and said, "How exciting. Our first marriage ceremony."

"Oh let me do it," said Brittany.

"Brit Babe, this is our first ceremony. I think one of us who has had some experience leading a service should do this," said Candace.

Brittany slammed her coffee cup down on the table causing it to spill. "You guys have been putting me off for weeks. I should have a chance to lead for once."

Candace tried to appease her. "I'm not sure you're ready for this? Have you ever conducted any ceremony?"

"No. But you guys hadn't either when we started this church. How hard could it be?"

"Listen! You didn't do very well on that closing prayer a few weeks ago. Furthermore, you just don't look the type," replied Candace bluntly.

Brittany became angrier. "I suppose you think you look the type."

"I have more stage presence. No one would argue that…unless you," said Candace."

Hannah interrupted. "Wait a minute. I think it's only fair to give Brittany a chance."

Although skeptical, the group agreed to let Brittany try. Hannah reminded Brittany that although the ceremony was relatively straight forward, it should be performed with a reverent confidence and dignity.

"This is going to be so much fun," said Brittany as she wiggled about in her chair.

"I don't think it's meant to be fun," said Diana.

"Well, you know what I mean."

"What should we charge for performing this ceremony?" asked Allison.

Harry thought Diana should set the price since she was the treasurer. Diana said she'd give it some thought.

Brittany spent the next week preparing for her unique ceremony. She purchased what she thought would be appropriate to transform the theatre into something special for a wedding.

The ornate theatre provided a dramatic setting for a wedding. Allison and Diana helped Brittany decorate for the occasion. When finished to their satisfaction, they left Brittany alone to complete and contemplate the décor.

Jason agreed to play the organ but insisted on a personal remuneration of $200 from the wedding party. “I’m starting to get tired of doing so much volunteer work,” he said as he peered at the others.

Candace peered back. “Why are giving us the evil eye? You’re the one who needs to prove yourself reliable. You can’t expect us to trust you when you show up intoxicated or hung over for a church service. It was just lucky that your blunder worked out when you were so hung over that you couldn’t hold your head up.”

“That was a one time event,” he retorted.

“Once is too much. If it happens again, not only will you be out but there will be no future for remuneration.” The conversation ended.

There was a spirit of joy in the theatre as guests gathered to witness the ceremony. Jason arrived appearing sober. He played romantic music that the bride and groom had selected. The preachers took their seats on the stage.

It was their first view of Brittany who was dressed in a robe she had especially designed for the occasion. It was a short top made of white silk lavishly embroidered with gold threads covering almost the entire robe. To further complement it, she wore a modified miter, also heavily embroidered and resembling a cloth covered tiara. Allison whispered to Diana, “She’s gone overboard with this, don’t you think?” The others were thinking the same. Brittany wore her usual mask-like smile that Candace often said ‘drove her nuts’.

Their jaws suddenly dropped as they viewed a large banner hung from the balcony. ***Rest in Peace*** it read.

“Who’s responsible for that?” asked Candace.

“I wonder!” commented Allison.

“Is that Brittany’s idea of a joke, or is she just clueless?”

“I don’t think many people would think it’s funny.”

Candace fumed for a moment, and then said to Allison, “I’m going up to the balcony, and see if I can get it down before the guests turn around and see it.”

“Do you want me to come with you?”

“No. Do your best to keep everyone looking forward.”

Candace made her way to the balcony. She peered over the edge where the banner was hung. "How in the world did she attach this?" she muttered. There were complicated knots and nails securing it and making it impossible for a quick release. She leaned far over the edge and started to tear it off. At that moment, Jason pounded out a loud vibrating chord that startled her, and she fell over the rim hanging on tightly to one end of the sign. Her weight caused the banner to rip to its midpoint attachment. The preachers had been watching and gasped. The congregation looked up at Candace who was now dangling from the banner. With quick thinking, Candace posed, dramatically threw one arm into the air, and yelled out, "Let the wedding begin!" As if on cue, the sign ripped from the midpoint dropping Candace gracefully to the theatre floor. Loud applause from the congregation burst out.

Jason started the Bridal March. The congregation stood as the bride walked down the central aisle holding her father's arm. They approached the smiling groom. Recalling the request that a unique ceremony was desired, Brittany began. In an attempt to be humorous, she imitated the preacher in the movie, *The Princess Bride:*

"Maywidge is the weason we are heewah to…day." She giggled.

Candace, having survived her unexpected fall, now almost fell off her chair from shock. She was tempted to intervene, but held back when she saw no remarkable reaction from the wedding party or guests. They all sat calmly with smiles. She nudged Hannah. "Isn't anybody paying attention? Or maybe they think she has a real speech impediment and are being polite and not reacting. I guess we're lucky."

"After your introduction, nothing would surprise them," said Hannah.

Candace looked upward and murmured, "Oh please dear Lord, make her give it to them straight now." But Brittany didn't.

Brittany followed her initial imitation with another giggle. That was almost too much for Candace to bear. "No! No! No! Tell me this is a bad dream. She's going to be the downfall of us all. What should we do?" she asked Allison who sat stupefied. She looked over at her cohorts who all sat with their mouths open.

Before anyone reacted, Brittany further shocked the other preachers by pulling out a sparkling gold wand. She tapped the heads of the bride and groom and then did the same to all members of the wedding party. From there she went to the other preachers and tapped their heads as well.

"What in the Sam Hill are you doing?" asked Candace with a look of abhorrence. With her back to the congregation, Brittany stuck her tongue out at Candace.

"You're asking for it," said Candace. Brittany returned the comment with a giggle and said, "Ha! Ha!"

Someone had to do something!

Candace slowly rose from her seat. She walked to the front and grabbed the microphone. She quickly said,

"As the bride and groom join hands, we will hear a musical selection especially chosen by the wedding pair." Candace then tried to discretely push Brittany to the side. She was met with a firm stance and strong hold from Brittany.

As attention focused on the soloist, a push-shove altercation was occurring in back of the bride and groom.

"Move aside," Candace whispered as she maintained a forced smile.

"This is my ceremony," said Brittany.

"You're ruining the whole thing. Get out of the way."

"I was doing fine until you got up here. Leave me alone."

Candace tried to keep her voice low and spoke without moving her lips. She firmly said, "Move! We'll talk later."

Hannah, Allison, and Diana sat immobilized with a feeling of helplessness. The bride and groom blocked the conflict from the wedding guests who seemed unaware of what was happening.

As the soloist was concluding her song, and before Candace could further intervene, Brittany quickly moved forward and shouted, "Do you each want to be married to each other?"

The couple appeared startled but answered together, "We do."

"I now pronounce you man and wife," shouted Brittany as she waved her wand over their heads.

Jason appeared stunned. The ceremony was not following the printed schedule. He looked around for a clue as to what was expected next. Candace mouthed, *Recessional.* He quickly pulled some stops and loudly started the recessional music. The bride and groom kissed without being given direction. The ring-bearer tugged on the groom's sleeve showing him the ring on his pillow. The happy couple quickly exchanged rings and then marched out of the church followed by the bridal party.

Brittany disappeared from the church when the room cleared. When the new groom saw Candace in the foyer, he said, "Now that was a ceremony that everyone will remember—exactly what we wanted. That ceremony was perfect for us. How did you guys know that The Princess Bride movie was our favorite? You must be psychic."

"*Psycho*" is a better word for it murmured Candace.

Brittany smiled on her way home. "I don't care what Candace thought. That was fun!"

Candace was waiting to confront Brittany at the next organizational meeting but Brittany didn't show up. She knew what to expect from Candace and didn't want to give her the satisfaction of being berated.

~ 16 ~
A Merry Heart doeth Good

The next Sunday service proceeded much as the earlier ones with Candace putting on a good show using her projected voice accompanied by much animation. Allison smiled as she watched her perform. She leaned over toward Brittany and said, “She reminds me of a chicken—the way she struts about.” That struck Brittany as funny, and she started to laugh.

“Control yourself,” whispered Allison.

As much as Brittany tried to stop the laugh, she couldn’t. Each time she looked at Candace, she burst out with another laughing spree. She tried to look away, but now even Candace’s voice made her laugh. She pinched her leg to the point of pain to try to divert her emotions. That made it worse. She leaned over and bowed her head low so that the audience couldn’t see her laughing.

Candace ended her song. Now Brittany’s laughing couldn’t be hidden by the music. All eyes focused on her as she laughed hysterically.

Candace was indignant. She walked over to her. “Stop it this instance, bitch.”

Brittany laughed all the louder.

Allison couldn’t help smiling and it soon turned to a laugh. Then Diana started and then Hannah. Harry concealed his smile by leaning over and keeping his head down. Hannah although amused, managed to restrain her emotion as she watched the others.

The audience didn't know what was so funny, but the laughing became contagious. Almost everyone broke into a laugh—everyone that is except Candace, who sat there angry and with a sullen expression on her face.

Candace went to the podium. She spoke loudly and with boldness in an attempt to drown out the laughing. "The sermon today will be given by The Reverend Allison Miller." She scowled as she returned to her seat.

Allison went to the podium trying very hard to control herself. She blurted out the first thing that came to mind: "Laugh and the world laughs with you." She looked over at Candace sitting there with a solemn expression. She burst out with a laugh when she saw her and said, "Weep and you weep alone." This brought another wave of laughter. Allison's laughing brought tears to her eyes and she could hardly speak. When she gained composure, she said "I remember seeing the movie *Pollyanna* when I was a child. In it, Pollyanna mentioned that there were over one thousand verses in the Bible encouraging happiness or rejoicing or even laughter. This church was developed with that philosophy—that going to church should be a fun experience. And so you witness happiness in church today." Another idea suddenly came to her:

"Brothers and Sisters. Most people are happy when they learn that meetings or speeches are cancelled. That's because most are dull, not interesting or repetitious. I suspect the same would be true for sermons. Since we're all in a jovial mood, let's alter the program today. Instead of a serious sermon, let's have an open-mike meeting. I'm going to start by telling a religious type joke. After that, I invite anyone in the congregation to come forth with their favorite church joke…no x-rated ones please."

She looked around at the congregation. Everyone was focused intently on her—quite unlike the attention during formal sermons.

"Okay…first joke: There was a substitute minister visiting a church. He began his sermon by saying, 'everyone in this parish is going to die'. He looked at a man in the front row who had a large grin on his face. 'Why are you so amused?' he asked. 'I'm not a member of this parish. I'm just visiting my sister here this weekend." Jason got in the mood with an organ exclamation after the punch line.

The audience loved it. They laughed heartedly and smiled at their neighbors sharing in the humor. A line rapidly formed leading up to the stage. A large-framed man with a wide grin was the first to the microphone. "There was a minister in a small town who rode everywhere on his bicycle. One day, his bicycle was missing. He assumed someone in his congregation had stolen it. On the next Sunday, he decided to give a sermon on the Ten Commandments and work up to the eighth—Thou shall not steal. It was his plan to look at the congregation to see if he could detect the guilty party. He started going through the commandments and got to the seventh—Thou shall not commit adultery. He stopped abruptly. He remembered where he had left his bicycle." Jason played a groaner type organ response while the congregation roared.

One by one, the volunteer comedians were cheered by the audience. The time that had been allotted for the sermon was soon exceeded. Allison finally had to announce a time cut-off. When the last joke was told, she said, "Folks, I wonder if this is the first church service to ever end happily late?"

People were still happy— smiling or laughing during the social hour. One woman approached Allison and said, "I wasn't feeling well when I came here today, but your service cured me. I feel great now. Thank you!"

"The Good Book says that a merry heart doeth good like a medicine. I guess you verified that!" responded Allison.

Another man said to Allison:

"I just thought of another joke. Have you heard this one, Pastor? Two aliens returned to their planet after visiting earth. They presented their leader with a television set. 'We weren't able to capture any earthlings,' they told him 'but we did bring you one of their gods."

"Good one," said Allison. "But that's almost not a joke. In fact you gave me a good topic for my next sermon. Thank you. Perhaps you could be my lead-in with that." The man smiled and said he would be happy to serve in any way.

As she stood there, others came to her and made comments including:

"That was the happiest service I've ever attended."

"That's my kind of church."

"Joy to the World. That's what it's all about!"

Candace was not amused. She had been replaced as the lead entertainer.

~ 17 ~
The show Goes On

Diana's ex-husband became more talkative each time he came to take their children for his allotted visits.

"You're looking brighter," he said to Diana. "How's your new church coming?

"It's going well," she responded with coolness.

"Are you raking it in?"

"We're doing alright."

Her self-esteem had increased greatly, and she now recognized how she didn't need his attentions anymore, in fact his presence was starting to annoy her. She looked at him with a blank expression. "How's your new lady friend?" She knew that would be a conversation stopper, and she was right. He didn't answer. He turned and escorted the children to his car. As he was getting in, he looked back toward Diana, but she had gone inside.

The midweek meeting began with many complements for Allison on how she spontaneously and successfully led the previous Sunday service. The group was taken back by Hannah's comment since she was the most serious minded of the women:

"We've got to make open-mike comedy sermons part of our regular programs—at least once a month," she said. "I've never enjoyed a sermon that much."

Allison smiled in agreement. “Maybe that is the key to the door for future riches.”

Candace was the only one who disagreed. “Well, I think it was a disaster. And thank you everybody for making me look like a fool.”

Brittany tried hard to not start laughing again. She dared not look over at Allison for she knew what she must be thinking.

“Candace, we weren’t laughing at you. Brittany just had a laughing fit, and it became contagious. Surely you know what that’s like,” said Diana.

Candace gave Brittany a piercing glare. “Why did you start laughing during my performance, Brittany?”

Brittany did everything she could to dismiss the chicken image from her mind. She failed again and started to laugh. “Excuse me,” she said as she rushed to the restroom while laughing.

“Tell me what’s so F’ing funny?” Candace demanded.

“It’s just Brittany. You know how she’s always been goofy,” said Hannah.

Candace pounded her fist on the table. “I don’t like being laughed at. I quit! I’m not participating in any more services.”

“Oh come on, Candace. The show can’t go on without you. You’re the one with all the wonderful talent.”

The group worked hard trying to convince Candace not to take Brittany serious. She finally submitted. “I just wish that idiot wouldn’t show up at the next service.”

Brittany came out of the restroom appearing composed. When Candace spotted her, she said, “Here comes that laughing imbecile. Shall we all try to humor her more?”

Brittany stuck her tongue out at Candace. “Ooo. That was a brilliant come back. Come closer and let me smack you.”

“You smack me and you’d better be ready for a real fighting match,” Brittany said as she glared at Candace.

“Stop it, both of you,” yelled Hannah. “We’re supposed to behave as civilized people, let alone *Wearers of the Cloth.*”

“Tell that to Brittany,” said Candace.

“Enough,” said Hannah. “Let’s focus on the logistics of next Sunday. Who’ll give the sermon?”

In an effort to appease Candace, Allison said, "I think Candace should do it. She comes across so much better than the rest of us."

Candace's demeanor softened. After a brief hesitation she agreed.

On her way home, Candace reached into her bag for a joint, but she had used them all. Her habit was becoming expensive, and she needed them now more than ever before. She called Jason who was known to raise marijuana plants, and asked him to bring her some plants so she could be her own supplier and cut expenses.

Candace was fired up on the next Sunday and ready to let loose with the fire and brimstone. The number of volunteers had grown enabling Brittany and Allison to help with more administrative duties. Allison's husband was happy to be a volunteer greeter—part of the show.

When Harry arrived, Candace said, "I haven't seen any positive results of your *great* PR work that you claimed to be an expert at."

"You will very soon," he replied.

Jason walked quietly into the theatre holding a brown paper bag with small marijuana plants in it that Candace had requested. He placed it next to the organ as he started to warm up. As Diana was fluffing up her pillows and creatively moving the floral arrangements around the organ, her foot knocked over the plants in the bag. Jason was immersed in his music and didn't see Diana hold up the plants in admiration. Thinking Jason had brought them as part of the décor, she placed them on the stage next to the other arrangements.

The preachers positioned themselves on the stage except for Diana who chose to sit in the back of the theatre where she could observe the audience. Jason captured the audience from the start with his enthusiastic music. The choir appeared more energized this morning. Only Harry maintained his quiet, warm smile offering a spiritual balance to the loud, upbeat theme.

It was time for the sermon. Candace started to the podium with determination but lost her balance and tripped. As she did so, she glanced over and with horror saw the marijuana plants on full display. She quickly used her trip to bend over and subtly push the plants to the back and hopefully out of view. She appeared visibly shaken but tried to make light of it when she began her message. "I think that's the Lord's way of keeping your attention on me and what I have to say today." Quiet laughing occurred from the congregation.

"These are hard economic times for all of us," she began, using much intonation.

When Hannah heard her opening lines, she nudged Allison and whispered, "Candace's style of delivery reminds me of how the Reverend Martin Luther King spoke. Do you think she's purposefully trying to emulate him?"

"Maybe. Let's listen to the rest."

Candace continued. "The Lord has provided us with abundance and doesn't want us to suffer from lack of needs." Her style elicited frequent "Amens" from the congregation. "He told us in scripture what we need to do to prosper even in such times as these. He told us to give one tenth of all we have to the building of his kingdom. And if we follow his advice, he promised that we will have so many blessings in return that there will hardly be room enough to handle them. Has everyone here given that advice the test?" There was silence in the audience. She went on almost with chastisement. "Anyone who hasn't tithed should hold only themselves to blame for any lack of money now." Some people in the congregation could be seen squirming in their chairs.

She encouraged members in the audience to start on a road to economic recovery with the Lord leading them in all they do—especially with church donations.

During the sermon, Harry leaned over to Brittany and said, "That Candace! She thinks she's so great. Wouldn't you like to belt her sometimes?" Harry's comment fueled the animosity between Brittany and Candace.

When Candace ended, she smugly sat next to Brittany.

"That was the worst sermon I've ever heard," said Brittany. "You really took the prize."

Through clenched teeth, Candace said, "Shut your mouth, bitch."

Harry heard the exchange. He whispered to Brittany, "I wouldn't take that from anybody! Someone needs to put her in her place."

His words further activated Brittany. She gave Candace a hard elbow jab to the ribs. Candace let out a loud gasp, and immediately returned the assault with a strong push that sent Brittany flying off her chair. Brittany stood up, turned around and picked up a vase of flowers. She emptied it over Candace's head.

"My hair! You ruined my expensive hairdo. Damn you!"

In disbelief, the congregation watched while sitting motionless and with blank expressions.

Candace, with her straight and dripping wet hair, was in position to attack. Brittany got up and this time picked up a marijuana plant and shoved it into Candace's open mouth. "There! Put that in your pipe and smoke it!"

Brittany ran across the stage with Candace in close pursuit. Candace reached forward and grabbed Brittany's wide brimmed hat and proceeded to belt her with it.

"My designer hat!" yelled Brittany.

Candace, with a gleam in her eye, shredded the hat over Brittany's head.

"Now you asked for it," shouted Brittany. She picked up the closest object she saw—one of the decorator pillows. She took a wide sweeping swing at Candace hitting her in the stomach. Candace bent forward clutching her abdomen. Brittany clobbered her again over the head. The pillow ripped and its Styrofoam and feather contents went flying everywhere. Candace grabbed another pillow while Brittany did the same.

Allison looked on in horror. "Put down my pillows—my beautiful pillows." Her words went unheeded.

Brittany lost her balance and slipped on the Styrofoam pellets that were covering the floor. She let out a loud screech. Candace showed no mercy as she continued to belt Brittany. In the process, flower vases were hit and crashed, and their plant-stands fell over. The noise brought the congregation out of its stupor. They reacted with loud harsh gasps.

Jason had been almost asleep and oblivious to the battle. But now the congregation's reaction stirred him. He looked over at what was happening. Half awake, he instinctively played the theme from *Can Can* to complement the action. With a loud rapid beat he began playing with intensity that further energized the people—all except Harry who sat back and smiled as he watched the ado.

Allison tried to intervene and came between Candace and Brittany. "Give me my pillows."

"Here they are," yelled Candace as she threw one at Allison. Allison was caught off-guard and slipped. She impulsively acted in defense hitting Candace in the face with her pillow. Now Candace and Brittany acted together bombarding Allison with pillow hits. They raced back and forth across the stage.

Hannah repeatedly shouted, "Let's calm down everybody." She was ignored.

During the battle, Candace broke one of her well-manicured fingernails. "Uhh," she screamed. "Now I'm really mad."

"Let's stop and talk about this," yelled Hannah.

Diana ran forward to intervene. The congregation seemed to take her run as a signal to join the action. There was a stampede forward. In the frenzy, innocent bumps were returned with pushes, shoves, and blows. The widow, who had become a regular of the church, got into the action swinging her cane.

Every decorator pillow in the theatre became a weapon. As they were swung at others, most ripped and soon so many feathers and pellets were in the air that it looked like it was snowing. The floor became covered and many people slipped. Sneezes filled the air. The children were delighted with the action. They had a great time sliding on the floor and throwing the pellets at each other.

The mayhem ventured into the streets. Curious crowds began to gather, and they peered into the theatre. Some entered and joined the fights.

It wasn't long until sirens were heard. Several police cars arrived at the scene. Policemen emerged with their Billie clubs and sprays. As they made their way to the stage area, Candace inadvertently hit one with a pillow spraying him with Styrofoam and feathers. She turned and recognizing him as an officer was about to apologize when she was knocked over by another blow.

In the midst of it all, Harry disappeared.

It took more than an hour to subdue and clear the crowd. While doing so, the children were laughing. Their parents were eager to leave, but the children pleaded with them to stay longer. As they were being dragged from the scene, they asked, "Can we come here again next week?"

When the action was under control, Jason swung his feet over the organ bench. He bent over to pick up his plants that he had brought for Candace but found only the empty bag. He looked all around the area but couldn't find them. Diana noticed him searching. "Are you looking for those nice plants you brought?"

Jason looked at her not knowing what his reaction should be. "Ah, yes," he said with reservation. "Do you know where they are?"

"Yes. I put them on the stage with the other arrangements. During the fight, I saw two teenagers run to the stage and they ran out with them. I thought it was nice that they should enjoy plants that much."

Jason became pale, but said nothing more.

Twenty-nine people were arrested, and taken to jail including Candace and Brittany.

~ 18 ~
Aftermath

Allison hobbled to the breakfast table holding the morning newspaper. Fred was already seated. He looked tired and unhappy.

"I had a hard time sleeping last night," he said.

"Me too. I was hurting from the bruises I got in the fiasco."

"Allison, if you tried to make up a scene like that in your novel, no one would ever believe it possible."

"That's for sure," she said as she smiled and then sighed. "The church idea isn't working out as we thought it would."

"I guess we can be thankful that the money it generated helped us keep up with the rent and added a bit to our savings."

"True, but I think our dream has ended."

Allison opened the paper. She gasped. "Fred, look at the headlines!"

Pandemonium Erupts in Broadway Church
29 GOOD people arrested as Preachers Punch Pillows

"Well, there's the clincher! Our church is a thing of the past. Look at the photos. Somebody must have been photographing from their cell phones."

Fred looked at the photos. "Hey, I think that's you trying to save one of your pillows."

"And that's you joining in the pillow fight. Wow, don't we all look bedraggled."

Candace called an emergency meeting after she was released from jail. Customers in the café stared as the church leaders arrived one by one. Candace had two black eyes, a swollen face and bruises; Brittany had a black eye and an arm in a sling; Hannah walked with a limp; Allison and Diana had facial and arm bruises, and also limped. Harry arrived unscathed.

"Aren't we a sorry looking group?" said Candace. "We should rename our church *The Church of the Woeful Countenance!*"

"Now there's a catchy title!" said Allison. "Let's do it!"

"Did you all see the news accounts?" asked Hannah.

Brittany started to cry. "Those photos made my beautiful robes look terrible. They were ripped and dirty."

"Think about what happened to my beautiful pillows that I had worked so hard on," said Allison.

"What about me?" said Candace. "My hair was a mess and my makeup all smeared. I hope my agent hasn't seen those pictures."

Candace looked back at Harry. "Harry, why no injuries like the rest of us?"

"I'm an expert at ducking punches."

Candace looked skeptical. "Where were you? I didn't see you involved in the action."

"I didn't see you in any of the newspaper photos either," said Hannah.

"I'm skilled in defense maneuvers outside of the public eye. I was in that mode as I was trying to shield you ladies."

"Wherever you were, you were obviously unsuccessful," said Candace.

"Well, the Lord knows I tried."

"Sure!" Candace grunted. "Well guys, I guess we can all admit that we've really done it this time! Not only did we miss the opportunity to pass the collection plates, but we're stuck with legal fines for assault, disorderly conduct, and inciting a riot."

"What do you mean *we*?" said Allison. "It was you and Brittany who started the whole thing. You guys should be responsible for legal costs and lack of income for us this week. I was really depending on that money, and I had nothing to do with that fight."

"You selfish bitch," responded Candace. "We bore the brunt of the fiasco, and are now suffering the most. You should compensate us for that."

"Oh, cut the crap."

Hannah interrupted. "Let's stop arguing and come together for the good of the group. The big question is where do we go from here?"

"I think we've discouraged future attendance. Maybe we should just call it a day," said Diana. "We've made enough to at least decrease our personal debts."

Candace rose quickly shaking her head. "Not after all our hard work and all the time we've spent on this. It was just beginning to pay off. I vote for continuing on as if nothing happened."

"Me too, and we can still count on visitors to the city who would come unaware of what happened Sunday," said Allison.

"I agree. Let's just go for it," said Harry.

Candace had become increasingly annoyed with Harry. "Harry, I don't really value your input. I think you ducked out of the whole scene to avoid personal injury."

"You cut me to the quick," he responded as he hung his head low. "I was fighting for you in the very midst of the action. Apparently you were all too busy to appreciate what I went through. I'll never do anyone a good deed again."

Candace looked smugly at Harry, and forced a laugh. "Among your other assets, you're a great comedian."

Diana said, "I think we're getting way off the subject. So far, it seems everyone is in favor of continuing—at least on this coming Sunday. Let's see what happens."

Everyone nodded in approval and agreed to keep their old assignments.

"One other thing," said Candace. "I think any money we had in our treasury is going to be taken by Marc. He was really mad about the mess from the service. He had to pay professional cleaners to vacuum and make the theatre presentable."

"I guess that means we won't have money for me to make new pillows," said Allison.

"Let's hold off on any expenses that aren't absolutely necessary this week," said Candace.

"Since I don't bear the battle scars as much as you ladies, why don't I give the sermon on Sunday?" said Harry.

"That's a good idea," said Allison. "Who would want to look at battered and bruised women?"

"What would be your subject?" asked Candace. "I'll need to coordinate it with the music."

Diana said, "We needn't be much concerned about that. I don't think there'll be many in attendance next Sunday."

"I can make my subject generic so that any music would fit," said Harry.

Candace glared at him. "Just lay off your Ode to Socks speech!"

~ 19 ~
Harry Comes Around

Diana returned to her former habit of keeping an immaculate house. She was in the midst of vacuuming when she heard the telephone ring. "Children, please be quiet while I answer the phone." She brushed the hair away from her face and cleared her throat. She was surprised to hear Harry's voice.

"Hi Diana. It's me, Harry. How's it going for you today?"

"Everything's fine. How's it with you?"

"Great! I was wondering if you had any plans for Saturday night?"

Diana was puzzled. "Nothing special. Why?"

"I have two tickets to *Wicked* Saturday night and wondered if you'd like to go with me?"

Diana was speechless for a moment. She wondered why Harry would want to invite her. She had long given up on the idea of dating or romance in her life. Her ex husband had bombarded her mind with messages that she was dull, plain, uninteresting.

Her hesitancy gave way to Harry's comment, "I heard you say that your ex has the kids this weekend. You're free to venture out, aren't you? Don't you deserve a break? Can I pick you up at six for dinner before the show?"

"Harry, your offer surprises me. I don't feel ready to accept such an invitation."

"Diana, have you seen *Wicked*? If not, this is your chance. Please say you'll accept. I don't want to go alone."

"It's true. I've been wanting to see that musical for a long time, and dinner out sounds like a real treat." She hesitated for a moment, and then said, "Sure, I'll go."

Diana's hands were shaking as she put the phone back in place. She walked into the bathroom, and looked in the mirror. She frowned as she saw her mussed drab hair, her pallor, and her plain features. She recalled her husband's words as he frequently berated her and referred to her as ugly. She began to cry. Her sobs alerted her children. They ran to her and threw their arms around her.

"We love you Mama."

She wiped her face and hugged them for a long time. "I sure love you all too. You don't care what I look like, do you?"

"You're beautiful, Mama." Diana let a few more tears fall.

After she composed herself, Diana went to her closet to see what would be most suitable for a Saturday evening at the theatre. Her outfits were old and out of style. "I have nothing to wear," she said aloud as she slumped over onto her bed. She buried her head in a pillow and softly wept.

On Saturday afternoon, Diana altered the hemline of her simple black dress—the fit-in-anywhere kind of dress. She found her least scuffed black shoes, and set them aside. Her thoughts went to her family sapphire ring she had taken to the pawnshop. That would have enhanced her outfit. She wished that she had been able to afford to retrieve it but it was no doubt too late now. She showered, and considered herself again in the mirror. She tossed her straight hair into different styles trying to decide which looked best. A hot curling iron added enough of a wave to create a more flattering appearance. She tried lipstick but saw that it made the rest of her face appear more gaunt, so she wiped it off. A touch of blush added the color she needed.

The doorbell rang precisely at six. Diana felt shaky as she approached the door. *Stop being silly,* she told herself. *This is only dinner and a chance to see a great Broadway show. It's not a marriage proposal.*

Harry greeted her with a bouquet of roses and a kiss on the cheek. "Wow! You look good!" he exclaimed. Those words stunned her. She didn't believe them but answered with a polite but weak "Thank you. You look good yourself." After those words escaped her lips, she thought of how unimaginative they sounded.

Harry helped her with her wrap and gently put his arm about her as he escorted her to his Porsche.

"Is this your car?" she asked.

"Yes. It's the result of a business deal that came through for me. Do you like it?"

"Who wouldn't? What kind of work do you do, Harry?"

"It's top secret—sorry I can't be more specific." Diana looked at him suspiciously, but also worried that he might think she was prying too much.

Harry opened the car door for her and carefully closed it after she was seated. She felt like a queen. As they drove off, Harry kept glancing at her and repeatedly told her how great she looked. It had been a long time since a man had been so attentive to her—maybe never before.

Reservations had been made at a five-star restaurant. Diana felt awkward in such an upscale place. She wasn't sure about correct etiquette but Harry, with his smooth behaviors, calmed her. "May I suggest the filet mignon with the house red wine which is especially good?" he asked her.

"That sounds great." Rare dinners with her ex husband were usually at the Big Boy—no wines available there.

Diana grew to like Harry more and more as the evening progressed. She soon found herself easily laughing with him. Her reactions became almost silly. At times she batted her eyes at him and flipped her hair in a flirtaceous manner. The conversation slowly shifted from small talk to more deep, pondering subjects and feelings.

"What did our friends say when they heard we were going out tonight?" Harry asked.

"I didn't tell them. Should I have?"

"I thought you girls shared everything. Well, I'm glad you didn't. This is our night and shouldn't be shared by anyone except us." Diana blushed.

Sitting near such a man as Harry, made Diana feel special. She noticed the enviable glances from other women, and couldn't conceal her radiance. She felt like the chosen one.

After the intro music in the theatre, Harry took Diana's hand, kissed it and then held it throughout the performance. Diana felt her hand becoming wet with nervous perspiration. She became so overwhelmed with emotion that she hardly followed the script, her thoughts being on Harry and how much she was enjoying him. She was relieved when intermission came, and she could take a deep breath in the ladies lounge.

As they drove to Diana's home, they discussed the performance. "Do you think witches really exist?" asked Diana.

"I know that there are people with special powers that others can't explain," he answered.

"Do you mean like the ability to put curses on people?"

"Some people might be able to do that. Others might be able to defy the laws of physics, but I don't know if that makes them witches."

"Have you ever seen the laws of physics defied?"

"Yes. I've done it myself, but that's a subject for a different time."

They arrived at Diana's house. Harry started to get out of the car.

"Wait a minute," said Diana. "There's something I must ask you."

He sat down and turned toward her.

It took much courage for her to ask: "Why did you ask me out tonight?"

"I enjoy being around you and thought we'd have a good time. I've been attracted to you from the moment we met," he answered.

Diana frowned. "That's hard to believe. I'm well aware that I'm not beautiful. And I have a blah personality—not at all interesting. You must have been bored out of your mind with me tonight."

"Where did you ever get such a low opinion of yourself?"

"I've heard it all my life. And I see it in the mirror each time I look."

"But you are a beautiful woman," he told her.

"It's nice to hear that, but I know it's not true," she said.

"What do you mean, 'it's not true'? You are beautiful both outside and in. Why wouldn't you believe me?"

"All my life, I've been told that, at best, I'm plain—especially by my ex."

"You are anything but plain. Your ex and anyone else who gave you that impression is a fool."

Tears welled up in her eyes. The positive comments embarrassed her. "It's very nice of you to tell me that, but I'm realistic. I know that I'm not attractive."

"Diana, there's magic in belief. You become what you believe you are. You've been feeding yourself a lot of false information, and now you believe it to be true. Look at me Diana. Look into my eyes."

The tears now ran down her cheeks as she looked at Harry. Harry held her close to him.

"You are beautiful, Diana." Diana shook her head negatively.

Harry persisted. "Stop telling yourself such lies. Say out loud to me, 'I am beautiful'"

"I can't. It's not true."

"Say it, Diana. Say it."

Diana started to cry. She opened the door and ran toward the house. Harry followed her and grabbed her arm. "Admit that you're a beautiful woman."

"I can't lie."

"If you're not beautiful, it's because you tell yourself you're not. There's magic in belief. So start telling yourself you're a beautiful woman, and you will soon see for yourself that you are."

"Let me go. I don't believe I am or ever will be beautiful. I'm plain. Open your eyes."

"I'm not going to let you go until you say it." He held her close to him.

She sniffled. She knew he spoke the truth. He would not let her go until she said what he wanted to hear. In a quiet monotone, she let the words escape her lips. "I'm beautiful."

"Say it again."

"Please don't make me."

"Say it again."

"I'm beautiful," she sobbed.

"Can I come in now?" he asked. She nodded.

There was a mirror in the foyer. He again firmly held her in front of the mirror. "Look at yourself and say those words again," he told her.

Not wanting to prolong the agony, she said, "I'm beautiful. I'm beautiful." She then relaxed. She carefully studied the face in the mirror. "I am beautiful." She continued to look at herself and began to smile. "I'm beautiful even while crying."

"Yes, Diana. You're right. You are a beautiful woman." He gave her a long passionate kiss. He pulled out his handkerchief and wiped her wet face. "May I stay for a few more moments?"

"Yes." She regained her composure and smiled again. "I'll make some coffee."

Harry followed Diana into the kitchen. He kept his arm around her as she prepared a snack. They engaged in small talk and took their coffee and snacks into the living room. As they were chatting, Harry asked, "Did the group decide to give me a cut of the donations?"

"Not an equal cut, but something." She reached in her purse and pulled out her checkbook. She quickly wrote out a check and handed it to him. "I'm sorry I didn't get it to you sooner, and I'm sorry it's not for more." Harry appeared disappointed but accepted it without comment.

Diana became slightly restless and said, "Would you excuse me for a moment? I need to use the restroom. I'll be right back."

Diana left the checkbook on the table. Harry picked it up and carefully tore out the last blank check, folded it and put it in his pocket. When Diana returned, Harry was looking at some family photos on the wall.

"I assume these are your children. They got their mom's beautiful looks. I hope I can meet them sometime soon."

"I'd like that. Your check was okay, wasn't it?"

"Yes. Thanks. I hope to give most of mine to charity for disadvantaged kids."

"You never cease to amaze me. And I've had such a good time tonight."

Suddenly, he stared intently into her eyes. He put his arms around her. "May I kiss you?" he asked. She quietly nodded. His kiss was again passionate and long. Diana's heart was pounding and she became limp. A sexual yearning consumed her during that kiss. It was a kiss deeply etched upon her lips, and she knew she would feel it forever.

"Diana, I want you so badly. I know what the Good Book says about sex when you're not married. We need to practice what we preach, don't we?"

She wanted to say, *who cares*? But Harry sounded sincere. She didn't want to do anything to turn him away, and so she quietly nodded in agreement. They stood in a prolonged embrace.

"It's getting late. We'd better get some sleep before the big day tomorrow." He gave her another brief kiss and said, "Let's get together often, Beautiful."

Diana barely slept that night.

~ 20 ~
Return to the Pulpit

Hannah stopped by the funeral parlor to get flowers for the morning service. She was greeted with an exceptionally warm welcome.

"Good morning, Miss Hannah. Isn't it a beautiful day? I saved some of the nicest arrangements for you, and I have a car ready to take them and yourself to the theatre."

"That's so kind of you. Thank you so much." She looked at the abundance of beautiful arrangements. "These flowers look hardly a day old."

"Well, I did pull some strings for you. We want your service to look good." He smiled, hesitated for a moment, and then said, "By the way, did you once tell me that our parlor would be acknowledged in the programs?"

"Yes, we always do that. I can bring you one of the programs next week."

"Thank you. Actually, maybe I'll come with you today and help you place the arrangements."

Hannah was surprised that he would want to admit to any association with the church after what happened last week. "You don't have to do that."

"It's my pleasure."

When Hannah arrived at the theatre, she was surprised to see a crowd gathered at the entrance. As she stepped out of the hearse, clamoring reporters surrounded her, all besieging her with questions.

"Do you work for the church?"

"Were you one of the ministers who started the fight last week?"

"Was the riot a staged event?"

The funeral director made a path for her as he helped carry in the flowers. "Please step aside and allow the lady to pass," he told the newsmen.

Hannah tried to smile pleasantly but ignored the questions.

Allison, Brittany, and Diana arrived soon after; each wearing heavy makeup to conceal their healing bruises. They, likewise, were surprised by the restless crowd that had arrived before them. Brittany appeared delighted by the attention. She laughed as she answered one question—"No. What happened last week was not planned." Allison pulled her away before she could say anything more. As they made their way into the theatre, they were amused as they overheard conversations by members of the congregation and guests:

"Were you here last week?"

"Did you take part in the action?"

"Last Sunday was the most memorable day of my life—I'm so glad I was here."

"I wish I had been here. I'm so sorry I missed it."

"I can hardly wait to see what happens this week."

"If they charged admission, I'd pay more to see it again than I would for a Broadway show."

"It's the greatest thing to occur on Broadway ever!"

Candace arrived by taxi. On the ride to the theatre, she felt depressed thinking that the dream of getting rich was lost. She fought the feelings by wearing a white feathery boa, sparkling silvery high heels, and heavier makeup than usual. As she stepped out of the car, there were cheers as the crowd recognized her as a main entertainer at the church.

"How about giving us a few bars of one of your show stoppers?" yelled one of the reporters. Without forethought, she belted out as only Ethel Merman would have done: *"There's no business like show business. There's no business I know."*

Those nearby cheered louder and clapped with approval. Hannah, on hearing the commotion, ran out and pulled Candace into the theatre.

"We're going to give up our image of any semblance to a church if you keep that up," she said to Candace.

"We gave that up last week, didn't we?"

When Harry saw the reporters and cameras, he looked down and made his way through the crowd trying not to be noticed. When he found Candace, he said, "I don't feel very well today. You once said you could give a sermon without any prior notice. Could you do that for me today?" Candace agreed. Harry then said he'd feel better sitting in the back during the service.

No one seemed to notice the look of elation on Diana's face from her date the previous night. She walked about in a daze and hardly reacted to the church clamor.

Not a single empty seat could be found at the beginning of the service, in fact it was standing room only. Several policemen were scattered through the audience, ready to subdue the crowd should there be another riot.

The energy level of the crowd was high. Candace easily picked up on it. She began the service with the fore-planned winsome hymn that she had selected in the midst of her despair when she felt the church had failed. After the first two measures, she upped the pace, threw the boa over her shoulder, and soon was strutting across the stage in all her glory. Camera flashes went off throughout the theatre. The more the flashes, the more she strutted. The congregation stood and moved with her while clapping to the beat.

Candace gave a brief, unrehearsed sermon. She delivered it with much drama. Her words didn't seem to matter to the congregation—it was the spirit in which she presented the sermon. It became an audience participation sermon. When Candace laughed, the audience laughed. When she cried, they did likewise. It took little to elicit yells of *Halleluiah* and *Amens*.

When the collection plates were passed, they started to overflow with donations. Fred wasn't sure how to accommodate the unexpected abundance of offerings. He looked down at his shoes, and then removed his socks and passed them for the overflow of money. When they also were filled, several men in the audience removed their stockings, and gave them to the cause. When the containers reached the back of the theatre, Fred saw the same homeless man who had absconded with their initial collection sock. This time, Fred was there to intercept before it reached the vagrant. Not wanting to disappoint the man, Fred slipped him a five-dollar bill as he passed by.

When the hour was near the end, Candace invited all to follow her and join in with singing, *When the Saints go Marching In*. She stepped down from the stage and moved into an aisle. "Follow me everybody!"

As people moved into the aisles, a line formed around the theatre following Candace's lead as she took the position of a drum major. Everyone strutted with an animated march involving pumping arms or raising hands into the air. The scene once again rivaled the pandemonium of the previous service. Jason repeated verses prolonging the excitement of the procession. As Candace ended the song, she marched up to the stage. To her surprise, those marching behind her followed. They continued clapping and swaying as Candace went to the microphone.

"After the final prayer, let's all hug our neighbors as brothers and sisters," she yelled. The congregation crowded onto the stage and ran to Candace. They overwhelmed her with hugs. She barely made it to the foyer to greet the remainder of the audience.

Diana raced to the back to talk to Harry. He was rapidly making his way out to the foyer. "Harry, wait up," she yelled. He turned and waved to her, but continued his exit. Diana managed to reach him outside the theatre.

"What's the big hurry?" she asked.

"I have an appointment. I have to hurry so I won't be late." Diana couldn't conceal her disappointment.

"Just tell me something. Did the good attendance today have anything to do with your efforts at PR?"

Harry smiled a coy grin but didn't answer directly.

Diana read that smile and said, "I thought so! Will you call me after your appointment?"

"Sure. See you later."

Diana returned to the foyer where she saw hugs being passed out en masse as she had never before seen in a public setting. Men laughed happily as they received hugs especially from the police officers.

Almost the entire congregation stayed for the social hour in the foyer. The energy and happiness continued from the service. Conversations came easily between strangers. Men were seen smiling broadly as they lifted their pant legs showing no socks, having donated them for the collections. Reporters had them pose for photos, each smiling with their raised pants and sockless feet.

It was fortunate that Allison had solicited a great abundance of treats donated from the local bakeries. The collection plates for refreshments were generously filled.

~ 21 ~
More Free Publicity

Every major newspaper carried articles about the Heaven on Hold Church. Allison found one of the accounts Monday morning while drinking coffee at the breakfast table.

"Hey, Fred. Listen to this:

The Heaven on Hold Church was standing room only for yesterday's service at the off-Broadway Old Templeton Theatre. The church service didn't resemble any other church service known to this reporter, in fact the only thing suggesting a church was a unique opening prayer, offertory prayer and closing prayer. This reporter wasn't the only one with such feelings. An elderly woman in the congregation often yelled out, "Where am I? This doesn't look like a church".

The congregation had fun while being entertained. The ministry was indeed talented, and reflected professional backgrounds.

I didn't mind personally making a generous donation—more than I have at conventional churches. I got my money's worth. What will happen next, only time will tell.

"Great article, don't you think?"

"Yeah you couldn't ask for better free publicity."

Allison smiled as she looked at the accompanying photos. I think that's me there. Look."

"You're right. And look there. Isn't that me?"

"I think so. We sure look like we were having lots of fun in that aisle march led by Candace. Does this article qualify us as celebrities?"

"Either that or scoundrels."

"Candace is the one who really stands out. Look!" Candace was caught strutting in her priestly attire. "A black top hat, tuxedo coat and pants would have fit the image better, don't you think?"

"You're the only one who would think of that," said Fred. "That feathery boa and dazzling high heels couldn't be surpassed."

"The reporter said only time will tell what happens next to our church. Isn't that the truth!"

"I agree. Only time will tell," said Fred. He smiled. "Anyway, not only has the church significantly decreased our debts, but our savings account has started to grow. After the donations are counted from yesterday, we may be on our way to real riches!"

"Let's hope so. Riches and a home in the Hamptons! Should we start packing? And should I start buying baby furniture and clothes?"

"Hey, slow down. We need to have more in the bank before we take on children to provide for."

Allison held the newspaper up covering her face to hide her disappointment.

~ 22 ~
Cause for Celebration

Diana couldn't contain herself. She had to call all the group members and announce the take from the last service. She called Harry first. "Over $10,000 cash!" she blurted out. "I was beginning to think we'd never reach that figure, but here we are."

"I'm not surprised," he responded. "People react and want to be part of adventure and controversy."

"So! That was part of your PR plan."

Harry smiled. "Maybe we should get together again this weekend and celebrate the beginning of two great affairs!"

Diana was glad he couldn't see her blush. "Yes, let's do it!"

When Diana phoned Candace with the good news, she envisioned her jumping around with glee.

"Yipee! I couldn't have done better if I had been in a Broadway show."

And Hannah's reaction: "Finally, our hard efforts and bruises have started to pay off!"

"When do we get our checks?" asked Allison and Brittany.

"We need to get together and talk about how to disperse all the donations now," said Diana. "Let's decide at our next Wednesday meeting."

* * *

Diana seemed to become a new person after she started dating Harry. She was much more outgoing and radiated self-confidence and happiness. She was in love not only with Harry but with herself and everyone else whose path she crossed. "What happened to you?" other members of the group asked.

"I've finally put my bad marriage behind me. There are better things to think about now."

All members arrived early for the weekly café meeting. As each entered, there was applause from the other café patrons. The preachers were now recognized as celebrities and on their way to riches.

Candace looked at Diana. "Let's divide that money first."

Diana smiled. "That's been safely deposited in the bank. The question is how much of it should we keep in the treasury and how should the rest be divided?"

"Just divide it equally between us," said Brittany. "I'll take my cut now!"

Candace became livid. "Like you deserve an equal cut! All you do is show up for the services and sit there with an idiotic smile while the rest of us have been busting our butts in preparations."

"F-you!" responded Brittany. "I should get special credit since I was the one who first got the idea of starting a church," said Brittany.

Hannah interjected at that point. "Correction, Brittany. You spotted a clergyman who appeared wealthy. It was me who suggested that I had heard that a fast way to get rich was to start a new church."

Candace became more irate. "Big deal, both of you! Ideas by themselves don't last long. Action means more."

Harry joined in and felt he also was being slighted by his meager income. "I'm not satisfied with the current divisions either. I'm worth a lot more than you gals are giving me, that's for sure."

"Harry, the church wasn't even your idea. And you did nothing to work at developing it. You agreed to take a small role in the program—just sitting upfront and reading a prepared prayer. The rest of us work a lot harder preparing the whole service. Why should you get any more?"

"Don't you think that now I would be considered an equal participant? I've seen how the people like me. If it weren't for me, I think your church would fold."

"Oh, come on. That's not true," said Candace.

Harry went on. "Everyone would miss me if I didn't show. I know it! And I wonder what would happen to your church if I quit and started my own?"

Those words sent a shudder of fear through Candace. He might be right.

Diana quickly came to Harry's defense. "Harry certainly should be considered an equal partner now."

Candace suddenly realized it was important to have positive feelings with Harry. "Harry, we all love you and want you to be one of us. We'll think more about it. I'll talk to the rest and see if we can do more for you."

"Why not discuss it now? I'd like to be in on the decision," said Harry.

"That would be only fair," said Hannah.

Candace took a deep breath. "Okay. First, let's look at how each of us plays a role in the church now and whether we should divide the income according to the functioning of each member," said Candace.

Allison said, "I think there should be one share for each of us that were founders of the group and one share for each person involved in preparations for the services, and another share for everyone who actually performs in the service."

"I think there should be an additional share for those who give more time on stage. It's very stressful to be in front of a large audience, said Candace."

"And I think I should get more than one or two shares," said Harry. We need to take into account audience appreciation and the effects we individually have on audience attendance."

"This is getting way too complicated, and we haven't even discussed Jason and Marc and their wants of a cut," said Hannah.

"Let's put it to a secret vote. Each of us should write the names of all of us and what shares we think each should fairly have," suggested Brittany.

"Should the shares be based on the time each of us spends during the entire week for the church?" asked Hannah.

"That would be one consideration. Performance should be another criterion," said Candace.

"I knew you'd think that would be highly important," said Brittany.

"You don't have a right to criticize me," said Candace. "You not only don't perform any essential role but also don't do much work for the preparations."

"I'm sick of you trying to be a one man show," said Brittany. "And I think I'm not alone. Some of us have been talking about how you try to take over everything for your own glory. If I'm not performing, it's because you don't give me the chance."

"Would you like to see me quit," asked Candace.

"No. No," said Hannah. "I think we all recognize your talents and how you are necessary for this success."

Brittany and Allison looked at each other knowing that they would have the lesser returns based on the way the conversation was going.

"As Hannah said earlier, this is getting way too complicated," said Allison. "Some of the outreaching just can't be measured. Let's just divide the money equally. We all have equal interests in trying to make the church a success."

"Brittany said that some of you think I've taken over too much. Have you been talking about me behind my back? If so, why would I want equal division of funds when I'm the main entertainer?" said Candace.

Brittany's jaw dropped and she appeared indignant. "You've said enough, Candace. And the rest of you—I'm beginning to wonder if you're all just a bunch of greedy bitches."

"Thanks a lot, Brittany. Do you really believe that? And do you really believe you participate equally and deserve an equal share?" asked Hannah.

Brittany slumped in her chair and didn't respond.

Lengthy discussions continued as to how future income should be divided. Hannah stood. "Girls, we've had this discussion before. No matter how we try to divide up the income, someone doesn't think it's fair. We settled a long time ago for equal divisions without weighting them for importance or efforts. I think that's the only way we'll settle reasonably."

"I was never included in that equal division agreement," said Harry. "I think you all should know that my concerns aren't for myself. I plan to donate all the funds I get from here. My favorite charity is for kids with terminal diseases who can't afford to pay for expensive treatments. That's why I fight so hard for my share of the contributions."

The women all lowered their heads, feeling some shame for their selfish desires.

"All in favor of making Harry an equal partner?" asked Diana. There were no nays.

"So, let's start by giving equal cuts to the six of us preachers, and give some fair salary to Jason and Marc," said Hannah.

Allison wrinkled her brow. "That brings about another problem: how much do we give Jason? He's often hung-over and we can't depend on him to be at his best on Sunday mornings."

"Let's put him aside for the moment and settle on ourselves," said Candace. "And I'm still against doing much for Marc. That wasn't in the initial agreement, and he's been paid in other ways," said Candace.

"Okay. Let's leave him out unless he makes it impossible for us to stay here a little longer," said Allison.

Diana continued her questions about the money. "How much should we take out of the total for our salaries? We need to have funds available in the bank for various costs."

"Why don't we put half of the donations into savings for various necessary funds and split the other half?" said Harry.

Allison looked disappointed. "I felt so happy when I heard how much we took in. I had already planned how I would spend my share. Receiving only half is a let-down."

Candace said, "I feel the same way, but I think we should go with the half-half plan for now and adjust as we go along. Money in the bank could serve as a savings account for all of us." She hesitated briefly. "At first I was happy thinking about how much we made, but then I thought it's really far from the donations we should be getting."

"What did you expect?" asked Diana.

"There were probably at least 1000 people there. That means an average donation of only $10. That's pretty cheap."

"I think that the problem is that people are associating our services too much with other churches," said Hannah. "The people coming here don't yet feel they're significant supportive members, and give only a token contribution. We need them to feel more invested somehow."

Allison thought they should start more self interest groups. Diana thought they should get more people to act as volunteers. Both ideas were accepted. Allison was put in charge of developing plans for each.

Harry spoke. "I think we need to use psychology on the congregation during the collections. We need to place people as plants in various sections who take out large bills, like two or three twenties obvious to everyone around. Those nearby wouldn't want to look cheap and would contribute accordingly."

Candace was delighted. "Harry, you're the greatest."

"I thought you'd never notice," he said as he winked at Diana.

"Now we need to talk about how to keep our momentum going. Last week's good attendance isn't going to continue forever. I think we're going to need something spectacular to keep a standing room only crowd," said Candace.

Hannah appeared tired of the interactions. "Let's just continue with our upbeat show. Last week gave us the exposure we needed. I think that alone will guarantee continued attendance for quite awhile, and our souvenir shop has been a boost to our revenues."

"I hope you're right. But if we continue on as before, let's still all keep thinking of new ideas to keep our congregation and attract more," said Candace.

Hannah summed up the meeting. "It's been agreed that half of the collections will be kept in the bank and the other half divided equally between the six of us. Right?"

The others nodded and Diana began to write out the checks.

~ 23 ~
Another Plot

Attendance continued to be high for the next few Sundays. The leaders were pleased with the abundant revenue and growth in the treasury. They began to feel the riches that had been their goal. But as the excitement slowly diminished from the notorious brawl, there was a noticeable slow trend toward lower turnouts and less generous contributions.

Harry was absent for the next meeting. Candace frowned as she said, "I told you weeks ago that we needed a plan to keep up the momentum after our peak. We need to get on this quick before we're out of business." The others agreed. "Well, any bright ideas?"

Allison said, "Hugging seemed to be appreciated when the crowd was in the right mood. Maybe we should promote more of that. Hugs make people feel good, and happier people are more generous with donations."

Hannah hesitated and said, "I noticed that when we tried it before, there were people who appeared uncomfortable with hugging strangers. I was thinking about this when I went to a football game last weekend. There was a silly mascot dressed as a cougar. He was giving out hugs. You should have seen the lineup waiting for a hug from him. Many of them posed for photos too. I think many people are more comfortable being close to costumed characters rather than to recognizable people."

"How would people react to a cougar hugging them in church?" asked Brittany.

"Obviously, we wouldn't use a cougar. A lovable animal like a Teddy Bear or Shrek would be a better choice." Hannah paused and then her eyes lit up and she said, "What about an angel? Wouldn't that be a great reason to attend our church? A hug from an angel! Doesn't that sound appealing?"

The other women became excited by that idea.

"How would we charge for that?" asked Candace.

"We could say that the angel was here to earn money to get his wings," said Brittany.

"I see you've watched *It's a Wonderful Life*," said Diana.

"True, but wouldn't the same idea work?"

"Maybe a better plan would be that the angel has been sent to collect money for the building of a better place to worship," suggested Hannah.

"I think you're on to something, Big H," said Candace.

"Who could we get to dress as an angel?" asked Brittany.

Allison volunteered, "I'm sure Fred would do it."

"No. We need him to be a greeter and organize the collections," said Candace.

The others all seemed to get the same idea at once—"Harry!"

"Did anyone talk to Harry about his being dressed as an angel?" asked Hannah at their next meeting. No one had. Before they completed their thoughts, Harry arrived.

Harry detected an impish expression on the faces of the women as he approached. "What gives?" he asked.

The women told Harry about their idea. He looked stunned and blushed. "Me, an angel? I don't think anyone has ever thought of me like that before."

"No one would know it was you. You would just have to present yourself as an all-loving, jovial being," said Diana.

Candace forced a cough. "Let's not ask the impossible from him."

Harry scowled at Candace. "If you think I couldn't carry it off, why are you asking?"

"Just joking, Harry. You know I love you," said Candace.

"Your acting skills could use improving."

Hannah intervened. "Enough! Enough! Will you do it, Harry? I think it would be a great source of income."

"I'll only agree if it's unanimous that I'd make the best angel."

"You're the only one we considered, Harry," said Diana.

After a brief hesitation, Harry accepted the challenge. "Do you have a purpose in mind for the donations? Would I just stand there with a collection plate?"

Diana smiled at him. "We thought we'd propose that donations be made into a building fund. In return for the donation, the donor would get a hug from an angel."

Harry smiled broadly. "That might work."

Excitement escalated. Hannah said, "We need some type of chart to display the growth of donations towards our goal."

"What about a big sock design with a thermometer-like indicator displaying the progress?" said Allison.

Everyone thought that sounded great. Hannah said, "We could also put a sign at the bottom of the sock saying something like *Help the angel complete his mission by contributing for a better house of worship*?"

"Good idea," said Candace. "It's unique, enticing, and money catching!"

"We'll need some good PR to bring people in for this," said Diana.

Candace was so excited she couldn't sit still. "How about you and Allison start working on this. I think we've got a winner. What should we call our angel?"

"I've always liked the name, *Herbie*," said Brittany.

Everyone smiled.

"For once, I think you've made a good suggestion," said Candace. "Herbie. That's a great name for an angel. Everyone will be comfortable hugging a Herbie."

~ 24 ~
Herbie

Not even his mother would have recognized him after the women helped him into his costume and applied makeup. Harry, now known as Herbie, looked indeed like an angel on earth. His head was adorned with a long blond slightly wavy wig upon which was placed a white satin skullcap. A long sleeved white robe tied with a twisted golden waist rope covered his padded frame and disguised his sexy, masculine body. The women worked together and were happy, even laughing as they created their angel.

Diana had promoted Herbie's debut in several ways. She sent announcements to the newspapers, made posters and hung them in many sites near Times Square, and even arranged for radio announcements. Thousands of flyers were given out on the streets. She had admired them and made several edits before she was satisfied that they would be effective.

Come for a *once in a lifetime* hug from an ANGEL
The angel, Herbie, has been sent from above
to the Heaven on Hold Church.

Come and get the blessing of a hug
and help Herbie complete his mission

Donations will help raise funds for a new church building

Old Templeton Theatre/ Sunday, 11 am

Allison made a poster in the shape of a sock, and painted on it: ***Building fund Donations*** with lines indicating collection levels towards the goal. From one corner, she hung a large golden Christmas stocking to hold the offerings.

The next Sunday service was presented much like the previous ones. The entertainment was superb and appreciated by the gathering, but the focus of the congregation was clearly on anticipation of the entrance of the promised angel.

The lobby was crowded, and curious people entered from the street as Herbie appeared. A line quickly formed to get a closer view and a hug from an angel. The crowd of people pushed and shoved to get personal contact from Herbie.

Harry was good at hugs. He gave every hug as if each recipient were valued and special. Diana carefully watched him. Before her eyes, he seemed to become the angel he was role-playing. She felt he was a true angel for her as he brought about a miraculous change in her self esteem. It appeared he was doing the same for others. After a hug from him, the recipients radiated true joy. The other preachers were less focused on personal reactions but merely smiled as they kept watching the golden sock swell.

One impish boy ran to Herbie and squeezed him so hard that a wallet fell from his angelic robe. Harry quickly stepped on it to prevent others from seeing it.

"What fell from your dress?" the boy yelled out.

Harry tried to distract him, and yelled out to the surrounding crowd, "You're all helping me complete my mission. Thank you. All of your help will be returned to you in blessings ten fold, and that's a promise."

The monstrous boy kept persisting. He circled around Harry trying to see what the *angel* was trying to hide. Harry again tried to change the boy's focus.

"Angels can perform magic," he told him.

"Like what?"

"Like finding a quarter behind your ear." Harry pulled out the quarter.

"That's not magic. Anyone can do that trick."

"You're a very smart boy. Now run along and find your mother."

"No. I want to see what you're hiding."

Harry struggled to maintain an angelic image. He said as pleasantly as he was able, "You're just imagining things. Nothing fell out of my robe."

"Yes it did, and I saw you step on it. Are angels supposed to step on things to hide them?"

"You just *thought* I stepped on something. Your mind was playing tricks on you."

"I saw it for sure. You're a fake angel." He then gave Harry a hard kick on the shin. Harry winced from the pain.

"Ah hah! Angels don't feel pain," the boy yelled out.

The boy's mother grabbed him by his shirt and pulled him away as he continued to yell, "Fake angel! Fake angel!"

"He'd make a great poster child for birth control," murmured Harry.

At that point, the widow came up to Harry. "That's you, Sylvester, isn't it?" She laughed and said, "That boy gave you exactly what you deserved, you bastard. You're going to have to do a lot more than give hugs to earn your wings."

Harry looked carefully into her eyes. "I'm sorry I wasn't a better husband. I wish I could make it up to you. You're still as beautiful as the young girl I married. I love you so much. Stay with this church that brought us together again, and give thanks with your donations. I'll put in a good word for you with that Man in the Sky." He gave her a long embrace. The scowl left her face and she departed in peace.

The crowd remained undaunted from the accusations of the brat. They continued to gather around Harry giving donations and seeking blessings from hugs.

When the crowd finally dispersed, the women excitedly looked at the bulging collection sock.

"We'd better take it into the office and count the take," said Candace. She led the others into the adjacent room, but Harry didn't follow. He stood very still.

"Aren't you joining us?" Diana asked Harry.

"No. I'm anxious to change clothes. You go ahead without me."

He remained still until everyone left the lobby. He then started to walk with an awkward gait towards the dressing room. As he did, several wallets fell to the floor from his robe.

~ 25 ~
A Rose by any other Name

The leaders laughed, cheered, and gave each other high fives when they learned that the total donations from the last Sunday service exceeded their expectations.

"Our angel turned out to be a true God-send for us," said Allison.

"I think news will spread and Herbie will become a well known attraction," said Hannah.

Candace put her elbow on the table and rested her head on her fist. "You're probably right, but it's really sad that it takes some stupid idea to be more valued than high quality performance."

"I can imagine how you feel," said Allison. "Anyway, let's go with the flow and pay our bills while the show goes on."

Marc saw the overflowing collection plates from the service. He joined the crowd in the foyer after the service and made his way to Candace. "I need to talk to you after everyone leaves," he said.

"Okay," responded Candace. *I wonder if there's a problem that will thwart our plans*, she thought.

She met him in the theatre office when everyone else had left. "How did you like our service today?" she asked as she flopped into the velvet covered armed chair across from his desk.

"It was your best yet. If you keep on progressing, you should be up for a Tony."

Candace relaxed in the chair and smiled dreamily. "That's my ultimate goal. I'm just waiting to be discovered and finally make it big on Broadway."

"There are hidden costs along the way, you know."

"Like what?"

"Well, you've fallen behind in your rental agreement."

"What do you mean?" Her initial puzzlement soon gave way to realization, and she abruptly sat up straight. "Oh. Is this a form of blackmail?"

"A rose by any other name... Should I lock the door now?"

Candace frowned as she once again started to unbutton her robe.

After the debt was paid, Marc said, "Your church services are costing me more than I expected. I'd like an equal cut into the donations."

Candace's entire body tensed. "Oh, sh...! You've got to be kidding! Our take is already divided between six people. That barely pays our bills. Now everybody wants to get into the act and capitalize on our hard work. Soon after all our hours of dedication, we'll be back to where we started." She grimaced. "I need a joint." Candace quickly buttoned her shirt.

"Boo-hoo! I've been watching those collection plates. You're more than paying your bills. A cut for me would be but a grain of sand in your pile."

"You're already getting paid in the form of tax cuts for use of your building by a non profit church. I'm sure that amounts to far more than we make from donations."

"I doubt that."

Candace started to rush out the door. "Maybe it's time for us to find a new place to hold our services," she yelled back.

"Good luck. I'll be generous and give you three months notice. I'll still expect our original agreement to hold—in fact I want more frequent payments from you."

"I thought we were friends, Marc. You've just given me a real lesson in life. When money is concerned, there are no friends."

"You're the one who doesn't want to share, Can Can. I suppose I could accept a little less than an equal share as a favor for all your favors."

Candace became more angry and sarcastic. "How very generous of you! I can hardly wait to see the reaction from the rest of my group when I tell them about your demands. Good-bye."

Marc laughed as he waved.

~ 26 ~
We want More

Candace's announcement about Marc's demands created anxiety at the next meeting. To make matters worse, Jason had voiced dissatisfaction with his meager payments, and was threatening to quit.

"Just when we started to rake it in! Why now?"

"Where can we find a new meeting place?"

"We're back to where we started."

"We've lost control of our business."

Harry spoke up: "Girls, nothing's impossible. It might not be as bad as you think. This might be a blessing in disguise."

"You mean quitting our business is a blessing? For who?" asked Allison.

Harry ignored the question. "Did Marc give you a time frame for us leaving if he doesn't get his cut?"

"Yes. Three months."

"Actually, that's not a bad deal. If worse comes to worse, we could give him a small share to extend the time until we relocate. He doesn't have to know what percent of a cut he's getting. We aren't obligated to show him our books. And Marc can't make any claims on our building fund collections."

Hannah supported Harry's comments. "Let's see if Jason would be satisfied with a small weekly gratuity."

"Another drain on our income!" said Candace. "What we earn now merely pays our bills, but that's not satisfying…at least for me."

"Me neither," said Brittany.

Hannah sat back and relaxed. "Aren't we all happy now with what we're doing and what we have? Do you really think more money would bring more happiness?"

In unison, the group answered, "YES"!

Candace pounded her fist on the table. "After all our hard work and energy that we've put into this business, we deserve more than being debt-free. We're entitled to the extras that have evaded us in the past."

Only Hannah quietly shook her head.

"Well gang, where do we go from here?"

"We've just started using Herbie for fund raising. News of him might spread and be our answer. I think we should put lots of efforts into PR work for him and keep his momentum going," said Allison.

Candace reminded the group that she had told them before that they should always be two steps ahead with new plans to keep up attendance. "Have you all been thinking of additional ideas?" she asked.

"One idea that occurred to me is that there are virtually no theatre performances on Mondays, and that's when we could hold some services without competition from other churches," said Diana.

"What about people with jobs? They wouldn't be able to attend," said Hannah. "Who would come to such a service?"

"A lot of those people may have been working on Sundays. We could have our service during the lunch hour. Workers would be able to come during their lunch break. And we would provide a great stress reliever for them? And those with jobs have money."

"I don't think the workers would like missing their lunches."

"They wouldn't have to. One of us could operate a hotdog stand just outside the theatre, and that could be another source of income."

Allison reacted with glee. "My husband just got his license for a pushcart food stand. He had to get some job, and that was all he could find."

"Wait a minute," said Candace. "I still have my waitress job and need to work on Mondays. I couldn't participate in the service."

"Me neither," said Brittany. "I wouldn't have time during my lunch hour."

"Yeah. We'd really miss you there, Brittany," said Candace sarcastically.

"Let's end those remarks now," said Hannah. "I could rearrange my schedule, I suppose, but it would add more stress in my life."

Candace frowned. "We need to think about Jason being available for music accompaniment. He's not completely happy with his small salary now. Also, I think people come because of the professional singing that costs them far less than going to a Broadway show. Without me there, what would be the big attraction?"

Brittany smirked. "Yeah, Candace. I'm surprised any of the Broadway shows are successful without you in them. You think that every service revolves around you, don't you? I'll bet that Harry, Diana, and Allison could perform just as successfully without you."

Candace gave Brittany the finger.

"You're not going to shut me up. I can say what I want to, whether you like it or not," said Brittany.

"Let's not forget that we need to work as a team for the wellbeing of all of us," said Hannah.

Harry interjected; "I'm not sure enough people would want to venture out during the noon hour, especially in the winter. But maybe we could go for a quick trial run without too much effort on our parts. It's possible we could develop a very different service that wouldn't involve so many of us there."

"Tell us about it, Harry," said Candace.

Harry calmly said, "First let's try continuing to use Herbie and the hugs program on Sundays. At the same time, why don't Diana, Allison, and I put our heads together for ideas for Monday services."

"I can help some of the time too," said Hannah.

"That brings up another problem. How will we split the donations from the Monday services if we all don't participate?" said Candace.

Harry assured everyone that shares would be equal providing that everyone have some input into the plans and working out details."

~ 27 ~
Herbie Lives

"Herbie! Herbie! Herbie!" The crowd chanted as they waited for their angel to materialize in the lobby after the next service. When he appeared, crowds gathered around him, some striving to merely get close enough to touch his robe. Every word from his lips was valued and interpreted as gospel by many. Many people thought they could see a distinct aura about him, and those steel-blue eyes aroused feelings likened to spiritual.

Candace confided to Hannah, "This may sound crazy but I swear that lately when I look directly into Harry's eyes, I feel something ethereal there. I'm beginning to think he might be legit. Am I losing my sense of reason?"

"Harry does indeed have powers that most of us haven't developed. He's complex. I don't know what to think about him at this time."

Church attendance increased because of the many who came to be blessed by Herbie.

Candace overheard others speaking to him. "When will you speak in church for us? We want to hear your messages." She recalled the success of his adlib sermon on the sock, and thought that he might be capable of giving inspiring sermons that would arouse generous donations.

"Won't Harry himself be missed if Herbie sits on the stage?" asked Hannah.

"We can make up some flimsy excuse if asked—such as he's on a sabbatical or something."

"We'd better announce it quickly before everyone starts to wonder puts two and two together!"

The first Sunday after their decision, they had Harry, dressed as Herbie, sit off to the side of the stage, which they thought added an air of mysticism about him. During much of the service, Harry sat with his head bowed and eyes closed as if deep in meditation.

All eyes of the congregation were focused on him as he rose to give his first angelic sermon.

With a soft ethereal voice, he began. "My brothers and sisters. You are truly part of my spiritual family. I am here on a mission to build the kingdom of my father that has recently been crumbling. You are aware that many people have fallen away from God. He sent me to change that.

Candace leaned over to Hannah and whispered, "I don't know if what I'm hearing is good or bad. What do you think?"

"Somehow, Harry has a way of making all things turn out right for him. I'm beginning to think his ultimate goal is to take control of the entire world! He may really be an angel."

Candace put her hand over her mouth to suppress a laugh.

Harry continued. "Also, this theatre is not acceptable for a place of worship of our Lord. He wants us to build a special edifice truly honoring his name. I have been concerned about this request. As an angel, I don't have the money to comply. Few of us could make a dent into the amount of funds necessary for a building truly fitting for the presence of our Lord. But, I have faith that if my father tells me to lead in this effort, he will pave the way. Those helping can be assured they will be blessed a hundred fold for all their efforts and time given to this project. We need to start today. We have our humble sock in the lobby available for your loving contributions to the building fund."

"Amen," was heard from several visitors.

"The Lord told me that you have demonstrated faith by your contributions to help me complete my mission. Those donations can be given directly to the building fund.

"You cannot yet imagine the blessings you will be given. One of the greatest that you can expect will be finding the way into a new dimension while on Earth." He looked at the congregation who sat with puzzled looks.

"That new dimension is Heaven! Yes! You heard me right! And if you prove yourselves faithful, you will learn how to set a foot into Heaven and see it while still on this earthly home. I have the keys that will open the door to this path. I can lead you in the steps necessary to start on this path that eventually will open the gates of Heaven."

Everyone in the theatre sat with partially opened mouths, unsure if they were hearing Herbie's words correctly.

"The first step in proving your faith is by giving generously to build our Father's kingdom. In my future messages to you, I will instruct and lead you into this new dimension. After seeing Heaven for yourselves, you will receive the blessing of never fearing death. You will be left with joyful anticipation of what comes after you depart this earthly life."

"What in the world is he talking about?" asked Candace of Hannah.

"I don't know, but it sounded like a promise to bring in a lot of moolah."

Loud chattering and general excitement was present in the lobby after the service. More people sought contact with a *real angel*. The donation socks were rapidly filled. When invited to join the congregation in enjoying the refreshments, Herbie politely declined. *Real angels don't need food,* he thought. *And I'm not ready to do more 'splainin!*

"Harry, I have underestimated your brilliance," said Candace at the next mid-week meeting.

"It wasn't my brilliance. The words that I spoke on Sunday were true revelation."

Hannah looked at him in disbelief. “Revelation from who, Harry?”

Harry looked at her sternly. “Don’t mock me.”

With a half smile, Hannah said, “I’m sorry.”

Candace broke in. “Well, to get on with business: How should we manage collections for the building fund, which looks like it could be a big treasure. We’ll need something bigger than socks to hold the donations.”

Allison had a suggestion. “Let’s make a really big sock for the lobby. Everyone can see each other contribute and do the same.”

The others thought her idea was sound.

“I don’t like the idea of so much cash being present in the lobby. There’s a risk of it being stolen and who will be responsible for the sock between services,” asked Brittany.

Candace rolled her eyes. “We wouldn’t be stupid enough to leave it there after the services.”

“Since Diana is our trusted treasurer, she seems the likely one to keep an eye on it all the time it’s in the lobby,” said Hannah. The others agreed.

Brittany commented, “Has anyone heard members of the congregation ask what happened to Preacher Harry?”

“I think everyone has heard of his *sabbatical*,” said Hannah. “I’m sure that deep down, they know who Herbie really is. I’m also sure they want him to exist so badly that they can’t admit to themselves that he’s only a happy dream.”

“And how do you know if I really exist as my usual charming self?” said Harry with a coy smile.

“Hey, we made you into the angel you portray. We’re in touch with reality,” said Candace.

“Time will tell, won’t it?”

“We don’t need time to tell,” said Candace in defiance.

~ 28 ~
Harry Calls Again

"Hi Dee Dee. It's me, your ever-luvin angel."

Diana's face lit up as she recognized Harry's voice on the phone. "Harry! Long time no hear from. I thought you'd lost all interest in me… which happens to be the story of my life!"

"Are you kidding? You've been forever on my mind. You know how busy we've all been with our church activities. You're the love of my life. Forget you? Never!"

"Church certainly has taken up much more time from all of us than I ever imagined."

"How about giving ourselves a break? Let me take you out for a good dinner Friday night. Can you get a baby sitter?"

"I already have one. My ex has plans to take the children at five on Friday."

"Great! Shall I pick you up at six?"

"Okay. What should I wear?"

"Nothing would suit me fine."

Diana was glad Harry couldn't see her blush. "I'll use my own judgment."

Precisely at six, the doorbell rang. Harry looked especially handsome in his well-tailored suit. He held out a bouquet of long stemmed roses, and kissed her on the cheek. That simple kiss, indeed any touch from him, aroused her erotically.

"I have reservations for us at a new seafood restaurant. I've heard that their lobster is close to Heaven itself."

Harry helped her with her coat. He then embraced her and passionately kissed her. She eagerly participated by throwing her arms about him. Her heart pounded so hard she thought it would jump out of her chest. She felt he had just sent her into a new dimension.

Small talk ensued during much of the gourmet meal before them. Harry was right: the lobster seemed Heaven-sent. She had to keep reminding herself to appreciate each morsel since her natural feelings and thoughts were so strongly focused on Harry.

After enjoying dinner, Harry drove her home in his sports car. He repeatedly turned his head to look at her and reminded her of how beautiful she was. When they reached her house, he turned off the engine and pulled her close. Diana felt like a teenager once more—making out with a boyfriend in his car outside her home. She wished those moments with Harry could last forever. The romantic moment was broken when she asked, "Would you like to come in for coffee and talk for awhile?"

They sat close to each other on the sofa. Diana said, "I'd like to know more about you. What you were like growing up."

"I'd rather talk about you."

"Come on Harry. I'm sure my life has been a cookie-cutter one compared to yours. You're still quite a mystery to me."

Harry looked deeply into her eyes and began to kiss her. "What you see is what you get."

"I love the feelings you bring out in me, but my eyes are clouded, and I'm confused by your behaviors. I want to understand you—like where you're coming from."

Harry released his embrace and stiffened. Diana realized she had touched a nerve.

"I didn't mean to upset you. You don't have to say anything if it's too uncomfortable," she said.

"I don't like to think much about my past. I like to live in the present." They both were quiet for a moment, and then Harry said, "If you're that curious, I'll tell you about my background.

"I was raised in a farm family. My parents worked me hard and were really strict. I had to get up early to do chores while my classmates were all enjoying at least two extra hours of sleep. If I complained, it was a hand or belt against my backside. Boy, did I rebel against my father especially. So many times I wanted to run away from him. I used to dream of ways to escape. I read as much as I could about ways to make myself invisible. And would you believe I found them?"

Diana looked skeptical. "Ways to make yourself invisible? Really?"

"Yes. And it was no trick. It was real. It started when I delved into magic. When I was a young kid, I was small and skinny. I was the class geek—complete with big black-rimmed glasses. My parents were too poor to buy me new stylish tennis shoes, and I grew out of my pants so they were usually too short for me. The other kids used to laugh at me and say things like 'I didn't know we're expecting heavy rains—you're wearing your floods.' I found that learning magic tricks was my way of making friends with my classmates. I became quite good. I always won at card games. My new friends accused me of cheating, and I did through magic, if that can be regarded as cheating. They could never tell how I did it."

"You said you learned how to make yourself invisible. Did that involve cheating too?"

"No, it wasn't a trick. Have you ever heard of quantum jumping?"

"No. I've heard the word *quantum*, but that's about it."

"It's not easy to explain. You need some background in physics. I'll tell you more about it after we get to understand and know each other better. For now, I'll just tell you, like I told the church congregation, that I've found a way to enter another dimension that others can't even imagine."

"I can't imagine it either. Can't you give me a few details on how you do it?"

"Later. I have to know you completely trust me first."

"I'm confused. I thought you were making up the new dimension when you gave your sermon. Why can't you tell me now what it's all about and how to enter it?"

"That requires a long answer and it's getting late. I think I've told you enough for one night. You know where I came from, what it was like growing up and how it led to my discoveries—how it made me what I am today."

"You gave me a brief outline, but what you told me just opened up more questions."

"Just take your time and digest what I've said for now."

Diana relaxed. It was clear that she should not pursue the subject any further. She circumvented the topic by saying, "Tell me though, since starting the church, do you feel your spiritual beliefs have become stronger?"

Harry hesitated a moment before answering. "Sometimes I find myself offering quiet prayers—for help or guidance mostly. That's something I never did before."

"My life has turned around a lot. I really feel closer to God now," said Diana. There was a moment of silence before she asked, "Do you really believe there's an afterlife, Harry?"

"I not only believe there is, but I know there is."

"You continue to be a man of great mystery. I can hardly wait for later. What do I have to do to gain your trust?"

"Just keep being yourself," he answered. He looked at her intently. "I have another gift for you. The roses I brought you tonight were real but mortal. This gift is immortal—a delicately blown glass rose."

"Harry, it's beautiful. Each petal is so fragile. I love it. I'm going to put it up high on the shelf where my kids can't reach it."

"Make sure you can always see it though. When you look at it, I want you to remember my immortal love for you."

Harry drew her close and held her tightly. "I love you, Diana." He passionately kissed her. She was at his mercy.

"Which way to your bedroom?" he asked.

~ 29 ~
Noon Hour Services

Harry was there! And his presence made it difficult for Diana to concentrate on planning the lunchtime services with him. Allison and Hannah kept the task centered. Diana was glad to attend these meetings, since they provided more excuses for her to be close to Harry. She watched him intently with stars in her eyes. *He indeed is a Greek God,* she thought. *A god who visits other dimensions!* Not only did his very appearance arouse her, but every movement of his muscular arms and legs made her flush. Harry, on the other hand, focused on the discussions.

Concerns were voiced about whether the lunchtime programs would be successful.

"I doubt whether working people will be eager to give generously from their hard earned pay they're getting that day," said Hannah.

Allison raised her brow. "I thought we decided that workers would appreciate a break from the tension of their jobs. Office workers and salespeople are often willing to pay for expensive gym memberships to work out stress during the workday, and besides, there will still be hoards of NYC visitors looking for entertainment during the noon hour."

"I think that's where we'll draw the most audience," said Diana as she glanced at Harry.

Harry appeared to be deep in thought. "If by chance, our program doesn't work out well, I have a no-lose idea. I think Candace will be open to it, especially if she sees us fail," said Harry.

"What's the plan?" asked Allison.

"Later," was his only response.

It was Harry's suggestion that Hannah take a more active part in the program since she was especially trained in stress reduction—the primary goal for employees on their lunch breaks.

When the preachers arrived at the theatre for their first service at noon, they were aghast to see Jason sleeping on the front step. He was unshaven and disheveled—certainly judged to be homeless by passersby.

"Oh no!" gasped Hannah. "What a way to begin our new program!"

Allison threw her arms up. "I'm not really surprised. We did talk about such a possibility, and how we should be prepared. Are we prepared?"

"I'm not," said Hannah.

They tried to arouse Jason, but he was in a deep stupor and didn't respond except for a few slurred words.

Harry studied him. "We don't have time to sober him up before the service. Let's just leave him here."

Hannah started wringing her hands. "But I need music for my relaxation exercises. What are we going to do?"

Fred spoke up: "I used to be in a boy's choir in high school. I could hum something during the exercises if someone else would manage my food cart…maybe you Allison."

Hannah appeared frazzled and just quietly said, "I guess we have no other option."

"What about prelude music?" asked Diana.

"Why don't we all sing some hymn together acapella?" said Harry.

"I can't sing a note on key," said Hannah.

"Me neither," muttered Diana.

"No one will notice. There's great power in believing. We all just have to believe we're part of a great choir like the Mormon Tabernacle choir. We'll sound great!"

The others looked at Harry with skepticism but said nothing.

When the first people arrived, Harry, Diana, and Fred started to sing the hymn, *How Great thou Art.* The attendees stopped in their tracks at the sounds. The sound system hadn't been tested, and the voices emerged with extreme blasts and with piercing shrills as the equipment tried in vain to meet the wishes of the vocalists. The singers stepped back from the microphone, which helped some, but it didn't correct for them being out of tune and nonharmonic. At the end of the hymn, the vocalists admitted defeat and slumped away from the stage. Fred continued on his own quietly humming.

Hannah turned toward Harry."What happened to the great power in belief?" Harry ignored her.

Only a few people came to the first noon service. The paucity was emphasized by the large theatre with many empty seats. Many of those attending took advantage of Fred and Allison's hotdog stand and brought the sandwiches and drinks into the theatre.

Hannah led the few attendees in guided imagery relaxation. Almost everyone relaxed so much that they fell asleep. Unhappily, many were holding drinks in their hands as they fell asleep, and many spills occurred on the recently cleaned carpet.

Unbeknownst to the preachers, Jason had stumbled into the theatre holding a bottle of whiskey. He sat down at the organ and suddenly blasted out some loud deranged chords. This shocked everyone and they jumped in their seats and gasped. Hannah tried without success to calm them. The agitated attendees rapidly cleared the theatre without leaving offerings.

When the last of the guests left, the preachers became solemn. Hannah facetiously said, "Well, that went well! I think we started to relieve their stress, but in the end we unnerved and frazzled ourselves as well as the congregation."

"I wanted this to work, but it's obvious now that our time and efforts would be better spent in soliciting donations for the building fund as we have been doing, or in some other fundraiser," said Allison.

Fred commented that they didn't sell as many lunches as he had hoped. He'd have to spend more hours on the street to sell the remainder to try to break even.

"Furthermore," said Hannah, "we're now left with a huge amount of work. It'll take hours to clean the carpets from the food and drink spills and Jason's vomit."

Just then a loud snore was heard from the organ area.

"Jason!" said Allison. "What are we going to do with him? He can't stay here all day."

Harry looked at him with disgust. "Let's pull him out to the front steps and let him sleep it off like we found him."

"We can't do that," said Allison. "It would be inhumane."

"So is Jason a good example of humanity?" questioned Harry.

The others took more pity on Jason. Allison and Fred offered to take him in a taxi to their apartment and let him finish sleeping it off there.

Candace expressed disappointment on hearing about the poor attendance and what happened with Jason. "I guess it's time to come up with other ideas before the congregation tires of Herbie and we lose everything."

Allison blurted out, "Harry told us he had some new ideas that he had confidence would be successful."

"I hope he'll share at our next meeting."

~ 30 ~
Does anyone need a Healing?

Candace sat rigidly in her chair at the midweek meeting. The others could see the obvious concern on her face. She began, "I hate to admit it but it seems obvious that Herbie is our big ticket for keeping the big bucks coming in for us. Without him I'm not sure if we would still be paying our bills. But, even with Herbie I've noticed that every week there are a few more empty seats."

"We still have lots of money in our treasury. We'd be rich now if we divided that up, wouldn't we? said Allison.

Hannah said, "We'd have extra money now, but it wouldn't last long, and then that would be the end of our business and we'd be right back where we started."

"None of us wants that to happen," said Diana.

Allison frowned. "Couldn't we divide up most of the money and each of us spend it as we wish while still participating in the church programs? I guess I'm paranoid about something happening to that money and losing it all."

Harry overheard the comment as he entered and joined the women. "Keeping money in a central treasury is the smartest thing to do. As the amount builds, we'll all be assured of ample future money if we decide to ditch the church."

"Once more, I agree with Harry. Our treasury is our forced savings plan. How many of us had any savings when we started?" said Candace.

"I vote for keeping things as they are for now," said Hannah. "Let's move on with different plans to increase our income."

Allison slumped in her seat, but gave no further objections. Candace took a long sip of her coffee and looked at Harry. "I understand you've been thinking of different ways to increase our incomes."

"How did you know?"

"Ha! News travels fast among this group. Anyway, now's the time to share, so shoot!"

Harry smiled as he straightened up in his chair. "Healing revivals notoriously bring in big bucks. People will pay anything to gain hope for the cure of an illness or loss of pain. When the docs give up, where is their hope? Well, here we are!"

"And why do you think we could help them when conventional medicine has failed?"

"There's magic in belief. That's all we need to do. Help people believe they are better and they will be," said Harry.

Candace looked at Hannah who had remained quiet. "As a psychologist, do you agree?"

"We try to do that to some extent in therapy sessions—both in trying to eliminate negative beliefs while suggesting the positive ones. For example, when people have poor images of themselves, we try to help them erase those as we point out all the good qualities about them."

Harry interrupted saying, "That's the beauty of our plan. When people have illnesses, they want very much to believe that we are the ones to change their plight. It makes our work easy."

"That may very well be true, but I for one have never had experience treating large groups of people in one session," said Hannah.

"Have you, Harry?" asked Candace.

"The same principals would work for one or one hundred people…the pay of course would be much higher treating many at one time."

"Well, I'm not convinced that any of us are prepared to handle such a complex plan," said Candace.

Harry looked sternly at Candace. "You don't believe it because you're not a dreamer. You don't dream the impossible dream."

"You're right about that. I dream but my dreams are realistic."

"And that's why you aren't a star on Broadway. Your own *realistic* negative thoughts limit you."

"You're so full of it, Harry. Does everyone or anyone here think Harry could successfully heal the masses?"

"He's amazed us before," said Allison.

Candace didn't like the idea of Harry taking over all the leadership roles. "I think there's room for doubt. Why don't you tell me the plan, and let me be the one to lead in the healings. I've captured many a soul with my music from the heart."

"I don't like this," said Diana. "I don't like the thought of robbing people of their last savings through deceit when we know we can't perform miracles."

Harry said, "Ah, but we can help them. Hannah has already alluded to the fact that the mind is a powerful tool and has much influence over the body. Right, Hannah?"

"You're right about that, Harry," said Hannah. "There is a big effect of attitude on the course of an illness. The mind controls more than people imagine—even the time of death. You can verify that by looking at the statistics. The greatest percent of people will die after their birthday or a major holiday than just before a major event. And some people know for a long time how old they will be when they die."

"But what about people with terminal cancer? What will we promise them? A cure if they pay us enough?" said Diana.

"Let's not get cynical. If we can give them faith and hope, their lives will at least be more comfortable. Isn't that worth a lot?" said Harry.

"Are you so sure we'll really help them in some way," said Diana.

"Would it be worth it to at least see them happy if only for a moment in time?"

"Perhaps."

"I think it's worth a try," said Hannah.

Candace became more animated with exaggerated arm gestures. “Would people give even more to look younger? I’ve sure paid a fortune for that! Could we offer them hope for that as part of healing?”

“Same treatment!”

“Well, how do we start?”

“What about Harry taking charge of the healings? People seem to have great faith in his words,” said Diana.

Candace defended her original position. “Harry inspires people as he acts out Herbie. Healing is quite different.”

“Are you so sure that I don’t have great healing skills given to me from above?”

“Harry. You’re getting carried away with your angelic role and powers therein,” said Candace.

“It’s not that. I seriously have worked miracles outside of my angelic role.”

“You’re a real mental case. Nevertheless, I’ll try to work you into a minor role that will give you one chance to prove yourself.”

Allison said, “Another thing... we should discuss Jason. We can’t depend on him to be there and perform appropriately. He was a real disaster at our noon hour service. He was the one who made the program fail. Has anyone talked to him about his alcohol problem?”

“I plan on speaking to him,” said Candace. He’s a talented musician and we can’t find anyone who would play at a more reasonable rate. I think I can get him to commit to arriving sober.”

Hannah cringed at the thought of what had happened at her service. “Lots of luck,” she told Candace.

When Diana was alone with Harry, she asked, “What do you think of Candace wanting to run the healing show?”

“She has no idea of how to do it. If she persists, it will be another disaster.”

It was decided that Monday evenings would be a good time for healing services since most Broadway shows weren’t scheduled on that day, and visitors would be looking for other forms of entertainment.

Harry was called upon to get some effective PR out for the service. Marc felt the need to be home with his family during the weekdays, so he entrusted Candace with the keys and simple lighting techniques for what he was told would be a reverent milieu.

Announcements were made during a regular service inviting those in need to attend, and the women and volunteers passed out hundreds of flyers on the streets.

~ 31 ~
Let the Healings Begin!

Hannah thought white signified purity and healing, and so she and Candace tried on their professional white suits tastefully adorned with gold jewelry.

"Do we spell out success or what? We ought to be able to heal anyone just by looking at them!" said Candace as she checked herself out in the theatre foyer mirror.

"We do emanate a calming spirit. That's for sure," said Hannah.

"I still wonder if we should go the microphone-earplug transmission route to really dazzle everyone with our great *insights*."

"We agreed not to take deceit to extremes. We want to instill faith, hope, peace, and some level of happiness, but let's not get carried away."

Candace seemed to be ignoring Hannah's advice as she continued to examine herself in the mirror. She practiced facial expressions that she felt to be convincing of her powers.

"You don't have to look anything different than yourself, Candace. You're convincing in your own way."

"And what's my own way? I'm an actress. I've been acting my way through my own life. Sometimes I wonder who I really am." Candace closed her eyes and her head bent over.

"Everyone behaves differently in different situations and around different people. I'm often reminded of Shakespeare's observations. Do you remember when he said that the world is like a stage and everyone is an actor playing many roles? I think that's true. And it doesn't imply the diagnosis of a multiple personality disorder as some psychiatrists label it!"

Candace relaxed and smiled. "So, I'm not the only one acting my way through life."

"By no means. It's just sad that some people are stuck with only one role. That makes for a very dull life."

Much publicity went into preparing for the service. Brittany designed black T-shirts and jackets for all the clergy and staff to wear. They each bore the logo:

HEAVEN ON HOLD CHURCH
HEALS ALL ILLS

While wearing their designed shirts, the group passed out flyers advertising the healing service to be held Monday evening. In addition to announcements made in church, newspaper ads were placed, and Candace won local TV interviews. She was determined to be the star of the show, continuing her role as she had been for the regular church services.

On Sunday afternoon, a feeling of panic came over Candace when she felt pain on swallowing and difficulty speaking. Laryngitis rapidly progressed to complete loss of her voice. She paced around her apartment thinking, *No! No!* A salt-water gargle only made her gag. She e-mailed Hannah to tell her what had happened. *Is there any thing I can do for a quick fix?* she asked. Hannah could hardly speak herself. She had been suddenly plagued with a sore throat and fever. *Just try aspirin, plenty of fluids and rest. That's what I'm doing,* she responded.

Neither of the women felt better the next day. Complicating the scene was that Brittany sent word that she had slipped and fallen, breaking her wrist in the process. Her arm had been put in a cast.

Candace sent e-mails to everyone: *I think we have no choice but to cancel our Monday night service. There's no way we can hold a service with three of us healers sick and in bad physical shape.*

When Harry opened the e-mail, he smiled and thought, *My prayers have been answered! There is a God!* He phoned Candace immediately. "We can't cancel at this late time. There are too many people planning to attend and looking forward to our help. I can lead the service. I've had healings experience."

Candace whispered, "But you said that was never done in a public setting."

"I never did it on a large scale, but I've healed individuals when physicians couldn't. I'm confident that I can successfully handle the service."

In a barely audible and raspy voice, Candace said, "I can only hope you're right. I guess we don't have any choice at this time." Candace was certain that the evening would be a disaster without her being there to engage the audience. After thinking more about the situation, she e-mailed Hannah again: *I can be there on the stage and act like a silent cheerleader. If you can drag yourself out of bed, we can put some blush on your cheeks and encourage you to play healthy too.*

It was thus decided that Candace and Hannah would sit on the stage and act as supporters to Harry. Diana, Allison and Fred could assist Harry on stage during the healings.

The piano was chosen for accompaniment rather than the organ. Jason thought he could elicit more striking energy from it. He selected music meant to be bold and inspirational for those entering the theatre. His first piece was his own arrangement of *Stout Hearted Men.* He knew the words were not relevant to the service, but most of the people attending would be too young to be familiar with the song, he reasoned. The strong beat was what was important.

Allison and Fred handed out programs as they ushered the visitors to their seats. They tried to prime the audience by saying:

"You can really feel the spirit here tonight. I believe we're going to see many miracles."

As the last people of the congregation was seated, Allison slipped as she began her walk to the front. It took all her effort to keep from screaming out in pain. She quickly took a nearby seat. Her ankle was rapidly swelling. She motioned to Fred to come to her. "I've sprained my ankle. I can't even walk up to the stage. Go tell Harry."

Harry and Diana waited off stage in the sidelines. Harry was dressed in a white sequined sport coat adorned with rhinestones. Complementing his outfit were white cowboy boots. Diana stood beside him, also dressed in white. She had makeup on and her hair was slightly curled. They looked the part of seasoned performers.

When Harry learned of the latest injury, he turned to Diana. "It's you and me, Babe." He instructed Fred to ask Allison to help by yelling loudly in responses to his sermonettes, and told him to try to locate Brittany to do the same. "Come back here on stage after. We'll need you to assist with the healings."

When Fred went back to give the message to Allison and Brittany, Harry said to Diana, "You've got to take the lead to arouse and inspire the audience before I enter and start the healings."

Diana was visibly shaken. "I can't do that. I can't even inspire myself."

"Diana. I've shown you the magic of belief. Believe that you can do it. You must do it! There's no one else that can. Talk to yourself, and tell yourself you are the ringmaster of the circus. Keep believing that."

Diana felt flushed and started to tremble. She moved the curtain apart enough to see the congregation. It was a full house. Most people appeared ill or depressed but at the same time hopeful. As her eyes focused on the congregation, she saw her ex husband. *Oh no! What's he doing here? I can't flub up in front of him. I have to show him!* Her mind worked quickly as she recalled attending a revival as a child. She closed her eyes. *I am in charge. I am a great ringmaster*, she repeatedly told herself.

Candace gave Jason the signal to end his music. Diana felt disengaged from herself as she grabbed a microphone. She had emotionally changed into a ringmaster! She skipped across the stage and began the service with the enthusiastic question: "Are you ready to see some miracles?"

The attendees yelled out their *amens* and clapped loudly.

Candace, determined to still be a focus of attention, brought a cowbell and rang it whenever a point needed to be emphasized. Hannah found a large drum in the dressing room and beat on it to further arouse the audience.

"Do you have the faith?" Diana yelled out.

The congregation responded with, "Yea!" "Yes!" "Yahoo!" "Amen!"

Diana yelled out, "I didn't hear you. Once more, Do you have the faith?"

A louder and more enthusiastic response came forth. Candace stood and skipped back and forth across the stage as she loudly rang the cowbell. Hannah felt too ill to stand but she was able to sit and beat on the drum.

"You've got to have the faith before the miracle comes. You've got to believe. Do you believe?"

"We believe," was heard throughout the room.

Diana knew that a prayer should be given, but she hadn't given forethought to who should give it—not Harry or herself, she knew. Fred was the only other person on stage. Without a warning, she announced, "Brother Fred Miller will give an opening prayer of healing."

Fred was shocked, never imagining he would be called on to speak. He had never given a prayer, and had no idea what constituted an acceptable plea. Now, he was backed into a corner with no escape! *The only way out is through,* he told himself. He proceeded to speak from his heart. He didn't have much time to be nervous but still his voice quivered and became high-pitched—almost comical. The congregation looked up from their bowed heads wondering what was happening.

"My friends," he began. "You've come here tonight to be freed from your ailments." He hesitated, not knowing what else to say. The congregation feeling a need to support him, yelled out loud *amens* and *halleluiahs*. That gave him encouragement to continue. "Well, you've come to the right place! Amen." Fred's face was bright red as he sat down.

Diana invited all to join in singing a rousing hymn. She looked out again at the congregation and saw increased hope on the faces of those who came to be healed. When Jason had played his last chord,

Diana said, "And now, I introduce you to The Man of Miracles…Preacher Harry."

Harry ran onto the stage and grabbed the microphone. "Brothers and Sisters, tonight will be a night of miracles. I feel the Spirit around me. But in order for the spirit to come through me, I need to first humble myself. We know how humble is the sock, and so I am taking off these restricting boots to allow the spirit vibrations to flow more easily through the socks and through me."

The boots were indeed restricting. Harry had failed to realize just how restricting they were. He struggled as he pulled and contorted. Finally Fred ran over to him and yanked on them for release. So strong was the suction force that once released, Fred fell backward onto the floor.

"You just saw for yourselves how strong a hold the devil has on us. He was doing his best to prevent the spirit from coming to me. But we overpowered that demon, and tonight we will release his hold on us and free ourselves from our pains and sufferings."

The cowbell and drum sounded wildly. Diana then gave an invitation to the congregation:

"Any of you suffering from any ailment are invited to come forward and present yourselves to Preacher Harry."

People began to come down the aisles. Fred assisted them onto the stage.

Harry looked at the first woman with his intense penetrating gaze. He said nothing for what seemed an eternity to Diana. He just kept staring at the woman until she became uncomfortable, restless and could no longer stay still. She shouted, "I can feel the force! I can feel the healing starting."

Harry finally spoke. "Sister, what illness are you suffering from?"

"Arthritis in my shoulders. I can hardly dress myself."

With much drama, Harry asked, "Sister, do you want to be healed?"

"Yes, I do."

"Do you have the faith?"

"Yes, I do."

Harry stared into her eyes and then put his hands on the woman's shoulders. He dramatically threw his head back and yelled,

"Lord, let your healing pass through my hands to this lady. Take away her pain."

The woman appeared near a faint. Fred put his arms about her to prevent her from falling.

"Where is your pain now, Sister?" Harry asked.

"It's gone. It's gone. Thank the Lord." She lifted her arms above her head and again repeated, "The pain is gone. Praise the Lord."

The audience cheered. Harry dramatically raised his arms into the air. Candace ran across the stage while ringing her cowbell loudly, and Hannah beat on the drum. The line grew longer waiting for a chance to be on stage and be healed.

The next woman was hunched over and bore angry facial lines. She initially looked defiantly at Harry, but Harry's piercing stare was no match for her. She looked down to avoid his dominating eyes. She relaxed and her stressful facial lines diminished.

"Where's your pain, Sister?" Harry asked.

"It was all over my body," she replied.

"Where is it now?"

"Some of it has gone already!"

"Are you ready to say goodbye to all that pain?"

Harry shoved his palm firmly and quickly onto the woman's forehead as he yelled, "Out! Out, you demonic pain." The woman looked startled from the unexpected blow.

"Where's your pain now, Sister?"

"I don't know. I don't feel it." Again, there were cheers and the sounds of the cowbell and drum. The woman walked more upright as Diana led her off stage.

Person after person submitted to Harry's deep stares and gestures for relief. Each person had his own style of reaction, some almost fainting, some jumping around for joy, and some laughing. Each brought rousing reactions from the congregation.

The lineup for healings appeared never ending. Both clergy and congregation performed their roles well. It was entertainment at its best! "It looks like everyone wants to get into the act," Diana whispered to Fred.

"I was thinking the same thing. And even the ill are acting out their parts."

Harry had been ignoring a child in the line supported by his parents. The child was bald, thin, and pale. Others in the line stepped aside and guided the child forward until he couldn't be overlooked any longer. Harry slowly bent down and looked him in the eye. The women preachers held their breaths. How could Harry help this obviously ill child?

He placed his hands on the boy's head. His voice resonated compassion as he said, "Feel well, my child." The boy smiled and turned eagerly to his parents. "Mom! Dad! I feel better!" There wasn't a dry eye in the theatre. A mad rush to the line followed.

Harry patiently tended to each person. During a lull, Diana cut the line off. Harry took the microphone. "I want to now give a special blessing to those of you that couldn't come up to the front today." He slowly looked over the congregation, and stared out intently seeming to make eye content with everyone.

Harry then abruptly turned and stared intently into the eyes of Candace. This caught her by surprise. She initially thought, *What the... He's not going to outstare me*...but he did! She yelled, "Enough! Enough!" Her voice had returned.

It took only a glance at Hannah from Harry to make her rise with renewed energy. She cheered loudly and with enthusiasm. Fred looked back at Allison and saw her on her feet jumping up and down in the aisle. *What is happening?* he thought .

As Harry was ending the service, he announced, "These very socks that have served to bring about my healing abilities will be available for auction after the service. Proceeds will go to our building fund to make more services like this available."

After the service in the foyer, the audience clamored about the clergy with many ardent requests for more similar services:

"When will the next healing service be?"

"I want to bring my mother to the next service. She really needs the help."

"My neighbor is depressed and suicidal. I know you could relieve his suffering."

Candace designated herself as auctioneer for the *spiritual* socks. She aped the stereotypic auctioneer with rapid speech: "What am I bid for this sock worn on the left foot of Preacher Harry? What am I bid? What am I bid?" She was a natural for the job. She hyped the congregation into spirited participation.

As the bids were increasing in amount, one person yelled, "Will you accept a check?" This was cause for a halt by Candace. *Should I insist on cash as a sure thing or take a chance with a higher check that might not be good?* She reasoned that few people would have much cash on their person.

"Checks will be honored!"

The first sock went for $355. The second for $401… and went to Diana's former husband.

~ 32 ~
Who dun it?

"Well, what do you think?" Candace asked three of the women after the last guest had left the theatre.

Hannah wiped her brow. "I was in a sweat the whole time—and not from feeling sick. I kept waiting to be exposed by someone who felt no better for having come here. Or worse yet, I feared someone would have a seizure or something and we wouldn't know what to do."

"That's how I felt," said Allison.

"I feel guilty about that sick boy who came forward. He and his parents looked so desperate," lamented Diana. "Changing his beliefs can't possibly cure him."

"Why feel guilty? Didn't you see how he really seemed to feel better after meeting Harry?" said Allison. "And wasn't it worth it to see him smile?"

Brittany, who joined the group for the conference, commented, "I think Harry really has special powers. My arm suddenly felt healed halfway through the service."

Candace rolled her eyes as was her usual response to Brittany. "Special powers? Phooey! Can you be any less profound?"

"Brittany didn't deserve that, Candace," said Diana. "And how do you explain your voice suddenly returning, and Hannah feeling better, and Allison's sprain disappearing so quickly?"

"Coincidence. Just coincidence," said Candace.

Brittany laughed at Candace, which further angered her.

Hannah tried to change the subject. "I think we helped a lot of people feel better tonight, including ourselves. And Diana! You were a totally different person. You were a natural—truly amazing! Where did that come from?"

"Harry just told me I had to believe I was that confident leader or ringmaster. So that's what I kept telling myself."

Not wanting to give Harry or Diana any credit, Candace changed the subject. "Well, people seemed to feel better but will the changes last very long?"

Hannah answered, "Even if it wasn't a final cure, isn't it still worth something to be free of suffering if only for a moment?"

Everyone except Candace agreed with Hannah.

"Oh well, the end justifies the means no matter how you look at it," said Candace. "The end might be near though. When people find their conditions returning, they'll probably stop coming here." She quickly changed the subject. "Did anyone count up the money that came in tonight?"

Fred came running in at that moment. He looked excited and beamed. "Everybody…I think our lack of funds for paying our rent is a thing of the past."

"How much, Fred?"

"$7172.25"

Candace jumped out of her chair. "Yahoo! We're on our way to join the rich and famous. And I did it without auditioning for a lead actress role. Does that figure include the proceeds from the auction?"

"No. That was extra."

Harry entered the office and heard how much money was donated. "I told you I had the special gift of healing. The audience wasn't fooled, and they appreciated what I did for them. Actually I'm surprised we didn't take in more. They got more than their money's worth."

Candace wryly smiled at him.

Brittany moved about restlessly. "Let's split it right now."

"What do you mean, *split it*? You didn't do anything at all except sit in the back and look stupid," said Candace.

"You're a bitch! I'm sick and tired of listening to your haughty comments." Brittany rose and left the room. The rest of the group was stunned by her reaction. She had no smile and no giggle as she left.

Candace took a deep sigh. "Finally, that idiotic smile left her stupid face. Well gang, let's turn our attention to how the program could be even more profitable."

As they relaxed, they shared a bottle of Piñot Noir and discussed more events of the evening. As they were about to leave, Diana rushed back into the room with a harried expression. "I can't find the donations pouch for deposit."

"Fred, where was it when you came in after counting it?" asked Allison.

"I left it on the table in the other room."

"Brittany!" Candace exclaimed. "Oh no!"

"It probably wasn't a good idea to infuriate her so, Candace," said Hannah. "Now what do we do?"

"I told you Brittany was a stupid good for nothing. Now we know she's a thief too."

"I find it hard to believe that Brittany took it," said Diana. "Although she is a little different, I never thought of her as being dishonest."

"Fred, are you sure you left it on the table? Maybe you placed it somewhere else for safe keeping," said Hannah. "Did you check your pockets?"

"I know I left it on the table. I was so excited with the amount that I left it, and ran in to report to you." He patted down his pockets to reassure himself and others that he hadn't misplaced it. The others all accompanied him to the other room and looked in every conceivable place but without luck. The money was gone.

Allison asked, "Is it possible that someone else slipped in while we were talking and took it?"

"Unlikely. We would have heard them, I'm sure," said Hannah.

"Hannah, tell me. Do you think Brittany was capable of stealing the money?" asked Allison.

"I can't say. Maybe it'll turn up. Let's not count it as gone yet," said Hannah.

Candace arose and started nervously pacing. "What do you mean? If it's not where Fred left it, somebody stole it, and all signs point to Brittany."

"If Brittany did take it, she may have the intention to just give us all a good scare and then turn it back to us later," suggested Hannah.

"I'm going to call Brittany tonight and confront her. That amount of money will be hard to replace," said Candace.

Everyone paced around the room lamenting the loss. Finally, Hannah said, "Fretting about it isn't going to help. Let's get our minds off it for now, and plan another service soon to make up for it."

Candace looked at her angrily and yelled, "We'll never make up for such a loss."

"We have enough money to more than pay our bills now, and there's a substantial amount in the treasury for retirement," said Diana. "Even if we never recover it, the loss won't be devastating to any of us."

Candace scowled at Diana. "Yes indeed…Pollyanna."

Then Allison said, "I'm not going to think about it anymore. What can we do about it now? I agree with Hannah. Let's move on."

Everyone became quiet and then took a big sigh. After they settled down, discussion turned to the dynamics and analysis of the service.

"Why were people relieved of their suffering tonight? I know none of us has any special powers," said Allison. Harry was about to comment when interrupted by Hannah.

"I think that when people get on stage, their adrenalin flows, especially when all eyes are on them. It's that burst of steroids that truly relieves pain."

"So, people have a built in power for relief. The cure came not from us but within the people themselves," said Allison.

"That's right. Attitudes are of utmost importance when people get sick."

"A can't fail system! Had I known that, I wouldn't have been so tense before we started. From now on, I'll have even more confidence in our services," said Allison.

Harry appeared disgruntled. "You guys still don't believe I have special powers from on high, do you?"

"I believe you do," said Diana.

"But do you know for certain that I do?"

"Let's not get into that now," said Hannah. "Let's just revel in the success of the evening, and how many people felt so much better after the service. I think we should have regular healing services."

"Not so fast," blurted out Candace. "I think we need to give it some time. I'm afraid that soon people may not feel they had the cure they thought they did. Another service too soon might not be smart."

Harry looked up at Candace. "Oh ye of little faith."

Candace ignored Harry. She said, "But just wait until I get my hands on Brittany."

Diana and Harry left the theatre together. Diana was surprised to see her ex sitting on the front steps. He stood when he saw them.

"Congratulations, Diana. You were quite the star tonight." He leaned forward to kiss her on the cheek, but she backed away.

"Thank you. I'm not the same person you once knew."

"Well, you look great. And did you notice that I'm the proud owner of this special sock?" He looked at her for signs of approval, but seeing none asked, "Can I take you out for coffee?"

"Thank you but Harry and I have other plans."

"Maybe some other time then," her ex said with disappointment.

As Candace traveled home, she found herself suddenly depressed. She had to face the reality that she was no longer the person in charge of the church. Harry had usurped her role. The thought came to her at the moment he stared into her eyes during the healing service. She had never before felt so vulnerable. *I don't trust Harry,* she thought. *I plan to watch him like a hawk. He may be planning to take over so completely that we'll all be at his mercy.*

~ 33 ~
Harry Leads

There was an almost uncanny transition by the congregation from their acceptance of the angel Herbie to Harry. It was Harry to whom the parishioners now flocked and thirsted for personal contact. Herbie was all but forgotten.

Yes, the congregation was clearly drawn to Harry. It was he who brought tears to the eyes of many, and it was he who naturally uplifted spirits. Most accepted him as the closest man to God that they had ever known. Much to Candace's chagrin, he had established himself as the leader—the one in charge—the one in control—the one who was *in touch.*

Attendance at the regular services continued to grow and more people from the congregation began volunteering to serve. Volunteers meant more personal investment and thus more generous contributions. And it wasn't difficult to convince people that there were ways to relieve all suffering—even poverty. The answers were in paying whatever money was at hand to receive promised rewards in even greater abundance. That had been a promise made by God himself. They could read it in the Good Book.

The congregation wanted to hear the Sunday sermons from Harry, and they hung on every word from his mouth, almost ignoring the other preachers. Soon after the successful healing service, Harry gave the Sunday sermon by popular demand.

Harry glanced around at the congregation and began. "I revealed to you previously that there is a path into a new dimension that very few people have found while still living on this earth. My brothers and sisters, you can't just stumble upon that path. Finding it involves faith and work. And it involves guidance by one who knows how to enter it." Harry began to speak louder, and he used his hands to emphasize the important parts of his message.

"The first step involves an appropriate milieu. The Lord has said it's not right to hold services in a theater in which there are often performances unpleasing to the Lord. Construction of a real church or cathedral building will take efforts from everyone, but it will be well worth the sacrifice. That is the first step on the path to the dimension of Heaven. The Lord once told us to tithe in order to further his kingdom, and that's what he wants us to do now. That means paying at least ten percent of your income to the church. We have been given the promise that for so doing this we will be blessed a hundred fold. That is a far better return than any stock we could buy. And so I ask of you faithful that you start today with generous contributions.

"For those of you who feel ready to make a commitment, I ask you to come to the front where I will place my hands on your head. I will set you apart for good health and strength for serving in the growth of his kingdom."

Harry's words acted like a magnet. People immediately stood and walked to the front. Harry felt an immediate sense of power as he laid his hands on their heads and blessed them. Some appeared near a faint. Others appeared in a state of trance. He needed to say little. The people convinced themselves what they wanted to believe.

Audience participation always meant increased donations, and so it was on this Sunday.

Candace spoke with Allison at the conclusion of the service. "Preacher Harry doesn't resemble in any way the country boy image we first met in the market. I guess the joke's on us."

"I'm not ready to laugh about it. I think we need to put our heads together before he takes control of everything including our money!

Donations filled the plates and the socks. Hugs were appreciated more than ever at the conclusion of the service.

Most of the congregation gathered around Harry in the foyer during the social hour. They were lavish in their complements to him. Candace was almost ignored. She heard an occasional, “You did good too,” which she interpreted as an insult.

Candace left the church, again feeling depressed. She had tried to sing with everything she had to excite people and control their emotions as she had done early in the church services, but it was Harry who excited and controlled them the most.

Harry sought Diana after the social hour passed. “Could I take you for lunch today?” Diana was thrilled.

Harry again spared no expense in selecting an upscale restaurant for Sunday brunch. He spent the hour praising Diana for her intelligence and beauty. Diana ate his words as she did the brunch.

~ 34 ~
Hiked Revenues

"Do you think the building fund is the extent of Harry's plan for increasing our riches?" asked Candace.

Diana answered, "Who knows! But even without that fund, the donations from services have jumped since Harry took control. $4500 dollars take this past week. My cut has dramatically decreased my debts. If things keep going this way, soon it'll be me donating greatly to worthy causes. And I'll still have the security of a comfortable retirement fund."

Hannah rested her head on her fist. "Harry never ceases to amaze me. He's a lot smarter than we've given him credit for. Maybe we should just let him do his own thing now while we participate in reaping the benefits. I don't think we should question him too much. Remember how defensive he became when he asked for a more equal cut. If we pressure him too much, he may want a larger cut than any of us, or leave us, and then what would we do?"

"I think Hannah is right. At this point, I think we need Harry to make this operation continue to be profitable and grow," said Allison. "Let's leave him alone and let him continue to do his own thing, but I'd still like to get money out of our bank savings.""

Candace said, "I was initially planning on really letting Harry have it, but I can see now that it might not be prudent to do so. He appears to be the one with the greatest power now." Candace looked down at the floor. "My talents have recently been ignored…replaced by his cuckoo ideas. How sad is that?" Allison thought she saw Candace's lip quiver.

At that point, they stopped talking as Harry entered.

"Sorry I'm late," said Harry. "There was a long checkout line at the supermarket."

"So where are your groceries?" blurted out Candace.

"The store is holding them for me until after the meeting," he lied. "So what's on the agenda today?"

Hannah said, "We were just making arrangements for envelopes with receipts for donations to the building fund."

Allison put her hands on her hips and looked challengingly at Harry. "Have you thought of where we could build a suitable structure to suit our needs, Harry?"

"The Lord hasn't revealed that to me yet," he answered.

No one dared question his answer. At all costs they wished to avoid conflict. He was the one with the power, and none of the women wanted to be in disfavor with him. They weren't ready to give up their handsome incomes. And Harry offered the potential of much higher takes.

Harry announced to the group that he knew that offerings became more generous when people had an invested interest in plans for the future.

"I think we should offer more positions with some authority such as elders, deacons, and board members. This will make it easier to call upon them to be more generous in their offerings as a means to further the building of the kingdom." He looked at each of the women directly and portrayed an innocence that dare not be questioned. He knew that not only the "pastors" but the congregation as well wanted the church to succeed.

"Will the people called to such positions have access to church finances?" asked Candace.

Harry gave a smirk. "There can always be double sets of books."

~ 35 ~
Don't Rain on my Parade

Not only did Harry dominate during the regular church programs and healing services, but also he had become the number one requested preacher for counseling. He was often told that the congregation felt that he was the most spiritually in tune of all the pastors. Part of the attraction to Harry was no doubt how he dressed for the counseling sessions. After the church service, he removed his priestly robe and went to the office in his street clothes—Bermuda shorts and a sleeveless tee that exposed his muscular physique. Not surprising was that his clientele was almost exclusively female.

Diana had been aware of all the females attracted to Harry. She felt uneasy about him being alone with young women behind closed doors. To ease her concerns, she arranged to meet him at the church and assist him as a receptionist for his counseling sessions. She scheduled appointments. Young and attractive women were scheduled for sessions considerably shorter than other clients.

Diana also was in charge of collecting the counseling donations. When a therapy session ended, she would say, "There is no charge for the counseling time, but if you feel it has been helpful, you might want to contribute to our building fund. That is where your donations do the most good to advance the Lord's kingdom."

If the session ran over the allotted time, Diana knocked quietly on the door to indicate that time was up. That worked well until one day when Harry had almost ended his sessions for the day. An exceptionally attractive and well-dressed woman walked in. Diana tensed the moment the woman had entered the theatre. "I'm here to see the counselor," she announced.

"Do you have an appointment?" Diana asked her.

"No, but I need to see him."

Diana tried to be pleasant as she greeted her and said, "I'll see if he can fit you in for a 15- minute session. We're running late, but if he does agree to see you, it'll be for only a brief time."

"I'm sure he'll agree to seeing me," she smirked.

"Preacher Harry does have a good heart. He tries to help everybody. If he can make time for you, I'll knock to give a five-minute warning for closure."

Harry looked surprised as he held out his hand to welcome the woman. She entered his office without saying anything, and then Harry closed the door. After ten minutes, Diana knocked on the door as a signal to wrap it up. She put her ear to the door and heard nothing. After five more minutes, Diana knocked again, this time a little harder. Still no response. She waited for at least five additional minutes before rapping harder. This time she heard steps toward the door. Harry opened the door and said, "This is going to take longer than expected. You don't have to wait. You can go home now if you like." The door closed and then came the sound of the door being locked.

Diana began pacing the floor while biting her nails. *What's going on in there? That woman looks like a siren if ever I've seen one! I should never have let her in.* She kept checking her watch frequently…half an hour past time…40 minutes…an hour. Diana felt she might go completely crazy wondering what intimacies might be occurring behind the closed door. She checked for cracks around the door and the keyhole, but found no adequate openings to spy through. *I've got to do something,* she thought.

She recalled some sound making devices back stage. She rushed back there and found a large, flexible metal sheet used to make thunder noise for storm scenes. *This might do.* She ran with it to the foyer area and started waving it loudly outside the office door.

They're sure to think there's a storm and quickly end the session. She tried this off and on for ten minutes, each time moving closer to the door and then retreating to hide the sheet behind a chair. No matter how loud the thunder, there were no signs of movement inside.

Diana's heart started racing and she felt a panic attack starting. *What else can I do?* Her eyes settled on a fire extinguisher and a nearby alarm. Without much forethought, she pulled the alarm. The blast of noise was so loud, Diana was sure it could be heard for miles. With the alarm came a heavy rush of water from the sprinkler system. In a second she became totally doused. She quickly ran inside the main theatre to avoid being seen by Harry. She heard the office door open, and Harry and the woman came running out while talking excitedly. Diana hid behind a chair in the special needs section of the theatre. Harry ran into the theatre. "No sign of fire in here," he yelled. It wasn't long before sirens were heard. Firemen ran in carrying hoses and axes. *I wasn't counting on this,* thought Diana. Amidst the downpour, they disconnected the alarm and checked for heat from the ceiling, walls and floors. They ran up and down the aisles. They ran onto the stage and backstage.

"Just before the alarm went off, I heard loud thunder. Could that have had anything to do with setting off the alarm?" Harry asked a fireman.

"Lightening can sure do it. It's a bright sunny day out, but that doesn't mean anything. Lightening can strike without a cloud in sight. That's probably what did it. We couldn't find any sign of fire or hot spots in the theatre. We'll keep vigil over the place for awhile until we're sure there's no danger."

Diana heard Harry and the woman client leave. A few of the firemen remained to be sure there was no sign of trouble. Diana stayed cramped behind the theatre chair. She longed to get up and stretch, but knew she couldn't without being suspect and ending up in much trouble.

The remaining firemen seemed to enjoy being in the theatre. Some went on stage and performed as if there was an audience. They sang, laughed, and danced. One of them began a striptease. The others whooped and hollered. "Take it off! Take it off!" He stripped down until totally naked and used his fireman hat to cover his privates. Another fireman ran up to him and grabbed the hat away. His audience clapped and threw coins. One of them yelled, "Hey, what happened? I think that cold sprinkler shrank something."

Diana covered her mouth to prevent her laugh from being heard. She raised her head to get a peek. As she did, she was spotted by a fireman.

"Hey! What are you doing here?"

The stripper scrambled to dress and the others surrounded Diana.

Diana said the first thing that entered her mind. "I was here meditating and praying when the alarm went off. I was scared and almost paralyzed."

The firemen looked at her with suspicion. One of them smiled and said, "We won't tell if you don't!"

Diana smiled awkwardly. "Agreed!"

A fireman offered her his hand and helped her out of her cramped position. He escorted her to the door as they all left.

Passersby stared at her as she walked down the street sopping wet on a beautiful sunny day.

~ 36 ~
Consequential twists

Diana's answering machine was flashing when she arrived home. There was a brief message from Harry: "Call me when you get in—something interesting to tell you."

Harry, you don't know the meaning of the word, interesting, she thought. She called him nonetheless.

"Where've you been?" he asked.

"I had some errands to run on the way home." Before he had time to respond, Diana blurted out, "By the way, did that last lady give you a hard time?"

"She had a lot of problems that I needed to help her with. Anyway, let me tell you about what happened after you left."

Diana was hoping he'd share more about the attractive woman in the office, but he told her instead about the ado. She tried to act surprised. His conclusion was that it was the theatre ghost that Marc had told Candace about who set off the alarm.

"Hmm. That is an interesting thought."

After a pause, Diana changed the subject by saying, "We didn't collect much money for those hours in counseling. Again, people don't donate anywhere close to what they'd pay a therapist. I wonder if we should drop the counseling or train volunteers to sit and listen."

"That's a good thought. There are less time-consuming ways to get money. I've been thinking about some ideas myself. People like the individual attention, but we can give it to them in a different way. I know you didn't feel completely good about the healing session. Instead, we could have an evening where people can line up to get personal contact with me. I could deeply look into their eyes and then give them a warm hug. That prolonged stare is very therapeutic for any ill, you know. Actually, an intense stare is even more therapeutic than the hug. It's like an intense beam that gets right to the soul and unleashes power."

"That sounds like hypnosis."

"Voila! That's my specialty."

"Is that what you've been doing to me? I feel like I'm under your spell."

Harry laughed. "Ah, my sweet little innocent Dee Dee. It's you who possess the ultimate control and power."

"I'm not so sure about that. Anyway, your plan sounds like a winner."

Diana continued to wonder about the woman who came unscheduled for counseling with Harry. She could wait no longer before saying, "By the way, did that last lady you saw today leave a generous contribution?"

"No. We were in such a hurry to leave that I guess she forgot."

Marc was pacing back and forth in his office when Candace entered. "I knew I was making a mistake by letting you guys invade my theatre. Now look what my good deed has done. It's going to cost me a fortune in repairs and cleaning."

"Marc, it wasn't our fault. It was what insurance companies call 'an act of God'. And I'm sure you have insurance that will cover the expenses."

"Your people were in the theatre at the time it happened, and as far as the insurance…I have a high deductable."

"How much?"

"$10,000".

Candace took a big gulp. "Again it wasn't our fault, but we'll do what we can to help you."

"Why oh why did I agree to your use of my beautiful theatre? I want you out of there ASAP."

Candace began to cry. The tears were real. It was no act. "Marc, I beg you. Give us time to find a new building. We've been saving for one for several months, but don't have enough yet for a down payment. We'll do anything you ask. Please just be patient with us."

Marc was agitated and didn't want to prolong the discussion. He didn't even ask for one of her favors. "Leave my office now. I'll get back with you later."

Candace called each of the other preachers, and shared the conversation she had with Marc. "He hasn't been happy with us for some time. He wants us to pull out even though the water damage wasn't our fault."

Harry spoke up. "I have some business acquaintances who owe me. I can have them come in and clean and repair for nothing."

Candace's eyes lit up. "Really?"

"For sure. Go tell Marc and if he agrees, I'll call them right away."

Marc agreed to Harry's offer, but made it clear that if the job wasn't done right, the preachers would be responsible for the total bill of having someone else do it.

Relocating was the focus of discussion at the next meeting. Candace said, "We've needed to do this for a long time. It's getting more complicated having to rent from Marc. Renting a building is an option, but I think we should take what we have in our building fund and start a church building that we own and have control over?"

"That's a good thought for the future, but I think we need to first pour on the steam and collect as much money as fast as we can to start the building," said Harry.

"What more can we do than we've been doing already?" asked Hannah.

"Diana and I were just talking about a more profitable therapy program where I could see a lot of people in a short time and get generous contributions."

"Can you be more specific?" asked Allison.

"It involves a different type of healing service. I'm still working out the details. I'll let you know more soon."

Candace frowned suspiciously.

Hannah raised her eyebrows. "How can we help?"

"I'll let you know soon."

The others realized that Harry's plans had worked out well in the past.

"Go for it," said Brittany.

Allison added, "May the force be with you."

~ 37 ~
Sunday Church

Diana awoke early Sunday morning. She anticipated a hectic day. First she needed to get the children ready to go with their father for his scheduled visit. Then it was her turn to gather floral arrangements and bakery treats for the service.

In the midst of helping her children look presentable, the doorbell rang. It was her ex.

"Hi Punkin!" he said using his old term of endearment for her.

"Hi Jack. You're early. The children aren't quite ready. You may come in and wait in the living room if you like."

He moved closer and smiled. "I'd like to help. Where's the hairbrush?"

"I can do that. Just give me a minute." *He never offered to help before,* she thought.

Jack hovered about her as she quickly finished. "I thought we might both take them to your church. I think they'd like to see their mom in action."

She backed away, feeling some repulsion. "I've tried taking them before. They're too young to enjoy it. They get really restless."

"Actually, I just wanted an excuse to be with you."

She looked at him sternly, and tried to brush him off. "Jack, I don't have time to talk to you now. I have a lot to do before the service."

"Could we meet after?" he asked.

"I'll talk to you tonight when you bring the children home."

As they left, Diana thought, *He must have all of a sudden tired of his cutesy secretary. Too bad for him. I've moved on to better things!*

While Diana was placing the floral arrangements, Harry entered the church. Their eyes met. Harry gave her a wink. She flushed. The others were busy dressing and preparing for the service, and failed to notice the exchange. Jason was already at the organ warming up and rehearsing.

Diana overheard Candace say to Hannah, "We'd better keep a close eye on Harry. I'm sure he's up to something devious, and not for our benefit."

Diana turned and said, "I really don't think Harry is doing anything dishonest."

"Whatever makes you think that?" asked Candace.

"No reason. I just think Harry is a good guy."

Candace and Hannah looked at each other but said nothing more.

It was another well performed service. Candace had her own way of trying to induce a group hypnotic state. She sang some heart wrenching hymns that stirred many to tears, and later changed the pace for more exciting beats that enticed the congregation to clapping of hands in unison as they stood and swayed. Her role now had changed. She had become the introductory act, making way for the main entertainer—Harry.

Harry, with his few words, stirred the souls of many. The volunteer ushers collected overflowing plates of donations.

There were a few counseling sessions that had been made two weeks before. It was Harry who had been requested, and he volunteered his services.

Candace, Hannah, and Diana all waited for the last person to exit. They tried to appear busy with small jobs but each was watching Harry. When he came from the room, Candace said, "How'd it go Harry?"

"Very well, as usual. Counseling is easy—more fun than work. I've come to the conclusion that therapists charge too much for their fun jobs."

The women tried not to watch as Harry took his box with donations into the office and put it into the collection envelopes.

"How much did you get, Harry?" Candace asked.

"I don't know. I didn't count it."

"I think we need a better accounting system to double check all donations." said Candace.

Harry said, "Good idea. I have nothing to hide."

Diana froze. Not only did she feel embarrassed for Harry but now feared close scrutiny of her books. If done, the others would find gross unidentified deficits that she couldn't explain to them. "I think we need to trust each other more," she exclaimed.

"It's hard to trust someone who just gets a new Porsche," Candace returned. She had seen him driving it earlier in the week.

Harry's body tensed. Then he turned towards the door and said, "Do what you want ladies. Watch and see how the donations change if I leave the group."

"Harry, please don't go," said Diana. "I trust you, and I'm sure the others do also."

"I have nothing more to say. Send a messenger to me and let me know what your plan is. I'm out of here." Harry hurried out of the building and walked briskly to his Porsche.

Candace turned to Diana. "Why are you defending that jerk?"

"You just don't know him like I do," said Diana. "He's generous and has a good heart."

"Hm. And just how would you know that better than us?"

Diana didn't respond.

Hannah said, "Harry might be right. Our church might fail without him. At present we're at least paying our bills and have leftover spending money."

Candace said, "That doesn't mean that we can let someone take advantage of us and literally steal from us."

"Some might look at our operation and claim we are taking advantage of many people—even stealing from them in the broad sense," said Allison.

"Oh, come on. We've been through this before. People are donating for services they need and are doing so happily," Candace returned. "You're quiet now, Diana. I'm beginning to think you have a thing for Harry."

"I'm not getting any further involved in this conversation," Diana responded. "Time for me to leave."

Diana hurried out of the building. The wind was howling as she pulled out her cell phone and tried to dial Harry.

"Oh, damn. The battery is dead," she murmured. She tried to reach him when she got home, but got no response. She tossed and turned through the night, unable to sleep. *What if Candace was right? Could Harry be a con man? There's no evidence. It's not possible,* she thought as she tried to reassure herself. *But where is he now? Why won't he answer his phone?*

~ 38~
Where's Harry?

"We didn't get as many Sunday donations as usual," said Candace as the women gathered for their weekly planning meeting.

"We can't point a finger at Harry. We all saw him put the counseling money into the big collection envelopes," said Diana.

"We saw him put some money in, but how do we know he didn't pocket most of the receivables?" Candace again asked with suspicion. "And there you go again, Diana—defending a guy we all know is a jerk. And why isn't he here now if he's so innocent?"

Hannah reminded her that Harry seemed quite insulted when he left after the accusations. "If he doesn't come back soon, he might leave our group. We might have losses instead of profits."

Allison said to Diana, "Maybe you could talk to Harry and get a better feel for his thoughts. We need him to return."

"I'll try." Diana didn't tell the group that she had been trying since Sunday with no luck.

"Diana gave me some more bad news, ladies," said Hannah. "Our bank checking account has been overdrawn. Have we had any big expenses recently?"

Candace's face turned red as she pounded her fist on the table and said, "Only Harry's car purchase!"

Diana felt suddenly ill and about to vomit. She remembered how Harry had asked her to write him an advance one week ago with the promise to repay it within three days. She had assumed he did. At the time, Diana didn't think it was that great of an advance. How could it have caused an overdraw? She said nothing about this to the other members.

When the meeting was over, Diana hurried out. When out of view, she tried to call Harry again. Still no answer. She hopped in a taxi and went to Harry's apartment. There was no answer at his door. His landlady told her she hadn't seen him for three days.

~ 39 ~
Good Ol' Harry

Diana paced the floor feeling nauseated and panicked. While wringing her hands and not knowing which way to turn, her telephone rang.

"Hi sweetheart." She recognized Harry's voice.

"Harry, where have you been? Everyone's been concerned."

"You might say I've been in another dimension. I told you that I had a lot of work to do getting the building project started."

"No one knew where you were. We were all worried, and our checking account hasn't balanced lately. Some of the group wondered if you were responsible."

"You know me better than that." He abruptly changed the subject and said, "I've sure been missing you."

All the doubts that had been creeping into her mind dissipated. "I've been missing you too."

"When can we get together again?"

"Soon, I hope. Right now I have some domestic problems that I need to tend to. Will you call me later?"

The bank account was the main point of discussion at the next meeting. When there was money missing that couldn't be accounted for, the women continued to suspect Harry.

"Ladies! Ladies!" Harry began. "After all your preparations for religious services, hasn't the spirit gotten to you yet? Surely, the Lord has touched your hearts in some way. Haven't you learned that money means nothing in the eternal perspective?"

"Let's not get goofy on us, Harry," Candice blurted out.

"Give us a break," Allison added.

"I think Harry is right," said Diana. I've been having those same feelings lately. It's nice to be out of debt and with some extra in the bank, but after that what really brings happiness?"

"Jewelry and shopping!" blurted out Allison.

"Very funny," said Diana.

Hannah agreed with Diana's thoughts. "Seriously, is anyone happier now with the extra money compared to a year ago when we just scraped by paying off our debts?"

"I'm happier. I don't have to spend as many hours on my feet waitressing," said Candace.

"Think about all the new conflicts that have arisen lately—new stressors," said Diana. "I'm happier but not because of the money…because I've found a new me and a quest in life."

"I'm glad I have someone on the same wavelength as me," said Harry as he smiled approvingly at Diana.

Diana blushed.

~ 40 ~
Harry, the Physicist?

After the meeting ended and the other four women left and were out of sight, Harry ran after Diana.

"Diana, wait up."

She turned and stopped. "Hi Harry. Are you doin okay?"

"Of course. Why wouldn't I be?"

"I thought some of the women were a bit hard on you."

Harry shrugged it off. "They don't bother me. They're always looking for something to complain about."

"I think it may a matter of jealousy. It's obvious that the congregation is closer to you than any of us. Some of our associates like to be number one in everything."

"Maybe." Harry didn't appear concerned.

Diana looked at him with a bewitched smile. "Well, I think you're wonderful. Your thinking is just so far above any of us. I'm sure Candace sees that but can't admit it."

After hesitating briefly, he looked into Diana's eyes as he said, "Remember how I told you I couldn't tell you everything until I knew I could trust you? I have to ask you now, can I trust you enough to not tell the others about my great revelations that I've kept guarded and secret?"

Diana's eyes widened. "You can tell me anything. I won't judge you or tell others, unless it could harm someone or unless it involves a big crime."

"Nothing like that—it's legit and harmless…maybe even helpful." Harry looked around, making sure there was no one close enough to hear their conversation. "Could we sit down somewhere and talk?"

They walked into a nearby park, and found a quiet bench. Diana braced herself for what she thought Harry might divulge. Harry again established penetrating eye contact with her.

"Do you remember when I told you I could make myself invisible?"

"Of course. You were kidding, right?"

"No, I wasn't."

Diana looked at him with skepticism. "How can you make yourself invisible? That just happens in science fiction movies, doesn't it?"

"Do you believe in personal revelation?" Harry asked her as he looked hopefully for a positive response.

"I'm not sure what I believe right now."

"I can tell you for sure that there is such a thing. The way into Heaven was told to me by a visit from Beyond."

"What was it that visited you? A ghost?"

"I suppose you could call it that."

"What did it look like? Did it speak? Did it touch you?"

"I could see it all right. It had a smoky, transparent appearance. I couldn't really make out eyes or a mouth." Harry stood and slowly circled the bench. "It looked more like a being covered by a smoky sheet. It floated around me." He raised his arms and waved them around to demonstrate the action. "I can't say it really touched me, but I felt it like a gentle breeze."

"Weren't you scared?"

"No. I felt a peacefulness like I'd never felt before." Harry sat down again.

Diana's curiosity was growing. "Did you hear it actually speak to you?"

"Yes. Very clearly."

"How could it speak to you without a mouth?" asked Diana.

"The voice didn't come from anything like a mouth. I just heard sounds that weren't human. They sounded more like hiccoughs."

"Hiccoughs? How did you know what it was saying hearing only hiccoughs?"

"That's where revelation comes in," he replied.

"Was the revelation in words?" Diana asked in all innocence.

"No. No. I heard it through strange vibrations, probably from the hiccoughs. It was more of a mental or spiritual message. I knew right away what the spirit was trying to tell me."

"That is so strange. I always thought ghosts just moaned or said *boo*. So was it the spiritual hiccoughs that told you how you could make yourself invisible?"

"That among other things. Have you heard that there are actually eleven dimensions in space?"

"I thought there were only three," she answered. "Aren't they width, height, and depth? How can there be more?"

"It's hard to explain. Anyway, by entering a state of super-hypnosis, I found a way to enter another of these dimensions—that of Heaven. I alluded to that in one of my sermons. Remember?"

Diana's eyes opened widely. "Are you for real? This is all too much for me to understand. How can an hypnotic trance send you into a higher dimension or Heaven?"

"It involves a transfer of energy into a higher conscious state. It's hard to explain unless you understand higher levels of physics."

"Can you simplify an answer?"

"If we were at a table, I could show you on paper some advanced mathematics and spatial facts that could help. For now, just try to believe what I tell you is true."

Diana gazed at him with admiration. "You have such a superior mind. You could be a professor somewhere. You are so far above me." Diana began to relax as she pondered Harry's ideas. "You know, I think the entire congregation is aware of the superior mind you have. They accept the fact that you know more about the spiritual realm than they or anyone else they know. Maybe that's why people look to you with such faith."

Harry nodded. "I'm sure I do know more. On some level, they may know I operate in a different dimension."

"I wish you could explain things on my level so I could understand better. For example, can you tell me what Heaven look like?"

"I can't tell you that. When I enter into that high of a spiritual dimension, I see how sacred it is. It shouldn't be described to others when they're not spiritually ready to receive it."

"Do you think I'm not ready?" she asked. "How long did it take you to prepare yourself?"

"Years of very intense focus and practice."

Diana frowned. "I don't know if I have that much time to invest."

"I've recently found a shortcut involving energy transfer through spatial wormholes."

"Can you help me go where you've been using your shortcut?"

"Diana, if I can be sure I have your trust, I'd like to share something I received by revelation that might help you to believe that what I say is true."

"You know your secrets are safe with me. I know you have everyone's best interests at heart."

"Good." He leaned back and closed his eyes. "I'm developing a system that operates beyond the laws of physics. It will take people who are ready into additional dimensions. It's a way to avoid the long preparation process that I needed to get where I am. Do you know anything about neutrinos?"

"No. What country are they from?"

Harry laughed. "Neutrinos are tiny particles—smaller than atoms. They are actually our first parents, if you can imagine that. I have found a way to capture them, lasso their energy, and use their power to pass through all matter like they do. This has given me the power to become invisible and to flow into other dimensions via wormholes with little effort from me."

"Passing through matter? You mean like you could walk through a door or a thick sheet of lead with no problem? Can you do that?"

"Haven't you ever heard that we are made up mostly of space?"

"I remember studying something like that in high school, but they never told us it was possible to move through solid objects."

"They lacked the knowledge that I was given through revelation. Anyway, until now, there was no known way to capture the higher energy."

Diana looked skeptical. "And you have found that way?"

"Yes, I have."

"That sounds like something you should be sharing with other scientists."

"They would only misuse the energy for earthly gain. My uses are much higher."

"And how do you plan to use that energy for the good of all?"

Harry looked at her intently. "I want to share this ability with faithful and good people. I want them to be able to face death not with fear but with excitement knowing what Heaven really is. More importantly, I want to capture this energy and its power to control evil in the world, and stop violence."

Diana looked at him with admiration. Her love was so great for Harry that he could tell her anything and she would believe him without question. And so she reasoned that his essence was so far advanced that he really held the keys to other dimensions.

"I'd sure like to get a glimpse of Heaven. When do you plan to help me into new dimensions?"

"I have to make sure you are spiritually ready to enter. You must be willing to give up all your earthly goods and those that you hold of others to enter spiritual dimensions free and unshackled."

"But what would I have when I return? I would return to this dimension again, wouldn't I?"

"I can tell by those questions that you don't have enough faith. Perhaps if you just start by releasing possessions you hold from others, you would feel the freedom and gain strength to continue."

"Do you mean like the money I control as treasurer of the church?"

"I hadn't thought of that, but…yes. I think that would qualify."

"I'll give it some serious thought."

"I can show you one small ability I have acquired by concentration and defying the laws of physics if you wish."

"I'd really like to see something like that."

"Okay. You stand here, and I'll move over to this place. Try to concentrate with me as I enter a new state."

Diana tried her best to cooperate as she watched Harry. His eyes closed, and he appeared to be in deep concentration. "Do you see anything strange happening, Diana?"

"No. You just look very relaxed."

"Wait a minute. I don't think your eyes are in a position to receive the right kind of energy. Maybe you need to stand more in the sunlight and take on its energy to see what I can do."

She shifted to another area and again carefully focused on Harry. She suddenly gasped when she saw him appear to levitate about a foot off the floor. Her eyes were widely opened and her mouth ajar. After a few moments, he relaxed and slowly descended.

"I can't believe what I just saw. How did you do that?"

"I told you. I have learned how to defy the laws of physics by entering another dimension."

"That was convincing! Wow!" She paused in contemplation. "Harry, are you from another planet? I don't see how any earthly human could do what you did."

Harry smiled. "No, I'm as human and earthly as you are."

Diana couldn't help wondering how Candace or Hannah would respond to Harry's feat.

"Well, I think your goals are worth supporting for the sake of humanity."

"I need money to get started. Will you unshackle yourself by writing me a check from our treasury?"

"How would I explain that to the rest of the group?"

Harry frowned. "I see you don't have the faith needed to follow me."

"But it's not all my money to give. I suppose what I could do is give you my share and your share now."

"How much is in the treasury now?"

"I'm embarrassed to say that I'm not sure of the exact amount. I wrote out one large check that I didn't put in my register and couldn't balance my books properly. I've racked my brains and can't figure out where that money went. That's what the group has been so concerned about. I'm sure I'll figure it out soon."

"Do they ever check your books?"

"No, they haven't yet although they have every right to do so."

"Well, mistakes like yours are understandable. The account is probably so large that no one would question it or a significant part of it to do God's will."

"I'm sure that's true."

"If you could write a check for half of what's in the treasury, it will help my research a little, but I'm afraid it's not enough to accomplish my complete goal."

"How much do you think you'll need all together?"

"It's not just the total amount given, but the faith that goes with it. For it to work, the Spirit has to be present and void of doubts."

"I'm going to have to pray about this."

"You'll get the right answer, I know."

Diana's adoration was obvious. "I know it too."

"My car is just three blocks away. Could I give you a ride home?"

"Sure." Diana felt her closeness to Harry growing. In her eyes, he could do no wrong. She just wanted to be near him as much as possible. They walked hand in hand to Harry's car. He suddenly almost blurted out without emotion:

"First, I hope you know that I've fallen in love with you. If I read you right, I think that these feelings are returned."

Diana blushed. She wasn't sure how best to answer him.

"You might think it's too early for me to be expressing such feelings, but when you know something's good and right like I do, it's not too early." He hesitated and seemed to be hoping she would express her love to him, but she was too shy to tell him how much she had fallen in love with him. When she didn't respond, he continued, "Are your kids at home this evening?"

"No. Why?"

"I'd like to enter another dimension with you in the bedroom."

~ 41 ~
Approaching the Eleventh Dimension

Harry and Diana met frequently to work on Diana's preparation for entering another dimension with. Diana reveled in the time spent with him. He could tell her anything and she'd believe him—merely for the chance to be close to him. She was his ideal subject. He had chosen well.

"We need you to relax so you can start on this path into a new dimension."

Diana willingly lay back on the sofa and closed her eyes.

"Let's start with a simple exercise. Keep your eyes closed. Relax. Let every part of your body relax."

Diana found it difficult to totally relax being in a horizontal position with Harry hovering over her. She did her best to focus on what he was saying although she wanted bed action rather than hypnotic action. She unexpectedly hiccoughed.

"Diana! Just as I suspected! You are very close to a new dimension."

"I'm scared, Harry. If I go any further, will I be able to get back. My children need me."

"You're fine. You'll be able to come back anytime you want."

After training her in relaxation techniques, he proceeded to work on visual imagery.

"Imagine yourself in a place that you've been before where you've felt at perfect peace. It may be a beach or a forest or anywhere you've felt safe and relaxed." He continued working with her until she did feel she had entered a different mental state.

After several hypnotic training sessions, Diana could enter a trance by a single word from Harry. While in that state, she was at his mercy.

"I think you're almost ready. I think it's time to help others learn the same truths that I am going to divulge to you."

"Who do you mean by *others*? I don't think Candace or Hannah would ever listen to you and follow your program to gain the knowledge you have."

"I realize that. I'm referring to our congregation. Their minds are much more open."

At the end of one session, Harry gave an assignment to Diana:

"Every morning before you get out of bed, you must keep your eyes closed, take a deep breath, and simply believe something to be true, no matter how impossible it might seem. I do it myself. It gets easier and easier with practice."

Those words sound familiar, thought Diana. *I must have heard them before from another wise man.*

~ 42 ~
The Plot thickens

Harry shocked the other preachers when he deviated from a prayer that had been written for him to recite in church. He looked at the parishioners with his penetrating gaze. He began:

"Brothers and Sisters: The Lord has blessed me with a powerful gift meant to bless all of you. He appeared to me in person while I was in deep prayer. He revealed to me answers to the keys of the universe—questions that Einstein had been seeking answers to for most of his life. The Lord further told me that when I was ready, I would be told how to use these keys to gain unimaginable power—strong enough to transport me and others who had the faith into new worlds where no living man has yet gone."

Not only the congregation, but the women preachers sat with their mouths open. "Did I really hear what I thought I did?" Candace asked Hannah who sat in a stupor next to her. "The end is near. I wonder if I can get my old full-time job back?

Diana glanced around the congregation and her co-preachers sitting near her. *I know it sounds weird to my partners here, but I understand Harry, and I totally believe what he says. I hope others will take him as seriously as I do.*

Hannah started up to the podium trying to think of a way to smooth out Harry's speech, but he went on before she reached him.

"At first I thought I was hallucinating. I asked the Lord, why he was telling me about this powerful knowledge. He said I had been chosen eons before my earthly life in the preexistence to bring about a great work. He added that now I was spiritually ready. I was to find the keys and use them only under his strictest guidance. At first I thought he was referring to a physical set of keys, but that thought was corrected under further revelation. I immediately felt strong forces and I suddenly understood. I had been harboring a headache and backache that disappeared immediately when everything became clear to me.

"I don't know how I will be directed to use this knowledge, but I was told only the faithful would reap the benefits of the power. Those of you with faith, I hope will follow me and share the unimaginable blessings."

Harry sighed and said, "Let us pray." He prayed for increased faith of all those in attendance and gave thanks for the recent blessing of healings that had occurred.

The parishioners sat motionless. Little of their attention was on the remainder of the service. At the conclusion, everyone hurried out to talk to Harry. His words didn't disappoint them. The parishioners looked at his convincing face, and asked many questions about the new dimensions of which Harry spoke.

It was almost pandemonium. Candace and Hannah called for everyone's attention. "There will be a meeting tomorrow night here at seven o'clock. Questions will be addressed at that time."

They hurriedly closed the doors. Then they glared at Harry.

"What's wrong with your head?" asked Candace. "You just ruined our lives. You just destroyed everything we have worked so hard for."

"You're crazier than any patient I've ever had," added Hannah.

Harry said, "What do you mean? Didn't you see how people wanted to take part in this blessing? Didn't you see how much money was donated today?"

"We may have the money today, but when they go home and start talking about it, we'll have no future voluntary donations."

"I'm sure you're wrong. I've been carefully watching people for several weeks now. They want to believe in magic. They want to believe in a God who is always there for them. They flocked to me today. They want to believe me."

Candace looked at him with contempt and said, "Harry, we don't want to be labeled as a cult. Please do us a favor, and don't say more about your revelations. Let's hope your sermon quiets down so we can concentrate on healings and entertainment."

Harry was silent.

Diana came to his defense. "I think we should listen to Harry. I know what he says is true."

"And just how do you know that?" asked Candace.

"He has shared some personal knowledge with me. We all need to trust what he says."

"What's been going on between you two? I thought I've seen you go limp in his presence. You've been having an affair, haven't you?"

Harry spoke up. "Diana has an open mind in considering new things not generally known or believed."

"And you're just the man to help her do that. Right?" said Candace.

"Sometimes it takes childlike faith to find the truth."

"Well I speak as an adult with reason. I'm not one to be easily duped, especially by guys who take me to bed for their own gain."

Diana started to cry. "Harry's not like that. Please believe me."

Brittany broke the tension from the conversation by asking, "Do you have the checkbook with you, Diana? I have some bills due now."

"Wasn't the money you stole from the healing service enough for you?" asked Candace.

"What's that supposed to mean?" said Brittany.

"The money from our healing service was never recovered and you were the last one near it."

"You owe me an apology," said Brittany. "I've never taken any of your filthy money."

"Yeah, sure."

Brittany tensed her entire body. "I don't believe what a psycho you are, Candace!" She slammed the door as she left.

Candace smiled and said, “That’s one problem solved. Does anyone else want out?”

~ 43 ~
Monday night

Candace paced around her apartment after the church service. She felt far more anxious than before any of her auditions. She wondered how Harry's proposals could be dismissed and how he could be silenced. She kept pacing, not knowing what to do.

There was much tension within all of the women church leaders Monday night. Candace was dressed in an all white suit and wore her nametag that identified her as Reverend Doctor Arthur. The preachers decided to lead a subdued and spiritual service. Appropriate and reverent music greeted the parishioners. The excitement however rose above the planned milieu and would not be quelled. The leaders immediately saw the excitement and anticipation by the parishioners. Harry entered and sat up front with an angelic smile as his cohorts sat in a sweat.

Candace opened the service with prayer and led the congregation in a heartfelt rendition of "Holy, Holy, Holy…Lord God almighty…" She tried to give a brief sermon on love. The congregation was restless. They weren't there to hear Candace. It was obvious to her that she was being ignored. They wanted to hear from Harry. He was the one they were there to see. She decided to let Harry be the one to squirm out of the predicament. Thus without further thought, she announced, "We will now hear from the Reverent Doctor Harry Hansen."

With great confidence, Harry went to the podium. He was silent for several moments, while he surveyed the audience.

"Brothers and Sisters: I know that many of you have questions about my recent revelations from God. Why should God select me to be his go-between between him and his earthly children? He told me the answer: because I was humble and ready to hear and accept his words." Candace loudly cleared her throat. Harry wasn't fazed and continued.

"He actually appeared to me in spirit form. It was no hallucination as some of you might think. He told me that he needed an earthly servant to perform righteous acts to help you, his children, to prosper and help build his kingdom. He told me that the pure in heart would believe and come to be blessed to have the strength to work for the Lord.

"One of the greatest blessings would be to find the path into his kingdom while still existing on this earth. It's not an easy task to find that path. It takes much faith and perseverance. But I'm telling you that I have entered the kingdom through a new dimension. The work getting there has not been easy but it has been worth it. The Lord wants all his children to come to him and experience the joy of heaven while we live on this earth. He revealed to me how this process can be simplified. We need to build a complex structure capable of energizing people who have prepared themselves for the trip. From the energy produced in this structure, we can quickly enter new dimensions where the Lord dwells."

"I want to go there now," yelled out one woman from the congregation.

"Me too."

"Let's get started. I'm ready."

"Hold on a minute. Your spirits need to be totally ready. We need to have preparation sessions," said Harry. "These sessions will start tomorrow night at seven and will continue every evening until everyone is prepared. And remember, it will take money to build the structure capable of energizing you to slip through the locked in dimension in which we are now living. The faster we collect the money, the sooner we'll be ready to travel."

Donations exceeded everyone's anticipation. They were placed directly into the building fund sock.

Candace gathered the other women pastors together while Harry was greeting the congregation on the way out.

"Do you realize what this is leading to? This is the beginning of the end of our endeavors to make a comfortable living. Harry is taking the congregation away from us. We'll be left with nothing."

"I think you're probably right," said Hannah." And I don't know how to stop him."

"Wait a minute," said Diana. "Harry is operating at a higher level than we are. What he's trying to achieve will bring unbelievable powers to all who go along with him. What he's doing will change the world for good and bring about universal peace."

Candace smirked. "He's really done a number on you, girl."

"No. Please open your hearts and try to understand. He has worked with me to the point of getting a brief glimpse of heaven itself. I'm almost there. The energizing principles of which he speaks will help others achieve the same much faster."

Allison and Fred had listened to Harry's words carefully. On the way home, Allison said, "What did you think of Harry's speech tonight?"

Fred, who had always been skeptical of Harry's motives, answered, "I'm sure he has an agenda, and his plans are coming to a head. We should try to get our money out of the treasury now."

~ 44 ~
Falling Off the path to Heaven—Whoops!

The next evening the theatre was packed with parishioners who were eager to start on the path into a new dimension. Diana recognized Brittany in the crowd. She approached her. Brittany told her that she was excited about Harry's work but wanted to avoid Candace.

"I believe in Harry and want to be a part of the action. I'm afraid that if Candace sees me, she'll have nothing good to say to me and spoil my enthusiasm. She still thinks I stole that money. I wish someone would believe me." Brittany became tearful.

"I don't know where that money is. I have no reason to believe that it was you who took it. And Candace, she's not exactly on Harry's side either. She's very suspicious of him. I'm sure those feelings now override any of those she might be harboring for you."

"Maybe. Anyway, I'm at the point now of not caring what she thinks or how she acts towards me. My motives are higher."

"Good for you. You're welcome to sit with us on the stage."

Brittany laughed. "I'm not that non-caring. Thanks anyway."

"Talk to me later after this service."

"Okay. Will do."

Jason used breath-spray to cover over his breath from his early morning imbibing. Candace had lectured him on his need to be in control during the services and to play appropriate music. He had been trying to decrease his intake, but his habit was now out of his control. He did his best to appear sober for this different kind of service. He decided on some Bach sonatas similar to the ones he had played before. They were always difficult selections, but Jason knew they were good practice for him. He sat down and began. The audience was busy chatting with one another and few were aware of music.

"Make it a good one," Candace whispered to Hannah as she rose to offer the opening prayer. Hannah did her best, but as she glanced up, few had their heads bowed. *Not a good sign,* she mused. The audience was there obviously to hear Harry.

Candace had selected a heart-wrenching version of *Rock of Ages* that she had hoped would steer the congregation into a more conservative mood, but this failed. There was much talking even as she sang with all the emotion she had. There was no point in delaying or de-emphasizing Harry's presentation. She succumbed to introducing Harry:

"And now we will hear from Porsche Harry…whoops, I mean Preacher Harry. He has some interesting things for us to think about." Candace had hoped those words would make the congregation wake up and think differently about harry and not accept his presentation as Gospel truth.

Not a sound could be heard throughout the theatre as Harry went to the podium.

"Brothers and Sisters: It has been revealed to me from on High that we must proceed in a stepwise fashion to be successful in walking that path into Heaven. It all begins with faith. We must faithfully prepare our minds, spirits, and bodies. They are all necessary to reach our goal and do so in a pure state.

"Tonight we will begin to prepare our minds and bodies by teaching them to be totally submissive to our wills. I want everyone to relax. Close your eyes, and picture yourselves in a place of perfect peace."

Harry worked with the congregation trying to achieve an induced hypnotic state. Each person had his own level of suggestibility. Some fell into a sleep-state quite soon while others achieved varying states of relaxation. When the hour was over,

Harry said, "I want you all to go home and practice this relaxation state until you can induce sleep quickly. I can work individually with anyone having a difficult time with this exercise."

After the service, most of the congregation appeared relaxed and claimed they felt in a state of pure peace. Even with a relaxed feeling, there was enthusiasm for the program and preparations to continue on along that path.

The building collection sock was in an obvious place to be seen by the parishioners as they filed into the foyer. Most donated generously.

As Harry was shaking hands and giving hugs, he startled everyone as he suddenly bent over in apparent agony while holding his abdomen. "Oh, the pain!" he yelled out. "The pain! The pain! It's unbearable. I can't stand it. Call an ambulance. Something's ruptured or something." His legs seemed to give out, and he knelt on the floor while still holding his abdomen.

Diana rushed to his side. "Can you go to another dimension to stop this?" she asked.

"I'm in too much pain to concentrate. Oh! Oh! Oh!" He started to roll about on the floor while grimacing.

People gathered about him. "We're praying for you Preacher Harry. The Lord will protect you."

As he rolled on the floor, his arms and legs began to jerk. His eyes gazed upward and various parts of his body shook wildly. Then his eyes started to rapidly move around in circles. Someone yelled out, "Put a stick in his mouth so he won't bite his tongue."

"No, don't touch him. Just clear the area so he won't hurt himself by hitting something.

Diana nervously clutched her hands and paced about him not knowing how she could help.

Candace and Hannah stood back observing the ado. Candace whispered, "I've never seen a person react like that to sudden pain. What do you think?"

"I don't see any beads of sweat on his brow. Hm. And I've seen seizures before that looked different."

"It's obvious he's faking," said Candace. "Let's have a little fun with this."

"Maybe he's not faking. I think we should leave it to the doctors to decide."

Candace tried to suppress a smile. She yelled out, "Step aside everyone. I've had some emergency medicine classes. The only way we can tell where the pain is coming from is to do a rectal. Hannah, hand me a glove." She hesitated a moment and then said, "Oh never mind the glove. We don't have time to find one. I'll do it without."

Candace started to unzip Harry's pants. He became suddenly more alert. "Don't touch me. You'll kill me. Stay away! Stay away!"

"Be calm. We need to find out what's wrong," said Candace.

Harry rolled over onto his stomach moaning while clutching his pants.

"Help me get his pants off," Candace yelled. A tug of war started with Harry tightly clutching his trousers.

Before any more action occurred, an ambulance arrived. The EMTs quickly examined Harry. With every touch, he screamed, "Don't touch me. It's too painful."

"It's either a ruptured appendix or a kidney stone," one of the EMTs surmised. A urologist happened to be present observing the action. "A kidney stone would explain that intense pain, but I'm surprised he hasn't broken out in a heavy sweat."

Several men from the congregation helped lift Harry onto a gurney and wheeled him into the ambulance. Diana started to enter the ambulance but was turned away. "Only relatives in here ma'am."

"But I'm his closest friend."

Harry looked at Diana and insisted she stay behind. Sirens blared as Harry was driven away.

While the congregation was in a dither, Candace spoke up to take charge. "Let us all pray that Porsche…I mean Preacher Harry will soon be healed."

Several of the women, including Diana were crying. The preachers tried to console them.

As Diana regained control, she said, "I don't know how Harry will pay for this. I know he doesn't have any health insurance."

"Don't worry, Preacher. We're his brothers and sisters and we'll see he gets the care he needs without financial ruin."

~ 45 ~
Con-valescense

Diana spent several days trying to track down Harry. She traced him to the hospital where the ambulance had left him, but the admitting office had no record of his admission. One of the emergency physicians recalled his arrival. "He didn't appear in acute distress when I observed him in the waiting room. I overheard him tell someone that he was going to his own hospital. I have no idea where that was. He left before he was evaluated by anybody."

After more than a week of trying to find Harry without success, Diana received a phone call from him. His voice was low and sounded weak.

"Harry! Where are you? I've been so worried."

"I'm home now. I've been too weak to use a telephone until now."

"Where did you go and what did they find that was wrong?"

"I went to a hospital in upstate New York. I know some medical people there whom I trust. That one EMT guy was right. I had a big kidney stone I was passing. They had to sedate me for five days until I finally passed it."

"I wish you had called me. I would have driven you there and helped to care for you. Do you need anything now?"

"Just rest. But I'm really worried about the big hospital bill. It cost over $35,000. I'll never be able to pay that."

Diana cheerfully said, "Don't worry about that. The congregation has already started a fund to help with your bills. Just save a copy of them for us. Everyone loves you and wants to help you in any way they can."

"I feel like crying," said Harry. "There really are a lot of good people still in New York."

"Yes, there are. Sometimes it takes a situation like yours to see that. Now, when can I see you? Do you need any meals or anything?"

"No, I'm doing fine and don't need anything. As you can tell, I'm still groggy from the sedation. I'll probably need three or four more days to recover…maybe by next Monday I'll feel up to getting out."

Diana took a deep breath as she hung up the phone. *$35,000! That's a lot of money to raise to pay for the hospital bill. I'd better come up with more ideas for fund raisers quick.*

The following Sunday, Diana was able to report to the congregation on Harry's status. She proposed many fundraisers to help pay his bills—potluck dinners, dances, bakery sales, white-elephant auctions, car washings for the teenagers. The congregation reacted with enthusiasm and was anxious to get started.

On Friday, a potluck dinner was held with generous donations given just for admittance. After the main meal, there was a bakery-goods auction. Church members had donated all the goods for the cause. Candace declared herself as auctioneer. She held up the first pie for all to see. It was a bit small and had burnt edges around the crust.

"What am I bid for this beautiful pie? It looks like it was made with healthy fresh fruit. This pie is beautiful enough to be photographed and submitted to a major foods magazine. Yum! My mouth is watering. You couldn't buy this in a bakery for less than $25. Come on! It's for a good cause."

The bidding was initially slow but finally sold for $30. People got into the mood as the auction progressed. The bids were greatly increasing when Harry slowly limped in. His posture was slightly slumped and he appeared to have difficulty keeping enough energy to walk to a chair. Everyone rose to their feet and clapped for him. "Thank you everybody. Please sit down," he said in a weak voice. Two men helped him to a chair.

Candace picked up the microphone again. "This is all for you Preacher Harry." She selected a small plastic bag with a few overly baked cookies made by one of the teenagers. "Now, here is a bag of cookies made with love. Who'll start the bidding at five dollars?"

Harry weakly raised his hand. "They look great. I'd love to have them for myself."

Candace smiled at Harry. "I'm sorry but your bids aren't accepted here tonight," she said.

There was a great outpouring of bids, the final selection going for $60. The recipient took the prize, walked over to Harry, and placed them in front of him.

Harry pulled a handkerchief from his pocket and dramatically wiped his eyes.

"Surely your rewards in Heaven will be great," said Harry to the woman who had won the bid. The teenager who had made the cookies was ecstatic.

He should get an Oscar for this performance, Candace thought while rolling her eyes. *By popular acclaim, he's the Broadway star here tonight.*

After everyone had left except for the preachers and staff, Harry stood before the others and said, "How much money was made towards my bills?"

"In round figures, it looks like about $1000," said Fred.

Harry frowned in disappointment. "Is that all?"

Diana smiled at Harry. "You'll be happy to know that $1000 is the biggest take for a bake sale auction that any of us has heard of."

"Maybe so, but at this rate we'll never get enough to help me pay my total bill."

Trying to comfort Harry, Diana said, "We have three other major events scheduled this weekend."

"I can at least make a payment towards the bill with this," Harry said expecting to have the money turned over to him.

"Wait a minute, Harry," said Candace with a firm voice. "Nothing is turned over to you until we see the hospital statement."

“I need the money now. The hospital is starting to hound me already.”

Candace looked at Harry, and said firmly, “Sorry, but no!”

“This is just going to prolong my stress and delay all healing.”

“Couldn’t we give Harry a small advance to help him out?” asked Diana.

“I said NO. What part of that sentence did you not understand?”

Harry and Diana left together. Diana smiled at Harry and said, “Don’t worry, I can write you a check for an advance.”

“I knew I could count on you, my love.”

~ 46 ~
Raising Money for Harry

Almost every church member eagerly participated in fund raising to pay for Harry's medical expenses. The teenagers had fun with their car washes. They painted large signs inviting donations for the car washes: SAVE PREACHER HARRY. That attracted many well wishers who donated generously. Babysitting jobs were volunteered also on a donation basis. Several women cleaned offices and homes. Men did landscaping jobs. Volunteers collected donations on the streets with signs and flyers imploring passersby to give for Preacher Harry's huge medical costs. Although some of the women preachers had doubts about Harry and his disorder, they also worked on moneymaking jobs such as designing and selling unique jewelry.

Candace organized a Broadway musical extravaganza featuring many from the congregation. With little rehearsal, they performed before a large crowd who had been enticed to attend through extensive PR work. Candace was in her glory. She was the center of attention for all the acts either as a performer or director. There was no competition from Harry in this show. As she looked out at the audience, her eyes lit up as she recognized Broadway talent scouts and her agent. This show alone brought in over $10,000 in donations.

Great bonds were created between the volunteers as they worked together on the fundraisers. It was a happy time, and it didn't take long to exceed the requested $35,000.

"Where's your hospital statement?" asked Candace during the next business meeting.

"I have it in my apartment. Could you trust me and advance the money now so I can be relieved of the collectors hounding me?"

"That's not how we operate. You know that."

"I guess I'll have to suffer through more humiliation until our next meeting."

Without showing sympathy, Candace answered, "I guess so."

On the way home, Harry whined about his plight to Diana. "I feel so embarrassed having to grovel for my needs. It's really humiliating and stressful each time the hospital calls hounding me for payment. It's so hard to wait for that money. I wish Candace had more faith in me like you do."

"I can understand how you feel," said Diana. "Unfortunately, Candace spoke to me and told me not to release any money to you until all of the group approves it."

"If only Candace knew my word is good like you do. Could you just advance me $10,000 until I bring my bill to Candace for verification?"

"I'd like to but Candace made me promise."

Harry put his arms around Diana and kissed her. He looked deeply into her eyes. "She wouldn't have to know. I'll have the statement for her within the next four days."

Diana blushed. There was no way she could resist his charm and request. She pulled out the checkbook.

At the next meeting, Harry pulled out a paper from his billfold and handed it to Candace. "Are you satisfied now?" he asked.

Candace and Hannah both looked intently at the hospital statement. The header on the form looked legitimate, but suspicion was raised when they carefully examined the charges.

"I've never heard of this hospital," said Candace.

Harry put his hands on his hips. "Do I have to drive you upstate to prove its existence?"

Candace stared back at him. "A listing in the yellow pages would suffice."

"There seem to be a lot of unusual charges," said Hannah.

"Like what?" asked Harry.

"Room cleaning services? I've never heard of that as a separate charge, and nursing charges for accompaniment to the operating room? And what are Sepharanochium tablets—two pills for $350? I'm familiar with a lot of medications but that one doesn't even sound vaguely familiar."

"I'm no doctor. I can't answer for that."

Candace shook her head. "I'm sorry but I need to verify this before we release the funds."

Harry responded with an angry tone. "I don't believe this. How much verification do you need? I've been through so much, and now you're prolonging my suffering. Maybe I should skip town and leave you with all my money? Would that make you happy?" He put his head down on the table.

"Let's stop this bickering. Just give Harry the money and let's forget the whole thing," said Allison. "The contention isn't worth it."

Everyone was quiet for a moment. Candace then stood and stomped her foot. "Okay, I give up. Diana take out the checkbook and write Harry a check for $35,000."

"Wait a minute," Harry interjected. "The congregation raised a lot more than $35,000 for me."

Candace still standing grabbed her long hair with both fists and pulled on it with frustration. "What?" she asked in disbelief. "The congregation raised money to pay for your hospital expenses. They didn't intend for you to gain more and treat yourself to another sports car."

Harry abruptly stood and stared at her. For a moment, he looked like he was going to out-yell her, but thinking better, he said quietly, "I think I deserve more for all my suffering."

"Yeah, right! We all saw your so-called suffering."

"Look who's calling the kettle black! You're accusing me of what you're guilty of: taking money under the false pretenses of providing spiritual guidance."

The other women were becoming increasingly uncomfortable with the conflict. Hannah said quietly, "Let's remember we all want to work as a team to provide some type of benefit to others. The congregation was obviously happy making sacrifices to help Harry, and they've been happy with our services and inspiration too. Harry, we ladies did work to raise the money for you. Fair is fair, right? How about settling for the $35,000, and we could split the rest for our work in the cause?"

Harry listened with his arms folded across his chest. "You gals have a strange sense of fairness." He looked down at the floor and then said, "Let your conscience be your guide."

"At least we have a conscience," said Candace.

Harry let out a disgruntled, "Ha!"

"It sounds like we've reached an agreement, right? Diana write out the check to Harry for the $35,000, and we'll leave the rest in the treasury."

Diana blushed since she had already given Harry a significant advance. "Perhaps we should make it a partial payment of about $25,000 until everyone's comfortable with the amount."

"No, if we're going to do it, as some of you want, make it the full amount and we'll forget it. I'll even watch you write it as a witness that he's been paid in full," said Candace.

Diana sheepishly wrote the check for the full amount and handed it to Harry.

"Harry. Have fun with your money," said Candace in disgust. She stormed out of the room.

Harry appeared forlorn. "I'm sorry. I didn't mean to upset anyone. I've been under so much tension lately. The doctors told me to expect that. What they didn't tell me was that others wouldn't understand."

"I understand, Harry," said Diana as she moved closer to him and put her arms around his shoulders.

"Thank you, Diana. I needed that."

Harry and Diana left together. “Diana, don’t worry. I’ll pay you back later for the money you advanced me.”

“Forget it. We both know that the congregation wanted you to have it all.”

“That’s true. What else is true is that I love you very much.”

~ 47 ~
Preparing for the Trip

Backstage, before the next church service was about to begin, Candace noticed that Harry was wearing a handsome Rolex watch. "Is that your reward from the hospital for being such a good patient?" she asked.

"No. Just an unexpected gift," he replied.

"Are you going to thank the congregation for it?"

Harry looked hurt. "Here we go again. I resent your implications."

Before they could finish their comments, Diana walked towards them with a big smile. "The theatre is packed tonight. Everyone's anxious to hear Harry and learn more about entering new dimensions."

Harry began his message with introductory comments:

"I brought with me today the specimen that was the cause of all my distress." He took a plastic vial from his pocket and held it up for all to see. In it was a rather large, multifaceted, hard concretion. The congregation gasped at the size and sympathized with what he must have suffered as he passed it. Harry overheard a woman remark, "That looks just like one of my gallstones that I had removed last year." Another cried out, "Mine too."

"Ah, a stone is a stone is a stone," said Harry. "So much for me." Harry smiled.

"The Lord asked me to give you a commandment that might be the most difficult for you to follow. He said that only the pure of heart would be able to enter the dimension leading to his kingdom. That would require giving up all earthly possessions and monies. The amount you are able to give will determine how far into the dimension you can go. If you never give anything additional, you won't be able to even find the path to start upon. If you give a significant amount, you may get a quick peek into heaven. If you give everything, you will get to enter into the presence of God himself. It's your decision. He wants you to make a commitment tonight."

Allison put her hand across her mouth as she whispered to Diana, "Harry is going too far. I'm embarrassed for him. No one is going to go along with such extremes. His request is so unreasonable that we may very soon find an empty church to preach in on Sundays." It soon became apparent that it was the preachers rather than the audience who felt Harry was going too far with his requests.

Harry reviewed his visual imagery exercises with the congregation. The parishioners relaxed more easily and appeared at peace. "You're making good progress, and will soon be ready for the next step."

After the preparatory session, donations were collected. The sock was beginning to bulge much to the surprise of the women preachers.

When alone, Candace took Hannah aside and frowned. "I think Harry is going to pull a fast one on us. I tried to check the hospital that was named on his statement and couldn't find any such listing in any directory. Also, why isn't he discussing all these plans with us beforehand?"

"That all does sound suspicious. We need to be en guarde."

Later that afternoon, Diana's ex-husband came to her home.

"Your church is getting more and more interesting, isn't it? I'd like to talk to you about it and talk about us. How'd you like to go to dinner with me tonight?"

Diana had long wished to hear him express love for her. But now his words failed to excite her. She stood up straight, and stared into his eyes.

"No thank you. Since our divorce, I've found my real self. I know who I am, and I like me. I've moved on. I can only thank you for leaving me, because by so doing you made my new life possible. I'll just say goodbye now. I wish you well."

In her heart, she whispered, *Thank you, Harry.*

~ 48 ~
Camera…Action!

Jason looked alert and healthy as he sat at the organ for the Sunday morning service. Allison noticed the change and nudged Hannah as they sat on stage. "Jason sure looks different this morning. I wonder if he's given up the booze?"

"He's trying. I talked to him and got him enrolled in a rehab program. So far, so good!"

"I'm so glad. He's a good guy. It would be a shame to waste his talents."

Lively organ music carried into the street. The vibrations were felt through the whole city block. Contrary to what Candace had predicted, the seats were filled with an enthusiastic congregation.

As Harry walked on stage, loud applause broke out. The cheers continued even when Harry motioned for quiet. He smiled shyly at first, and then made exaggerated waves to the congregation and blew kisses. Jason ended the ovation by loudly starting the opening hymn.

Harry took his seat on the stage facing the people. As he surveyed the audience, he hesitated as he noticed a distinguished man in the back row. *He looks familiar. Where have I seen him before?* he wondered. Those thoughts were interrupted when singing of the first hymn began. He stood and sang, concentrating to avoid the drowning voice of Candace.

At the conclusion of the hymn, Candace turned to Harry and whispered, "What's that big box near the mike…covered by a black cloth? What's in there, Harry?"

"You'll see soon enough…props for my sermon."

Candace groaned. "What now? Another magic trick? I'm not sure I can handle any more of your surprises."

After the opening prayer, Harry rose to give the sermon. He began his presentation with a magic trick… something that always got his audience's attention. He pulled colorful scarves from his clenched fists and seemingly from the air. The congregation loved the show and again applauded loudly. They became silent only when Harry began his message.

"Perhaps some of you think these scarves came from another dimension. You saw no physical evidence of them before they suddenly appeared from nowhere. We can liken this to the new dimensions which those of you who have been faithful will soon enter. But first, let us consider just why each of us has been placed on this earth."

As he glanced around the room, he felt uneasy as his eyes kept hesitating on the austere man in the back row. Suddenly the theatre doors opened. There stood a woman he immediately recognized. His face flushed and he tensed. Diana tensed as she also recognized her. It was the same woman who had recently appeared for an unscheduled and prolonged counseling session with Harry. With the entrance of the woman, Harry suddenly recalled the identity of the man in the back row—John Murray.

John had been a successful businessman in Albany, where he was highly regarded in the community and known for his generosity to charitable causes. Harry presented him with false records of phenomenal growth in a business. He convinced John that it was sure to bring great wealth to investors. John was easily taken in by Harry's charm. Harry urged him to put a large portion of his assets into this venture. Then with John's money in his pockets, Harry ran, leaving John almost broke.

John now sat in the theatre staring at his enemy. Then Harry saw him glance to the side and nod towards two other men in the back. One of them held a phone to his mouth.

It was clear to Harry what was happening. The plain-clothesmen were there to arrest him. He experienced a moment of panic. *They're closing in. I'm trapped!* He could barely continue his sermon because of his intrusive thoughts of impending capture. He worked to compose himself. *Wait! Me trapped? What am I thinking? I've been in tighter situations than this. I'm the great escape artist,* he thought to himself. *This time I must make myself invisible and it must be for real.* He knew the setups for zeroing in on a criminal. There would be men at all exits waiting to prevent his escape. *The only way out is through,* he thought as he used a common self-talk phrase that always had proven true for him.

The women preachers were unaware of Harry's plight. As usual, they sat braced, wondering what novel idea Harry was about to divulge to the congregation.

Harry began to perspire as he continued his sermon, but he quickly put a different slant on it. Just as he had used the sock fiasco for donation plates, he thought he could use his planned magic trick to his advantage. "The Good Book tells us that when the end is near, the lion will lie down with the lamb in peace. The same is true for other animals that we know to be predators, but in the last days they will live in peace with all their former prey. Take the hawk as an example."

At that moment, Harry in one dramatic sweep, threw off the black sheet from the box. Inside was a large hawk tethered by a small line. The congregation gasped.

"Another Harryism!" said Candace to Hannah. Diana sat watching him in admiration.

"Don't worry. Just as the Lord has control over all wild creatures, I have control over this beautiful beast. In fact, I am the creator of the spirit of this beast."

Candace subtly shook her head. She whispered to Allison, "Now he thinks he's God himself!"

Harry saw the lawmen rapidly moving in on him. He spoke louder and more rapidly. "Fear not the beautiful animal." Harry took the hawk in his hands, cut its tether, and released it into the air. "Fly hawk! Fly!"

The congregation screamed as the bird of prey flapped its wings closely over their heads. They grabbed nearby decorator pillows and used them to fend off the hawk.

"Be careful with my pillows," yelled Allison. She ran into the aisle trying to save her precious works of art without concern for the hawk. She gathered armfuls. In a frenzy, people tried to grab pillows from her and fights broke out. Many people dove to the floor to avoid a collision, and many ran to the exits.

The hawk flew throughout the theatre frequently swooping down to grab any interesting tidbit. Several people swatted at it to scare it away. It landed on a woman's head and pulled off the flowers in her headband. She madly waved her hands and ran about in a frenzy, all the time screaming.

Harry crouched down and crawled between the rows and in the aisles. One of the officers had made his way very close to Harry and was about to pounce on him when the hawk glided in and grabbed the officer's toupee. In a dramatic upward glide, it flew around the ceiling chandelier as if proudly displaying a trophy. The embarrassed officer pulled his coat over his bald head and crouched low. John Murray had been keeping a close watch until the hawk flew over the head of the woman sitting next to him and gracefully deposited its duty. The other agents were concentrating mostly on the bird, themselves trying to avoid attack. In the pandemonium, the officers lost track of Harry.

"Where did he go?"

"Did anyone see him leave?".

The women preachers were totally perplexed; none of them having any idea as to what was the cause of the commotion.

Realizing that Harry was nowhere within view, one officer yelled, "You're all under arrest. Don't anyone leave." No one seemed to hear him as they forced their way out. The officer took out his spray gun, and used it to try to gain control and to keep people from leaving.

The hawk was confused also, and flew out of the theatre clutching the toupee in its talons. "Follow that hawk," yelled the bald officer.

As the room slowly quieted, Harry was not to be found.

"That bastard escaped again," yelled John.

~ 49 ~
The Cruelest Deception

The women preachers stood in a daze when the theatre finally cleared. Their stupor was broken by the appearance of the woman who had entered the theatre just before the turmoil. She walked briskly to the front where the other women were standing. Diana squirmed as she approached.

"Well…our Harry has escaped again!" the woman said.

The others appeared puzzled. "What do you mean?" asked Hannah.

"The feds are forever on his trail, but he always outsmarts them."

As the woman extended her hand to greet them, Diana caught sight of the beautiful blue sapphire ring on her right ring finger. Diana gasped as she recognized it as the one she had pawned to help the group get started. It was gone when she had tried to redeem it. She blurted out: "That ring! Where did you get it?"

"It was a gift from Harry for our twentieth wedding anniversary. Why do you ask?"

Diana quickly sat to avoid a faint. "I had one like it once," she answered with a weak voice. She couldn't hold back a sob. The other women gathered around to comfort her. She looked up at the attractive woman and stammered, "Harry is married?"

The woman looked at her with compassion. "I think we need to talk." She extended her hand and helped her stand. "Let's go somewhere quiet. I think there's a lot you need to know."

"There's a lot we'd all like to know," said Candace. "He's a wanted man by the Feds?"

The group sat around a table in the corner of a small café near the theatre. Allison put her arm around Diana who was pale and trembling.

"Where would you like me to start?" the woman asked.

Candace almost interrupted her. "At the beginning! Just who is that guy who charmed us while cheating us?"

Harry's wife answered abruptly. "He's a big lie! Even the name he uses isn't his real name. He chose to be called *Harry* after his idol, Harry Houdini. He worshiped him. He did more than just want to be like Houdini—he practiced night and day to become him—his clone, you might say."

Harry's wife leaned forward. "He became so skilled that he even impressed adult magicians. He could have made a good living as a professional magician, but he thought it was more profitable to use his skills in other deceptive ways. He once told me that the world was full of suckers holding their money out just to be taken by him."

"I guess I was one of those suckers!" sobbed Diana. She looked directly at the woman through tear-filled eyes: "I had no idea Harry was married. He told me he loved me, and I thought we would soon be married. How could he be so cruel?"

"Oh he can be charmingly cruel. I know the pain you're feeling. You're not the only one who has experienced his deceit, including myself."

Harry's wife spoke softly to try to calm her. "Harry was a genius and an expert at making people trust him. Don't look down on yourself for being another of his victims."

Diana covered her face with her hand. "I believed so easily everything he told me. I never doubted him."

"I'm sure Harry spotted that trait in you and took advantage of it to meet his own goals. He's an expert at reading people."

Diana grabbed another tissue from her purse and dabbed her eyes. The women continued to discuss Harry at length. Diana's mood slowly changed as she found herself becoming more angry with what she learned about Harry. "He must not have any conscience," she said.

Hannah nodded. "A clever sociopath."

Harry's wife seemed eager to continue. "I read about the big brawl in your church and saw a photograph in which I thought I recognized Harry. We had been apart for a long time and it was that photo that led me to him. You probably think that the brawl happened by accident, but I guarantee you that it was somehow part of Harry's plan."

Hannah thought for a moment. "I think you're right."

"I'm not at all surprised, and I'm sure he profited by it."

Allison smiled. "Actually, we all did."

"Federal agents were forever on his trail, but that guy always eluded them."

"Is that who was after him at our last church service?"

"Of course. But as usual, Harry disappeared before they could apprehend him."

"I think he was right when he said he knew how to make himself invisible," said Brittany.

Harry's wife laughed. "He's smart enough to elude all officers after him. I don't think anyone will ever catch him."

"He sounds like a genius, always a step ahead of his pursuers."

Diana started to relax as Harry's wife described his upbringing and her life with him. She said, "You know, Harry wasn't completely a taker. He gave a lot too. I grew a lot. As I think about it, Harry's the only one who hasn't grown or matured. That's the saddest thing of all. And overall, I'm sure he's lonely—always in hiding."

"I can't believe all his tricks weren't magic," said Diana with a puzzled expression on her face. "One thing I don't understand is how he levitated. I saw him rise above the floor right in front of me. I really saw it!"

"I told you he was a master magician. Levitation was a trick that I worked on with him to perfect. It was just an illusion. Just another deceptive trick."

As the group stood to leave, Harry's wife removed the sapphire ring from her finger and handed it to Diana. "This belongs more to you than me."

Diana cried again as she accepted the ring. "Thank you. This is a family heirloom. You're a good person and you deserve a good man!"

"So do you! By the way, if your book club resumes, I'd like to join it!"

As everyone was leaving, Diana still was shaking and tearful. Hannah asked her if she wanted someone to go home with her, but she declined saying she would be okay and just needed time to process the news.

Diana's mind was on Harry, and she wasn't even aware of walking to her home and entering.

One of the first things that she focused on was the delicate red glass rose that Harry had given her. She remembered how he'd told her he was giving it to her as a symbol of his eternal love for her. She reached up, grabbed it from the shelf, and hurled it against the wall causing it to shatter. She stomped on it and laughed.

~ 50 ~
Settling Affairs

The raid on the theatre brought an end to the church services. Police officers roped off the theatre entrance with crime scene tapes, and the preachers had no access to the building.

Diana walked into the café slowly. Her face was gaunt. The five women had arranged to meet together a few days after the incursion to review the business and records. Hannah was the only one there when she arrived.

"You look like you've seen a ghost," said Hannah.

Diana sadly shook her head. "I've had more than one huge shock this past week. I haven't been able to sleep since Sunday."

Diana then told Hannah how she had been taken in romantically by Harry. "I really loved him and trusted him. I had no idea he was using me. I haven't told the rest of the group, but I advanced him money that he never paid back. I need to confess that to the others." Under her breath, she added, "and more." She sadly shook her head. "I'm so embarrassed about it that I was thinking of not coming today. How could I have been so blinded—so stupid?"

"Diana, love makes fools of everyone. Educated women are no exception. We're just plain goofy when it comes to love. Maybe you should begin your confession by admitting how you had fallen head over heels in love with Harry. I think the group could understand how that influenced your judgment."

Diana sat silently looking at the floor.

Brittany was the next to arrive. She brought her boyfriend, Charley, with her on this day, thinking that Candace wouldn't belittle her as much or try to give her proportionally less of the money left in the treasury if her boyfriend were present.

When Candace arrived a few minutes later, Brittany proudly introduced Charley to Candace.

"So this is our modern day philosopher," said Candace. She looked at his long straggly hair and beard and his attire with his low-rise pants that looked like they were going to fall off at any moment—indeed he often held them up with one hand. Candace didn't hold back her thoughts and she said, "Aren't you afraid you're going to lose those pants if you release your grip?"

Brittany interjected, "Get with it Candace. Charley knows what's hot and what's not in men's wear."

"So he's a real style king, huh?"

When the others arrived, Candace took charge of the meeting. "Diana, let's have the treasurers report. How much is there to split?" she asked with great expectation.

"Is everybody sitting down?" asked Diana.

The others braced themselves. "Oh, oh," said Candace. "Let's hear the bad news."

Diana looked like she was about to cry. She hung her head low, and quietly said, "I went to the bank to close the account. All that was in it was $25. I know we had over $250,000 there when I balanced last week."

"There goes my house in the Hamptons," said Allison.

"There go all our dreams," said Hannah.

Candace's face turned red. She rose from her chair with clenched fists and stomped around the table. "So how do you explain the missing money?"

Diana looked down and her voice started to crack. "Harry's wife told me how Harry was an expert at forging checks. He must have somehow made a copy of a check he received or got hold of a blank check. That's the only explanation I can think of for what happened. Nobody had legitimate access to the account except me." Diana took a deep breath. "I have to tell you that I advanced Harry a small amount which he never paid back, but it was almost nothing compared to the total we had in the bank."

"What?" screamed Candace. "I told you not to give him money without an okay from us first. See what happened! How could you be so stupid? It's all your fault." She stomped her feet hard and raised her hand as if she wanted to strike Diana.

Hannah stood and came between them. "Candace, there was no maliciousness on the part of Diana. Her judgment was off and she didn't realize how cunning was Harry. She simply felt she was helping someone in need at the time."

Allison and Brittany also came to her defense saying that they could understand her predicament.

"Understanding doesn't make it okay," returned Candace. "All our hard earned money gone! No, no, no!"

"There's nothing we can do about it now. Let's try to move on," said Hannah.

"Move back, you mean." Candace beat her fist on the table. "That bastard is somewhere enjoying our money while he's busy with more cons, I'm sure. Well, I'm not going to let him get away with it."

Diana looked surprised. "What are you going to do? Harry's wife said that professionals have been after him for years without success. We don't stand a chance."

"When we started the church, no one thought we could succeed. But we did! We know that we're all smart women." She then looked at Brittany. "Well, maybe most of us are." Brittany stuck her tongue out at Candace while Candace looked away. "Let's use our smarts again to get him!"

"I think Harry's out of our league," said Allison.

"I don't agree with that. We just need to come up with a plan for revenge. Start thinking everyone!" said Candace as she sat with her chin resting on her fist.

Hannah strongly stated, "Although it's tempting to think of putting a bomb in his car, we can't consider that kind of violence—

especially when one of us could get hurt. Our revenge must be subtle and not traceable."

Brittany's boyfriend spoke up: "According to Nietzsche, the best revenge would be living successfully."

"Charley has a good point," said Brittany as she looked at her boyfriend with admiration.

"Yah, like that's going to make Harry sorry," said Allison. "I agree with Candace that Harry needs to be put in his place by somebody."

"Should we run out and let all the air out of his tires?" asked Diana.

"Not good enough," said Candace. "Not worth $250,000!"

Hannah had been deep in thought. "I was just thinking that Harry is a great con artist, but would he be able to spot someone conning him?"

"I'm sure he could. You know the old saying: *You can't BS a BSer*," said Allison.

"But I think we could De-con a con artist," said Candace.

"What could we do that would bring us satisfaction?" asked Diana.

"Get our hard earned money back!" yelled Candace. Her face again turned red as she fumed. Then she turned towards Diana. "Diana, we all know that you were dating Harry. Do you have any idea where he kept most of his money?"

"Money was never a big part of our conversations. All I know is that he only used cash—never a credit card."

"Where did he do his banking?" asked Allison.

"Harry's wife told me that Harry didn't keep money in banks. He didn't think it was safe there."

Candace sneered, "Our money sure wasn't safe in a bank!"

"Harry's wife thinks he hid his money somewhere, but she never found out where."

Candace glared at Diana. "Did you ever go to his apartment?"

"Well, yes…once, but I didn't see any money there."

"Think, Diana. Think. Think of anything unusual that could have been a clue as to where he kept it. You need to make up for your poor judgment that resulted in our huge losses!"

"I can't think of anything. Of course I wasn't looking around with that in mind." Diana frowned as she tried to think of any likely hiding place.

Hannah said, "Wherever he kept it, I'm sure he was smart enough to think of a place that would be fireproof, and a place where others would never guess he'd hide money."

"The idea that he hid it in his apartment is becoming more than a good guess," said Diana. "He mentioned that he chose an apartment in an area that was not upper class—one that would not reek of money increasing the chance of break-ins."

"You've got to search your mind for clues. Was there anything in the apartment that drew your attention?"

Diana suddenly sat up straight. Her eyes opened wide. "I just thought of something. Harry always paid bills with cash. Once at a restaurant, I noticed a white powder on some of the bills. I jokingly asked Harry if that was cocaine. He laughed and said he'd never been into the stuff; in fact he said he never took any mind-altering substance including coffee. Those things would interfere with his escape into other dimensions, he told me. Then he looked at the powder and said it was probably baking powder that he spilled earlier that day."

"Eureka!" yelled Candace. "He hides his money in food canisters where others wouldn't think to check for money during robberies."

The others laughed and gave Candace a *high five*.

"Do you remember how to get to his apartment?" asked Hannah.

"Yes, but I don't have a key."

Brittany became excited and jumped up. "Charley, here, learned to pick locks from a locksmith. He's an expert at unlocking doors, aren't you Babe?"

Candace laughed with glee. "Brittany, I think we've at last become friends!"

"Now we have to think of how we can go there when we're sure he won't be home," said Hannah. She looked at Diana. "Any ideas on the best time for us to break-in?"

"I know he used to have some meeting just before our book club met."

"Let's plan on going to his place next week about an hour before our scheduled meetings," said Candace.

"I'm a little nervous about breaking into someone's apartment. Couldn't we go to jail for that?" asked Allison.

Candace snickered, "Harry wouldn't dare to press charges against us. He knows that the minute he flaunts himself in public, the law will find him, and he'll immediately be arrested for all the warrants out against him. We're safe."

~ 51 ~
Taking it to the Mattresses

At noon on the next Wednesday, the five women, Charley, and Fred met at a corner near Harry's apartment. They huddled around Candace for a last minute briefing.

"Diana, you know what you have to do—stay within site of the apartment and the road entering the neighborhood and be the lookout. Hannah, you stay outside at the back of the building to watch in case Harry approaches from the rear. If either of you see Harry coming, call my cell phone. Charley and Brittany, you enter the building first. After you get in, call the rest of us. We'll come and help search for the money."

Candace, Allison, and Fred waited at the corner for a call from Brittany. It only took minutes until Candace heard, "We're in." They walked briskly into the building and up the stairs to Harry's room. The dimly lit apartment with its shabby furniture and worn carpet presented an eerie scene upon entering.

Candace went immediately to the kitchen area. She opened the cabinet doors in search for the baking powder can. It was large and easy to spot even though half obscured by smaller spice containers. She quickly opened it. As she did, powder sprayed over the counter. She reached in with wide eyes and a big smile said, "Voila! That was easy."

There was a big wad of bills in the can. Candace unfolded them. Most were fifty-dollar notes. "Wow! There must be several thousand dollars here. Who would have thought so much would fit into a canister this size! But he must have more hiding spots. Keep looking everybody."

Candace stayed in the kitchen area, and looked through more containers for possible money while the others looked elsewhere. They looked under the mattress—nothing found there of course. Harry was no fool! Stuffed pillows? No…too obvious. No loose floorboards under the carpet. No hidden safe behind the paintings. While in the bedroom, Allison stopped suddenly.

"I didn't know Harry was religious. Didn't he say he had no religion per se? Look in here!" Over his bed was a reproduction painting of Jesus' mother, Mary, holding a rosary. Allison lifted the painting and examined the back. The frame appeared broken and loose in one area. She easily removed it and then the backing. There it was! Another *voila*! Several thousand dollars cash in there!

"Great," said Candace, "but don't stop looking. There's got to be a lot more to find."

Soon after, Candace came across a large coffee can. "Didn't Harry tell Diana he never drank coffee?" She pried off the lid. At the bottom of the can were more fifty dollar notes. She chuckled, "It's starting to add up, but we can't stop until we find at least double this amount."

The others found stashes in pockets of pants hidden back in the closet and taped under the sofa.

"I'm running out of ideas," said Allison. "Where can I look next?"

"How about the freezer?" said Fred.

Candace quickly opened the freezer door. There were several TV dinners, frozen pizza, frozen burritos, and a large tub of ice cream. She pulled out the tub and examined the contents. The ice cream appeared old and to have melted and been refrozen. She scooped it out into the sink, and cried out in delight, "Eureka!" There in the midst of the contents was a plastic bag stuffed with large bills.

"Has anyone checked his sock drawer?" laughed Allison. "He sure had a special interest in socks." She opened the drawer and squealed in delight. In the back were four large socks stuffed with money.

Suddenly there was a quiet knock on the door. Everyone froze. "What should we do," whispered Allison.

"Be quiet," instructed Candace.

Another quiet knock followed. "Mister Hansen, is that you in there?"

"It must be the landlady," said Candace. "You all hide. I'll handle this."

Candace brushed herself off. "Who's there?" she asked.

"It's Mrs. Martin, the landlady."

Candace looked around making sure the others were out of sight. She then opened the door halfway. A strong whiff of alcohol greeted her along with an unkempt, elderly woman. With a confident voice, Candace said, "Hi. Can I help you?"

"I heard some noise in here. I didn't think Harry was home. So, what's going on?"

At that moment, Fred bumped into a plant that had been placed on a high stand. It went crashing to the floor. Candace shuddered. How was she going to explain that? Before she could answer, the landlady said, "Oh, that must be Mr. Davenport in the apartment above. He's always stumbling around and breaking things."

"That explains it. For a minute I thought there was someone else in the apartment," said Candace. "Harry's my good friend. He should be home soon. He told me to wait here."

"He's a good man. Always pays his rent on time and in cash. Never causes me trouble. Are you his lady?"

"You might say that we're a team."

Suddenly Candace's cell phone rang. She quickly dismissed the landlady and answered the phone. She whispered to the others, "Harry's on his way. Let's get out of here."

"We need to clean up our mess," said Allison.

"Don't be ridiculous! Burglars never clean up after themselves. Gather the money and let's go," said Candace.

Brittany and Charley started towards the front door. "We can't leave that way," cautioned Candace. "We might meet Harry on the way up. Open the back window."

Everyone hurried to the window. “We’re on the second floor,” said Allison as she nervously peered out. “We’ll kill ourselves if we jump.”

Hannah appeared below them. Seeing their predicament, she pointed to a dumpster below the window that was filled with bags of trash. “Jump here,” she said. “It’ll help break your falls.”

Fred grabbed Charley’s arm. “Why don’t we go first. We can help catch the girls when they jump.”

Charley appeared faint. “I can’t jump. I’m scared of heights.”

Candace pushed the men aside. “I’ll go first. I’m used to falling in my dance routines. I know how to roll with the jumps. But, the rest of you better come quickly after.” She grabbed hold of the windowsill and turned allowing her legs to dangle downward. Without hesitation, she released her grip. She landed safely in the dumpster below. Hannah helped her climb out. After making sure Candace was alright, Hannah commented:

“Ooh. You don’t smell very good. What’s that brown stuff over your pants? Never mind. I think I know. There are babies living in some of these apartments!”

“Yuk! But no time to worry about that now. On my way down, I passed the first floor window where I saw the landlady watching her television. Her back was towards the window so I don’t think she noticed me. Still, we need to be quiet.” She signaled quiet to Allison and Fred who stood at the open window both considering their jumps.

“Do you want me to go first and then catch you?” asked Fred.

“No. Please hold onto me as long as possible before I drop.”

Fred held Allison as she slid her legs over the sill and held onto Fred’s grasp. She looked up and nodded to him to release her. She landed quietly just missing the soiled diapers. Fred quickly followed. Only Brittany and Charley remained to escape.

“I can’t do it,” said Charley. He was visibly shaking.

“We have to,” said Brittany. “I’ll go first. You hang onto me so I can get as low to the ground as possible.”

Brittany jumped and was guided by the others into a soft landing in the trash. “It’s easier than it looks, Charley. You can do it. We’ll all help catch you.”

Charley appeared petrified as he eased himself out the window. As he hung out the window, he could no longer hold onto his pants. They started to drop. The more he wiggled about, the more they fell until they came completely off and fell to the ground. Those watching from the ground couldn't stop laughing at his bareness from the waist down. Allison laughed so hard she almost spit up her cucumber salad. Candace laughed so hard, she rolled on the ground, but quickly regained her composure, and called to him in a loud whisper, "Charley, jump now or someone will arrest you for indecent exposure."

The landlady hearing the commotion outside, walked to her window just as Charley released his grip. When the landlady saw Charley fly by without his pants, she yelled, "That does it. I'm tired of these hallucinations." She then hurled her whiskey bottle out the window, barely missing Charley who lay quivering on the dumpster.

~ 52 ~
Resumption of the Book Club

The door of the café swung open, allowing a cold rushing wind to sweep through the room.

"Oh, the weather outside is frightful!" Diana sang out causing heads to turn. She looked like a stunning movie star, and was wearing an attention-getting bright red, shiny raincoat with a matching umbrella that she dramatically shook and folded.

"Is this the drying out station?" she asked the hostess as she wiped her shoes on the foyer mat.

The greeter smiled and said, "It is for you! Good to see you again. Your club members are waiting for you in the back."

Five women smiled with amusement as they watched Diana make her way back to them.

"Now we have two drama queens who make their arrivals obvious," said Allison.

Brittany giggled. "Yes we have."

Diana talked with almost everyone she passed. "I like your sweater," she said to one man as she gave him a wink.

"Hello. Hello. Hello," she sang out as she approached the women who were waiting for her.

"Hi Diana. That was quite an entrance. I think we've created a monster," said Hannah as she laughed.

Diana looked at the club members. Her eyes lit up as she recognized her former book club friend. "Mona! Good to see you again. How've you been?" She walked around the table and gave her a warm hug.

"I've been doing great." Mona smiled. She took a long look at Diana. "Diana! You look and act like a different person. Your business enterprise must have done wonders for you."

"It wasn't just our business that changed me. Would you believe that it took faith in the words of a con man to bring my changes?...or was he an angel in disguise?"

The group all reacted with loud "noes". "Let's not start deluding ourselves. Without question, he was a true-blue con man," said Hannah.

Diana smiled. "Even a con man can be a great teacher. He taught me a lot about myself. That's for sure." She then looked intently at Mona. "You haven't changed—still your attractive self!"

"Flattery will get you everywhere," Mona responded.

Candace gazed at Mona. "We could have used your expertise in our healing services. We did what we could. Although we were amateurs, we saw many people get relief from our hands-on actions. But we could have expanded that lucrative service with you there. If we start our business again, will you join us?"

The others sighed when they heard that proposal. "It'll take me years to get back my energy after all the stress we went through," said Hannah.

Mona smiled. "Thanks Candace, but I'm happy with my job. I got a promotion with a significant increase in salary, soon after you started your church."

Candace smirked, "But how exciting is that? Aren't you sorry that you missed the adventure with all its excitement?"

"I get my excitement from the people I help everyday."

"Ooo. Exciting!"

"Can you still relieve a headache with acupressure?" asked Allison. "I've had a pounding headache for a week and haven't found any way to shake it. I almost didn't come today."

"Give me your hand," said Mona.

Within minutes, Allison's headache was gone, and a warm smile replaced the tension lines in her brow.

"It really worked, Mona."

"Better and cheaper than a joint, right?" said Candace.

Mona looked at the others and asked, "Did you meet your goal of getting super rich quick?"

Everyone was quiet for a moment. Then Candace pounded her fist on the table. "Let's face it. We did make some money but hardly became rich, and it didn't come as easily as we thought it would. We would have made tons more if it hadn't been for that con man."

"By the way, it was fortunate that Fred broke that plant pot in Harry's apartment. We recovered another big wad from it," said Allison.

Diana told the group that she went back to the apartment a few days later and found that Harry had moved. "I'm sure he knows it was us that broke in."

"I don't think that had anything to do with his move," said Hannah. "He probably was evading the feds again."

Diana held her head low and spoke quietly. "That's true. I feel sorry for him in a way. He lives a lonely life—always on the run."

"His way of life was a choice. With his skills, he could have had a successful career and stable family," said Allison.

"I feel a little guilty about the whole business," said Diana.

"Guilty about what?" asked Candace. "We only recovered what he stole from us."

"I still feel guilty not only about breaking into Harry's apartment, but in taking so much money from so many people who thought their donations were going for a spiritual cause."

Candace assumed a defensive posture. "We gave those people so much more than they paid for. How can you put a price tag on taking people out of their ruts and relieving them from their humdrum lives? We gave them some invaluable entertainment and excitement."

"That's true," said Hannah. "Candace, your music provided an escape from the continuous roar of taxis, sirens, and other commotions in New York City. It made our congregation hear sounds from another dimension. Our services made them stop for a moment and reflect and hopefully they were inspired to look beyond the routines of life."

Allison thoughtfully pondered all that Hannah said. She looked up and smiled. “You know, people in the congregation weren’t the only ones helped out of ruts. Consider us. It seems each one of us was stuck in some kind of routine before we started our church. Even though we didn’t get as rich as we had hoped, we did gain something far more valuable. We captured that holy grail.”

Everyone relaxed and smiled as they understood how their endeavor was a true success.

“So what’s our next grail to go after?” asked Candace. “We still need to pay our future bills.”

“I think we need a breather before we talk about that,” said Hannah. The others nodded.

“Moving right along, where do you suppose Harry is now?” asked Allison.

“Miles from here, no doubt. I’m sure he’s the biggest shyster the world has known. And yet, for some strange reason, I can’t help admiring him…even liking him.” Candace turned towards Hannah. “How can that be?” asked Candace.

“He was good at what he did. Everyone admires a person who is good at what they do, no matter what that might be. And Harry was a master at everything…mostly deceit. Besides that, he was a real charmer.”

Hannah looked at each member of the group. “He did what he had to do to make it to the end of each day, just as we do. I think Harry needed to find his way by entering his different dimension.”

Candace grunted. “As Harry thought he escaped into a new dimension, he took our money with him.”

“But we found out how to get into that dimension and get that money back,” said Hannah.

The others laughed.

It was then that Brittany looked out the window. She stood and became excited. “It can’t be! It’s déjà vu!” she exclaimed.

“What?’ the group asked.

“Look at that Porsche sports car that just parked in the lot across the street. The guy that stepped out is wearing an Armani suit and expensive Italian shoes, just like the preacher who prompted us to form our church.”

They all stood by the café window and looked out.

Diana gasped, “That’s Harry!”

They watched as he hurried around the car to open the door for the passenger. He bent over to assist an elderly woman with a cane.

“It’s our widow,” said Allison. “And look at her big smile. She looks so happy.”

They watched as Harry escorted the widow into an upscale restaurant three doors from the café.

“Should we call the police and warn our widow about Harry?” asked Allison.

Hannah smiled and said, “He’d be out of sight when the police arrived, leaving the widow alone and miserable. Right now, Harry’s giving her a way out of her routines. Let’s not spoil her chance at happiness.”

“Waitress!” Candace yelled. “Bring us your best Champagne.” She stood and said,

“Let’s toast Harry—the jerk who brought—and still brings joy and hope to so many!”

“And unknowingly helped some of us to reach our potentials,” added Diana.

Epilogue

Five women in protective overalls and wearing masks and gloves were working feverishly cleaning a crime scene area on a backstreet in New York City. A Porsche drove up to them driven by a man wearing a clerical collar.

"Hey gals. How'd you like to help me start a new church. You'd be able to make a lot of money fast."

The women recognized Harry. They angrily grabbed their brooms and mops and while yelling curses, chased Harry down the street as he sped away.

Acknowledgements

There are several people to whom I owe gratitude for their inspiration, encouragement, and ideas for enhancement of this novel. Foremost is my writing group in Ann Arbor: *Writers Unlimited.* Those members include Joy Rome, Mary Fancher, Larry Nathan Burns, Charles Duncan, Edna Morris, Don Skiff, Don Lamphiear, Susan Hansen, James Kane, Randi Hoffmann, and Alice Bingner.

I am indebted to Richard Mikat for the many hours of patient technical assistance including formatting. He also gave many hours to developing the book cover design.

CPSIA information can be obtained at www.ICGtesting.com
Printed in the USA
BVOW051055101111

275747BV00006B/1/P

9 781450 798266